MICHAEL BENNETT

RETURN TO BLOOD

SIMON & SCHUSTER

London · New York · Sydney · Toronto · New Delhi

First published in Great Britain by Simon & Schuster UK Ltd, 2024
This paperback edition first published 2025

Copyright © Michael Bennett, 2024

Original characters created and developed by Michael Bennett and Jane Holland
Kiri's poem and elements of Kiri's dialogue by Matariki Star Holland Bennett, adapted from works from her original poetry collection, *e kō, nō hea koe?* © Matariki Bennett, 2024
Guess How Much I Love You by Sam McBratney © Sam McBratney, 1994
'Till We Meet Again' music by Richard A. Whiting, lyrics by Raymond B. Egan © 1918
Recipe for mussel and courgette fritters by Elaine Jocelyn Bennett (née Westerman)
Māori design by Māhina Rose Holland Bennett

The writing of this book was undertaken with the support of
Creative New Zealand Toi Aōtearoa

The right of Michael Bennett to be identified as author of this work has been asserted in accordance with the Copyright, Designs and Patents Act, 1988.

1 3 5 7 9 10 8 6 4 2

Simon & Schuster UK Ltd
1st Floor
222 Gray's Inn Road
London WC1X 8HB

Simon & Schuster Australia, Sydney
Simon & Schuster India, New Delhi

www.simonandschuster.co.uk
www.simonandschuster.com.au
www.simonandschuster.co.in

A CIP catalogue record for this book
is available from the British Library

Paperback ISBN: 978-1-3985-1228-3
eBook ISBN: 978-1-3985-1227-6
Audio ISBN: 978-1-3985-2281-7

This book is a work of fiction. Names, characters, places and incidents are either a product of the author's imagination or are used fictitiously. Any resemblance to actual people living or dead, events or locales is entirely coincidental.

Typeset in Sabon by M Rules
Printed and Bound in the UK using 100% Renewable Electricity at CPI Group (UK) Ltd

For Ngamaru Raerino.
Moe ma rā e te rangatira.

Tukua kia tū takitahi ngā whetū o te rangi
Let each star in the sky shine its own light
                         Māori whakataukī (proverb)

Praise for *Return to Blood*:

'The vivid picture of ethnic cultural life alone marks out the book as special, but it's Bennett's control of a tense narrative that is key' **Financial Times**

'Evocative' **Crime Monthly**

'A confident, convincing work in a crowded genre' **NZ Listener**

'A powerful novel that stays in the mind long after it is finished' **Jeff Popple**

'His deep understanding of marginalised communities, family tensions and the travails of our justice system enrich the novel ... *Return to Blood* shows a writer in full command of his material and which reaches deeper into our shared human experience. It also has a surprise ending few readers will be able to predict' **Greg Fleming**

'Even better (if possible!) than his searing debut – Michael Bennett's latest, *Return to Blood*, had me moved to tears of empathy and rage within the first fifty pages. Richly evocative New Zealand detail, a take-no-prisoners female Māori detective and a riveting crime make for a sizzling and culturally important page-turner' **Alexandra Sokoloff**

Praise for the Hana Westerman series:

'A compelling, atmospheric page turner with an authentic insight into Māori culture' **Val McDermid**

'*Better the Blood* touches on themes that have become increasingly urgent in recent years including the far-reaching impacts of colonialism and the often uneasy integration of identity and heritage into modern multicultural society. A tensely plotted, gritty crime novel that has the courage to force us all to rethink our relationship with the past' **Vaseem Khan**

'As page-turning as it is eye-opening. An excitingly fresh perspective upon a world you thought you knew' **Ambrose Parry**

'Stunning. *Better the Blood* is a tremendous debut, and Hana Westerman, the Māori detective at the center of the story, instantly becomes one of the great characters in crime fiction on any continent. This novel has it all: a gripping mystery, complex and memorable characters, and timely social and cultural commentary. Don't miss it' **David Heska Wanbli Weiden**

'Carefully crafted and beautifully written, intelligent and insightful, Bennett opens a unique window onto a fascinating Antipodean society as only world-class crime fiction can. I devoured it' **Deon Meyer**

'A cracking thriller; it also extends our sense of what crime fiction can do' **Liam McIlvanney**

'Bennett deftly illuminates the historical plight of the Māori people and its continuing effects in New Zealand. His action-packed narrative, blended with various cultural references, recalls the novels of Tony and Anne Hillerman, Craig Johnson, and William Kent Krueger' *Library Journal*

'Packed with intricate detail about Māori history and culture, this tense and involving story ushers in a remarkable new detective' **Geoffrey Wansell,** *Daily Mail*

'This thought-provoking debut is a compelling, insightful and highly addictive read' *My Weekly*

'So chilling' *Crime Monthly*

'A well-crafted story with a strong plot and characters which invoke sympathy' *Shots*

'Making his fiction debut, Māori screenwriter and director Bennett establishes himself as an excellent storyteller ... the book's immersion in tribal culture and history makes the greatest impact, lending complexity and sweep to the narrative. A striking debut and a significant addition to Indigenous literature' *Kirkus Reviews*, **starred review**

'[A] stellar series launch. Bennett is a writer to watch' *Publishers Weekly*, **starred review**

'A moving, timely and powerful thriller that brings to life a crime story deeply embedded in our history. Bennett, like North American crime writers S. A. Cosby and David Heska Wanbli Weiden, articulates the generational impact a history of trauma and injustice can wreak on a people' **Greg Fleming,** *Kete Book Reviews*

'Everything I look for in crime fiction – a tense, gritty, thought-provoking plot, top-notch characterisation and a fabulous sense of place. A cracking read' **Karen Cole,** *Hair Past a Freckle* **blog**

Michael Bennett (**Ngāti Pikiao, Ngāti Whakaue**) is an award-winning screenwriter, director and author. His first book, a non-fiction work telling the true story of New Zealand's worst miscarriage of justice, *In Dark Places*, won Best Non-Fiction Book at the 2017 Ngaio Marsh Awards. Michael's second book, *Helen and the Go-Go Ninjas*, is a time-travel graphic novel co-authored with Ant Sang.

Better the Blood, the first Hana Westerman thriller, was shortlisted for the Jann Medlicott Acorn Prize for Fiction/Ockham New Zealand Book Award, as well as for the Audio Book of the Year at the Capital Crime Fingerprint Awards and Best First Mystery Novel at the Barry Awards. It was also longlisted for the CWA John Creasey New Blood Debut Dagger and was a finalist for Best Novel at the 2023 Ngaio Marsh Awards, where it won the award for Best First Novel.

Michael's short and feature films have won awards internationally and have screened at numerous festivals, including Cannes, Toronto, Berlin, Locarno, New York, London and Melbourne. Michael is the 2020 recipient of the Te Aupounamu Māori Screen Excellence Award, in recognition of members of the Māori filmmaking community who have made high-level contributions to screen storytelling.

He lives in Auckland, Aotearoa (New Zealand), with his partner Jane, and children Tīhema, Māhina and Matariki.

Also by Michael Bennett

In Dark Places
Helen and the Go-Go Ninjas

Hana Westerman series
Better the Blood

1

THE GODS OF AUCKLAND

I'll start with that night.

It was a Saturday. The last night of the full moon over Auckland city. The night Dax broke me in two. The night that changed everything. Is there an emoji for 'it's completely fucked'? There should be.

Dax. So endearing. But such a dick.

He rides a shitty old scooter. Dax is a terrible rider, so it's good he can't go fast enough to do serious damage to himself or me or anyone else. I know a lot of things about a lot of things, but zero about mechanics, so I'm taking an entirely random guess that if his scooter has four spark plugs, only one of them is firing. It's a trash can with handlebars and two wheels. But he loves it. It's such a crazy sight when he turns up to one of our Youth at Risk sessions on his bike, fumes billowing out the rusted exhaust. His huge smile plastered over his gorgeous-slash-ugly face. Don't get me wrong. He's handsome as hell. But he's *unusual* handsome. One way to put it. Gingers get a bad rap, but I love freckles and pale skin and red hair. Opposites attract, maybe. And his nose is like a Roman statue or something. Which is to say, it's big. A bit bigger than is necessary for the size of his face. *Quite* a bit bigger than necessary. Dax says it makes him a better breather, whatever the hell that means.

I think it's dignified. I love it. The first time we kissed, it was his nose I kissed first.

There's one good thing about Dax's shitty old scooter. Its name.

The Gods of Auckland.

That was my fault.

When I was still at school, a couple of years before I met Dax, I got obsessed with the atua. The Māori gods. I went to a fancy school and out of nearly seven hundred girls, there was at most a handful of other brown faces like mine. They gave us a couple of Māori culture classes every term, something to look good in the email newsletter, I guess. You know. Diversity. In the classes they talked about the basics; how the Sky Father and Earth Mother were separated by their kids. The rain falling from the skies is the tears of the Sky Father, crying for his missus. The mist is the Earth Mother's heartbroken sighs. In the space left between mum and dad, the children became the gods. Tāne Mahuta, God of the Birds and the Forest, the one who pushed his heels hard up against his father and tore the parents apart. The God of War, Tūmatauenga, and his little bro Rongo, the God of Peace. I figure those two siblings didn't get on. Had to be arguing all the time, right? Which raises the question: if push comes to shove, when there's a full-on face-off and things get slappy, what does the God of Peace do?

At first, I was put off by the gods thing. Every time you see pictures or carvings of the Māori gods, they're almost always guys. There are goddesses, of course, but the ones that get all the attention are the men. Surprise, surprise. Then I thought it through, and I decided gods aren't actually male or female. How can the wind be a man? How can the stars or the forest or thunder or peace have an X and a Y chromosome pairing in their DNA? Someone just made that up, same as how all those painters decided that Jesus, a Middle Eastern guy out in the sun all day, was fair-skinned and blue-eyed. The moment I started imagining the gods as genderless, I fell in love with them. There's this one god, Rūaumoko, the youngest kid, still inside the mum when the parents were separated. So full of anger at what happened to the family that they became the God of Earthquakes. Rūaumoko means 'the shaking waves that scar the earth'. Rūaumoko also got the job of God of Tā Moko. A god for tattoos! That's so awesome.

One time I told Dax about the gods. He borrowed one of my spray cans and painted the scooter's name on the mudguards. *The Gods of Auckland.*

I love those kick-ass genderless gods. And I love Dax.

Or should that be 'loved'? The past tense–present tense thing is complex for me. As you'll see. I need a proofreader.

I love Dax and I hate Dax, equal parts. I hate how he can't walk past a clothes shop without falling in love with a shirt or a jacket, and he'll just have to go in and nick it, but then he'll throw it away a day later because he's decided he actually can't stand it. I hate the thing with the ciggie packet rolled up in his T-shirt sleeve. He got that from a movie he saw once, this really old movie, *Badlands*. This pretty, geeky, skinny girl and a good-looking bad boy. The bad boy always had a ciggie packet rolled up in his T-shirt sleeve. Dax doesn't even like smoking. But he wants to be a guy from a movie.

Such a dick.

But... the things I love about Dax. How he looks into people's eyes like he's looking into their souls. How he's kind to little kids. Maybe because no one was ever very kind to him when he was a little kid. I love how after I told him about the atua, Dax decided I was an honorary god.

'Your eyes aren't normal eyes. Māori don't have green eyes. You've got god eyes.'

It's not true about the green eyes, by the way. Something else I got obsessed with at school: biology. The genetics thing, alleles and genes. My birth parents, both Māori, had brown eyes, so how could I have green? I read and googled and bugged the bio teacher even more than I usually annoyed teachers and I worked it out. It's completely possible. The dominant-recessive thing is way more complicated than you think. There's not much chance I'd get green eyes. There's not much chance *anyone* will get green eyes, if you're not Swedish or Irish or Scottish. Only two per cent of the planet's population actually has them. But there is a chance. And that's what I got.

Dax wasn't interested in the science of it. He's a dreamer. He's living in a movie.

'You've got god eyes.'

After that we were two seventeen-year-old recovering junkies, trying to stay out of remand home by going to the Youth at Risk group. Riding around the city on a crappy old moped called *The Gods of Auckland*.

If Dax was a vape flavour, he'd be tequila and petrol fumes. Such a dick. But so endearing.

Anyway. That night.

A Saturday. The last night of the full moon. The night that changed everything. Dax wasn't being endearing. He was being whatever the exact opposite of endearing is. He was being the God of Fuckheads. I couldn't work out why. I had to push and prod the guy for an hour. More. He finally told me.

'I slept with someone.'

Boom.

Tangaroa, God of the Sea. Send a tidal wave. Wash me away.

He didn't love her, he said, as if that was going to make things even remotely better. Didn't even like her, particularly. Certainly didn't wanna be with her. But he knew what it meant, doing the thing he did. It was his fucked-up way of telling me we were over.

My boy with the beautiful over-generous nose didn't wanna be with me anymore.

I walked out the door. Out onto the street. I took a deep breath. Looked at the big full moon hanging over the city. Didn't know what I was going to do next. Didn't know how I was going to unbreak everything that was so suddenly, so unexpectedly, so completely broken. So completely fucked.

Dax keeps money in a jar by his bed, one hundred bucks. It's symbolic. The cost of two small bags of rock. After we got out the other side of rehab, the jar of money was Dax's way of saying, 'We're clean now. We made it. We can sleep next to the money we need to get a hit without giving in to temptation. We're stronger than that.'

I thought about that jar. I picked up a brick, went

back and threw it through Dax's window, climbed in, screamed at him to stay the fuck away from me, took his symbolic lame-arse money. And I walked off into the night.

So.

That was the night everything changed. It was Saturday. Seven days later, the next Saturday, in the wee early hours of the morning, a sickle moon would be rising over Auckland city.

But I wasn't going to see that sickle moon rise.

Or any moon, ever again.

By then, I'd be dead.

2

BLACK SAND DUNES

Hana runs down the wild, deserted beach.

There's firm sand from the receding tide beneath her feet, enough to give her solid footfall, and she really pushes up her heart rate over the last half kilometre. Hana always runs with her swimming togs under her running gear. She puts in a final hard sprint, knees high, arms pumping, lungs aching as she reaches the stretch of sand below her house. She pulls off her running gear and her shoes, dives into the waves in her swimsuit. She swims out a couple of hundred metres. Looks back towards where the sun is starting to crest above the mountain range, fifty kilometres inland. The morning rays reflect gold in her eyes, the water calm, the skies clear. It's going to be a stunning west-coast day.

This part of the coast can be a wild, tormented place. Over the millennia the prevailing onshore winds have whipped the iron-rich sands inland, forming rolling dunes as far as the eye can see. The green and silver grasses are backlit this morning by the first shafts of the new sun, a dramatic contrast to the black of the sand. A kilometre further north along the coast the big trees start, their early morning silhouettes like a line of old men marching along in arthritic pain, vertebrae twisted and hunched by the centuries of wind. The effect is majestic, like a baroque artist at the height of their gifts designed this place, rather than the random acts of brutal, unstoppable nature that actually did the job.

A lot of New Zealand feels the same.

Hana floats in the water. The twenty-minute lull before and after sunrise is her favourite time of the day. All year round, growing up here, she used to come down and plunge into the dawn waves; swimming in the middle of winter would usually be jump in and jump out, but it would be enough to give her a blood rush that lasted for hours. This time of year, now the ocean is warming, she's in no hurry to go back to shore, though dawn and twilight are also the times when the big animals of the ocean are in hunting mode and pose the greatest danger to humans. Sharks are out there all around this country; not in nearly the same numbers as in the warmer waters of Australia, but they're there. Statistically, almost every other way a healthy, fit woman in her late thirties can die is way more likely, Hana figures. She'll take her chances. If she becomes the victim of a great white on this stretch of beach, at least her final act will be to give nutrition to an endangered species.

She kicks her way back to shore. On the beach she rubs handfuls of black sand onto her shoulders, arms and legs, smoothing it more gently onto her neck and face. A mineral-rich exfoliant, the kind of skincare she might pay the equivalent of a week's groceries for back in the city, but scooped up here free of charge. After quitting the cops six months before – after Hana wrote her letter of resignation, handed in her detective senior sergeant ID, cleared her desk and took the elevator down from the eighth floor of Central Police Station in Auckland for the last time – she made a decision. She came back to this place where she grew up, found a home to rent just a few hundred yards from her dad Eru's house. Every morning since, she's run the roads and hills of the small town, swum in these waters. Scrubbed her skin with iron-laden sands.

One more plunge into the waves to rinse off the sand. Then she heads to her house.

Hana pauses, as she always does, at the concrete memorial constructed at the base of the dunes, well above the high waterline. It's simple, beautiful. A concrete cross with one word.

PAIGE

Hana brushes sand away from the memorial. She was in her second to last year of high school when Paige Meadows was murdered, twenty-one years ago; Hana was a year behind Paige. It was an early insight for her, one that was only reinforced when she left her little town to become a cop in the big city: compared to attacks by aquatic wildlife, you've got much more chance of dying due to the actions of a fellow human. In a car crash, say. From diseases caused by the greed of big tobacco and alcohol businesses.

Or, as with Paige, murdered.

She was strangled, her body found in a shallow grave in the sand dunes. The crime was quickly solved but it remained an awful, lingering scar for the local community.

Hana places a shining white shell at the base of the cross, adding it to other little treasures that locals have left. Shards of ocean glass made round-edged and translucent by years in the waves, a pretty starfish washed ashore, a piece of driftwood the shape of a heart.

Hana heads up through the silver and green grasses towards her house.

'Tīmoti. Bro, we're all waiting.'

A half dozen local Tātā Bay teenagers and kids in their early twenties are gathered in the rugby field across the fence from the marae.* Hana and her dad Eru get to the marae early every morning, put out a bunch of bright orange road cones around the rugby field to make an obstacle course. It's a project they instigated soon after she returned. Hana uses her own car, and she and Eru prepare young locals to get their drivers licences. Pretty much every one of the students knows how to drive already; it's rural New Zealand. Try and stop any fourteen-year-old from pestering their older siblings to let them drive down to the river for a swim, or go do doughnuts on the hard black sands when the tide's out. But there's a world of difference between knowing how to drive and actually getting a licence that lets you do it legally.

Tīmoti is seventeen years old. Lanky, with some DIY tatts and a carefully shaved mullet. He's the son of Hana's second cousin, Ngahuia. Ngahuia got the nickname 'Eyes' as a kid, because hers were so huge and soulful, and the name has stuck ever since.

Growing up, Eyes and Hana were close, but a rift formed in their teenage years, and has only grown wider since. Eyes regards Hana disparagingly as the cousin with the airs and graces. The flash one who took off from their small hometown the moment she

---

* Marae – the communal buildings and meeting place of a tribe.

could and went and got a big job in the big city, forgetting about the ones she left behind. When Hana came back, after quitting the cops, Eyes wasn't inclined to revise her opinion of her cousin or embrace her return. Just the opposite. Hana had left it to those like Eyes to be the ahi kā, the ones who keep the home fires burning. Now she thinks she can swan back in and enjoy the warmth? Whenever there's an event on the marae or a family get-together, or even if she and Eyes pass on the tiny main street, Hana is painfully aware of her cousin's frostiness.

And the familial tension has rubbed off on Eyes' son.

'I know how to drive already.'

Tīmoti leans against the rugby posts, his expensive-looking basketball boots tapping on the ground. The impatient rhythm is a message for Hana. He would rather be pretty much anywhere than at these driving lessons.

'I know you do, and you're a good driver,' Hana says, patiently. It's a conversation that happens with Tīmoti every day. That is, the days he turns up. 'But you don't have a licence. What happens when a cop pulls you over?'

The easy thing would be to tell him if he doesn't want to be here, go home. But for Hana, someone like Tīmoti is exactly the reason to do this. For young Māori in small rural areas with little employment like Tātā Bay, being able to drive means being able to get to where you need to in order to study, if that's your thing, or to find work on a farm or on one of the big forestry operations in the nearby towns. Getting busted for driving illegally, especially if you're driving an unlicensed or unwarranted vehicle, which is almost always the only car most young drivers can afford, means fines you can't pay. If it happens again, more fines you'll default on, and you risk losing your vehicle. In a place like Tātā Bay, a drivers' licence is much more than a licence. It's a passport to employment, to qualifications; to a life.

'Those fellas wanna do it. Let them,' Tīmoti says to Hana, gesturing dismissively with his restless basketball boot towards the others. 'This is their idea of fun. Not mine.'

Tīmoti left school the previous year. Hana has noticed he's not friendly with any of the others in the group. In the mornings when they arrive, Tīmoti always sits on his own; when the others are hanging out or laughing, he's on his phone texting. Hana assumes he has his own mates, a girlfriend perhaps. It's clear he thinks of the others in the group as losers, and the feeling is reciprocated.

When Eru asked his niece to enrol Tīmoti in the course, she was offhand. 'That daughter of yours, eh. Trying to be the bigshot again,' Eyes said. Eru isn't a man with a sharp tongue. But he was sharp with Eyes. Tīmoti had been pulled over by the cops a few months earlier for unlicensed driving, resulting in a fine Eyes struggled to pay. Eru told his niece he didn't care what raruraru* the cousins had with each other, he wanted her boy there at the driving course.

Watching the interaction taking place beside the rugby posts, Eru steps forward, puts a firm hand on Tīmoti's shoulder.

'The others will get their turn, nephew. Let's get you back in the car.'

When Hana's father speaks, Tīmoti's reaction is very different to when she is trying to talk to him. Eru is in his late sixties. Long, flowing silver hair under a battered felt bushman's hat. Hana inherited his smile, and his demeanour. Both of them calm, neither father nor daughter is the kind who fills silence with chatter. Eru is quietly spoken, but when he speaks it is with authority. He's an elder on the marae, and the attitude Tīmoti gives out to Hana disappears when Eru talks to him.

'Okay,' Tīmoti says, begrudgingly. 'Sweet, matua.'†

As Eru heads back to the marae to prepare lunch for the students, Tīmoti gets behind the steering wheel. Hana sits in the passenger seat. It's a parallel parking exercise, one set of cones representing a parked car, a second set of cones another vehicle. There's enough space between them to pull in.

---

* Raruraru – conflict, argument.

† Matua – term of respect for an older man.

Tīmoti drives the orange cone route around the rugby field. Pulls up next to one set of cones. He reverses, judging the distance perfectly, straight into the space without needing any back-and-forth. *Beep*, a text alert goes off in his pocket. Hana watches him thumb a reply and press send before he looks at her.

'All good?' he asks.

'Very good.'

'Told you.'

'Except you just failed the test. Twice.'

'Bullshit. What'd I do wrong?'

'You didn't indicate. And you used your phone. One strike, you're out. That was two. The assessors don't let you get away with anything.'

'I drove fine.' His foot bounces against the brake pedal. The rhythm faster now. Frustrated. He's starting to get angry.

'Tīmoti, it's nothing to be worried about. This is the time to make mistakes. That way you won't do it in the test. Let's go around again.'

'Let's not.'

He gets out of the car. Goes and sits under the goal-posts, his phone in his hand. Texting whoever he's texting. And Hana knows, that's all she's going to get from him for the rest of the day.

'Grandpa, tell PLUS 1 your stories. About Grandma Jos.'

A picnic is laid out on blankets down on the sands below Hana's house. Hana's daughter Addison and her best buddy PLUS 1 have come prepared: they've splashed out, nice cheeses and olives and crackers. Addison turned eighteen in the months since her mother left the cops and moved back to Tātā Bay, and she and PLUS 1 are renting Hana's house in the city. They're both at university, writing music together and playing gigs. They've released a few songs that are starting to get attention. And they've got a new project: a puppy called Boca, currently wobbling around the sand dunes, her paws still way too big for her body.

Boca is a rescue puppy of wildly indeterminate parentage; her head suggests a Staffy whakapapa,* her body and fur resemble a golden Labrador, and her oversized front legs have the ranginess of a Boxer. Her face is what made PLUS 1 and Addison fall in love with her. The black lines around her eyes look like really well-applied eyeliner, with little wings at the edges. And Boca is one of those dogs whose mouth naturally forms a friendly smile, whatever they might actually be feeling, so it's pretty much guaranteed that no one will ever be able to tell the amiable-looking animal off, no

---

* Whakapapa – genealogy, line of descent.

matter what she does. Like peeing everywhere, all the time, which is what Boca has been doing for the last few days. PLUS 1 and Addison are pretty sure it's a urinary tract infection.

It's a bit of a journey from Auckland city to Tātā Bay – a two-hour drive in a good car, with no distractions. They've inherited a particularly crappy old car from PLUS 1's big brother, and a couple of months after getting her licence, Addison still isn't the most confident driver. The trip today took even longer, Boca needing to stop every half hour or so for a pee, and more than once they didn't pull over in time to prevent an accident on the back seat.

Now, on the blankets on the sands, Addison sits cross-legged, her head smooth and clean-shaven, the way she's liked it for the past few years. She smiles, hand in hand with Eru.

There's a bit of a pang for Hana, seeing her daughter's fingers entwined with Eru's. Hana can't remember the last time her daughter held her hand. It would be entirely normal for a mother and daughter to walk hand in hand in lots of places. In Italy, for instance; in many Islamic cultures; South America. It doesn't happen so much with New Zealanders, and Hana feels that's a bit of a shame. It seems like the simple act of holding hands would be a way of expressing the aching love she feels for her daughter that 'Love you xx' at the ends of text messages just can't capture.

'The story about the gun,' Addison implores her grandfather.

'Addison's grandmother was the most capable person I've ever met,' Eru tells PLUS 1 as they pass around the food. 'Jocelyn could fix a carburettor. Had a two-octave vocal range.'

'Two octaves, Mum! The DNA skipped you, and Grandma handed it straight down to me.'

'I can sing,' Hana says.

'You can harmonize. Me and Grandma Jos are the leads.'

'Hey!'

Addison can't get enough of her grandfather's stories about the grandmother she only barely remembers; Jocelyn passed away of an undiagnosed arterial weakness when her granddaughter was very young. Mostly what Addison remembers is her laugh and her sparkling cobalt-blue eyes.

As the sun goes down Eru tells the stories Addison loves, about the pretty nurse he met when he was shipped back from Vietnam, injured, with a badly smashed leg that was reconstructed but still plays up on cold days. How the nurse turned out to be not only pretty, but his equal in most things, and more than his equal in many others.

'When my leg healed up, we took her deer-hunting, me and my brother. We thought she'd last thirty minutes tops and want to go home. We were out for six hours. Didn't get a deer, but when we did target practice with pinecones, she was by far the best shot. Put us both to shame. And—'

Addison and Hana join in with the final sentence they've both heard so many times. 'And she never let anyone forget it.'

Addison hugs Eru, laughing. 'These are the olives you like, right, Grandpa? And I made the hummus for you, from scratch.'

Eru piles hummus onto a piece of bread. He shoots a sideways glance at PLUS 1 as he eats. 'Gender non-binary. Have I got that right?'

PLUS 1 grins at Addison. It's another conversation that happens every time they get together, and PLUS 1 actually relishes it. A lot of PLUS 1 and Addison's friends' parents aren't at all sure how to approach the topic of gender, the minefield of which pronouns to use. And for most of their generation's grandparents it's downright bewildering, so the topic is avoided like it's a discussion about a disease, not about gender identity. PLUS 1 adores the fact that Eru just dives on in. Even if he dives on in in the exact same way every time.

'Yep. Non-binary, Mr Westerman. Same as last time.'

'Non-binary sounds kind of flexible. Like you might change your mind. Does that mean next week you might decide to be him? Or her?'

'Grandpa! That's not how it works.'

Addison and PLUS 1 are both laughing now. Hana

too, knowing that after Eru learned about PLUS 1 he took the time to do serious research online and fill in all the gaps in his knowledge; he understands exactly what a non-binary orientation is.

'When we meet next time,' Eru says, not ready to leave the subject alone just yet, 'do we shake hands? Kiss? Press noses?'

'We could do all three,' PLUS 1 suggests. 'Bump asses, if you want. Why choose?'

Eru barks a laugh, the kind of guffaw that makes everyone within hearing distance smile. Alarmed by the unexpected explosion of human noise, Boca climbs up onto Hana's lap.

Eru looks thoughtful for a moment. 'You know, I've still got my gun. They let me keep it after the war. Or maybe I forgot to mention I had it. Next time you're down, I'll take you two shooting.'

'We're pescatarian, Grandpa.'

'That's different to non-binary?'

Eru is poker-faced. Everyone else is giggling.

'We eat fish, not things with legs. We're not going to shoot a deer.'

'My days of killing animals are long gone,' Eru reassures them. 'We'll bring fire and fury down on a bunch of empty spaghetti cans lined up on a log.'

'Hell yeah,' PLUS 1 says, buzzing with excitement at the idea.

Out to sea, the sun is cut clean in half by the horizon.

Everyone's faces are drenched in the last warm yellow rays. Hana starts to pack away the picnic.

'Twenty minutes till dark. We should head home.'

Walking back through the dunes, as Eru describes the workings of a New Zealand Army rifle in far more detail than PLUS 1 will ever conceivably need, Hana falls into step beside Addison.

'The new living arrangements,' she says quietly, testing the waters on something she's been trying to work out since Addison and PLUS 1 moved in together. 'When I'm not up visiting, do you keep one of the rooms empty, for recording music, or ... ?'

Addison tries not to roll her eyes. The attempt isn't successful. 'You're asking, are we sleeping together?'

'The question was about music.'

'Oh my God, Mum, you're so transparent. No, it wasn't.'

'Answer whatever question you want to answer,' Hana says.

Boca is off the leash, trotting along with her easily distracted puppy navigational skills, doing her best to stay out from underneath people's feet.

'Stan came around the other day. He dropped off the bag of groceries you got him to pick up for us. But it was obvious he was just there to keep an eye out and report back to you.'

Hana knows she's busted. But she's unapologetic. 'If I wasn't interested, you'd be hurt.'

They lapse into silence as they continue walking. A few weeks earlier a big cyclone had rolled in, straight off the ocean, colliding with the Tātā Bay coastline. Hana had gone over to Eru's place. They cancelled the driving lessons and sat all day drinking hot chocolate, playing Monopoly and watching the broken vertebrae of the old man trees take yet another pounding. One tree came down in the storm. A bunch of sand dunes got eroded pretty badly.

As they head through one particularly beaten-up section of beach, Boca gets a burst of energy, taking off through the damaged landscape. Addison hands the picnic basket she's carrying to Hana.

'I'm a grown-up. PLUS 1 as well. You gotta cut the umbilical cord sometime.'

'The expression is apron strings.'

Addison kisses her mother. 'Stay interested, Mum. It's sweet. Except when it gets stifling.'

Hana watches as Addison hurries through the sand dunes after the puppy. Boca has decided it's the best game in the world to run further the more Addison calls. As her daughter disappears into the shadows behind a badly collapsed dune, Hana is no closer to knowing if she and PLUS 1 are living together, or *living together*. She looks out to the ocean. The sun gone, the last light fading in the sky. A seagull flies inland, heading ashore for a final scavenge around the village.

'*Mum?*'

Addison is calling her from somewhere deeper in the dunes. Hana hears the strain in her daughter's voice.

'Addison? Something wrong?'

'MUM. OH SHIT, MUM!'

Addison's evident alarm answers the question. Hana sprints in the direction of her shouting, to find her daughter standing before the far edge of a collapsed dune where something has been exposed from its lonely resting place in the black sands.

A human skeleton.

As PLUS 1 and Eru arrive, Hana looks at the bones. From the structure of the pelvic region, she can already tell the body was female.

And Hana sees something else.

There are the remnants of duct tape around the wrists and ankles. This death wasn't from natural causes.

Holding Boca in her arms like a baby, Addison stares down at the remains.

3

KARAKIA, HĪMENE

It's a clear, cold night in Tātā Bay. The beach is alive with battery-powered police floodlights.

Far beneath the black sand dunes lie the bones of dozens of warriors who fell centuries ago to the strike of a patu* or the thrust of a taiaha.† Before the arrival of the English on the tall ships, many deadly battles took place between rival Māori tribes contesting this region of the western coastline. Violent death has long been a visitor here; now it has made an unwelcome return.

'I miss you,' says Lorraine. 'We all do. The eighth floor isn't the same without you.'

---

* Patu – wooden club used in hand-to-hand warfare.
† Taiaha – carved, wooden fighting staff.

Hana is with two senior cops from the Auckland CIB*, where she worked until only a few months ago. Lorraine Delaney is Hana's age, and she holds the same rank as Hana did before she quit: detective senior sergeant. Jaye Hamilton is Hana's ex, in every sense of the word; he's her ex-husband, Addison's father. And he's her ex-boss, a detective inspector. When Addison discovered the bones, Hana immediately called Jaye. There's a small two-staff police station in a farming town some distance away, but she knew an unexplained death would immediately be pushed up the line to CIB investigators, so she cut out the middleman.

'Then again, since you bailed, I'm getting the good jobs,' Lorraine continues, smiling. 'So, thanks, mate. Don't come back any time soon.'

'No danger of that, Lorry.'

Hana and Lorraine have known each other from when they went through police college together, two women in a majority-male class entering a heavily male-dominated profession; there's still never been a female commissioner of police in New Zealand. Back then you could fit all the female detectives in the country into one medium-sized patrol van. In college and after graduation they were never exactly best mates. Hana, the young, ambitious small-town

---

* CIB – Criminal Investigation Branch, the section of the New Zealand police force that investigates serious crimes.

Māori woman. Blonde, blue-eyed Lorraine from a rough-round-the-edges South Auckland working-class Pākehā* family. But they had each other's backs. Over the years, in the rowdy police bars where the tough job of day-to-day law enforcement habitually turned into the consumption of way too much alcohol, young male cops with too many drinks under their belts would occasionally decide they must be the prize that Lorraine with her red lipstick or dark-eyed Hana had been waiting for. The women would try to defuse these situations with humour or with matching scary glares. More than once, when an unwelcome approach had continued, Hana and Lorraine had taken an arm each and hauled the wobbly young man in question out of the bar. As they rose up the ranks they remained cheerleaders for each other, and for the other women who were slowly changing New Zealand policing. When Hana resigned, Lorraine was the obvious choice to fill her role as the most senior investigating officer in Jaye's team.

The most intense concentration of floodlights is focused on the collapsed dune where the bones lie uncovered. Police photographers and SOCOs† examine the scene. A pathologist has arrived to see the remains in situ before they are removed for the post-mortem.

---

* Pākehā – New Zealander of non-Māori descent.
† SOCO – scene-of-crime officer.

Jaye and Lorraine wait with Hana, a distance from the site.

'It's good this is in safe hands,' Hana says. 'But you should know, this is going to be unwelcome news for the locals. Another woman murdered and dumped in the dunes.'

Both cops know about the young woman who was Hana's schoolmate, memorialized by the simple concrete cross overlooking the ocean.

'Paige Meadows was killed what, twenty years ago?' Lorraine asks.

'Twenty-one years. My second-to-last year at high school.'

'I remember you talking about it, at police college. The parents still live here?'

'They're just on the other side of the shops.'

Lorraine looks towards three streetlights, visible beyond the sand dunes, marking the total length of the small main street of Tātā Bay township.

'They're not going to welcome a cop knocking on their door,' she says. 'But I'd rather they didn't find out from the papers. Do us a favour?'

'I'll go see them first thing in the morning,' Hana assures Lorraine. She turns back towards where the SOCO staff are carefully sifting through the black sands surrounding the deceased.

'The remains don't look historic. The bones are intact, in good condition. To my eye, the body's been here maybe three to five years, max. What do you think?'

A glance between Jaye and Lorraine. It doesn't escape Hana's notice. She called them in, and they're her close former colleagues. But they are *former* colleagues. This is a police investigation, and Hana's no longer police. If she was Lorraine or Jaye, Hana knows this would be the point where she'd be saying, 'We'll let you get home,' or words to that effect.

The wind is rising. A few strands of Lorraine's blonde hair have blown loose and she captures them again, retying her bun into the slightly messy, tossed-together look that Hana knows is actually carefully planned, despite its casual appearance.

'Good to see you, Hana,' she says, heading back towards the floodlit dune. 'We'll let you get home.'

It's still an hour before dawn when the black shape of the hearse pulls into the car park at the edge of the sand dunes. When Jaye and Lorraine arrived earlier that evening, Eru told them that the locals would want to perform the necessary rituals of respect.

A low blanket of mist rolls in from the ocean as the body bag holding the remains is carried from the dunes and placed into the hearse, where Eru and another elder from the marae are waiting. Eru calls in all those present, the detectives and SOCO staff joining locals who have gathered. A semi-circle forms around the open rear door of the hearse. Eru speaks in te reo Māori,* acknowledging the land, the mountains, the ocean. Blessing the deceased, calling on her ancestors to welcome her spirit back into their care.

The elder finishes with a karakia,† half-spoken, half-chanted. When the prayer is finished, Addison takes her parents by the hand, leading Hana and Jaye to stand in front of the remains.

She starts to sing.

Tama ngākau mārie,
Tama a te Atua,
Tēnei tonu mātou,
Arohaina mai.‡

Others join her, their voices drifting through the slowly waving grasses, singing the mournful hīmene§ for the deceased.

Murua rā ngā hara,

---

* Te reo Māori – the Māori language.

† Karakia – prayer.

‡ 'Son of peace, Son of the Eternal, Here we are always, Show us compassion.'

§ Hīmene – hymn.

Wetekina mai,
Ēnei here kino,
Whakararu nei.*

As the hearse pulls away, Addison moves close to her mother. 'She was a she, Mum?'

Hana nods, *yes*. It was a woman.

'She was tied up. Someone murdered her. Is that what you think?'

'I think so, love.'

Addison keeps hold of her mother's arm, unsettled by the thought of the woman left cold and alone in a wind-swept unmarked grave.

---

* 'Wipe away our sins, And unshackle, The evils, That besiege us.'

4

EVIL AND WONDER

There's this park in Auckland, perched on a big hillside that looks out over the Harbour Bridge. In the middle of the park there's an outdoor swimming pool painted with kooky candy-stripes. They reckon in summertime you used to be able to climb the fence and swim at night, but there's barbed wire on top of the fence now, and security cameras and those guys who patrol in little white cars.

At some point, the world decided to ban fun.

I'm thinking it was probably about a day after I was born.

The park is full of pōhutukawa, these amazing trees with huge, twisted Lord of the Rings trunks and branches that explode into iridescent red flowers at Christmas. There's one particular family of pōhutukawa trees, a group of four on the edge of a rocky cliff face, that Trish and I adopted. Or maybe they adopted us. We'd sit in the circle of trunks for hours, laughing, smoking weed, playing music or just staring out through the branches as the sun went down. The city doesn't have stars, so we made our own stars from what we could see through the ancient branches. Lights from boats on the harbour, the glowing windows of the fancy houses across the water, the flashing beacons on top of the Harbour Bridge that stop helicopters flying into it.

It'd be awful if a helicopter flew into the Harbour Bridge.

But still. Imagine actually seeing that happen.

I like pōhutukawa. They've got to be the most resilient, undefeatable creatures in the entire tree world. These trees are cockroaches; you can't kill them. They grow in places it should be impossible to grow – on top of stony outcrops, their roots burrowing down through tiny cracks in the rocks. Or literally emerging sideways out of a sheer cliff, clinging on like a twenty-metre leech, the big trunks growing horizontal, defying the laws of gravity and physics, then twisting upwards to reach for the sun.

Tell a pōhutukawa, 'Don't grow here,' the pōhutukawa says, 'Go fuck yourself.'

Me and Trish are like those trees.

We find any available cracks in the rock. Burrow in. Grab hold.

Trish looks like porcelain. She's so white, she shines. Whiter than her own teeth. So white, I worry that looking at her might break my retinas, like staring at the sun.

After Dax did what Dax did, I found Trish. She's got a car, from when she worked the till at McDonalds for three entire years. No wonder she took drugs. Didn't take me long to hunt down one of the oily dudes I used to buy from. I bought two hits with the $100 from the jar by Dax's bed, there to prove he could resist temptation.

Couldn't resist fucking another girl though, could he?

Thanks for everything, Dax. I'm resisting putting a knife in your brain.

Just.

We drove to the car park outside the candy-stripe swimming pool. Went to our place among the tree family. Trish had rap on her speaker. Rap is all she listens to, which is kind of odd given how she looks. Opposites attract, again. The sun went down. Night-time belongs to Whiro-te-tipua, the God of Darkness. He's the guy responsible for all the evil shit that happens. In my limited experience, I've found that to be true. Bad stuff happens at night.

My mum and dad's car crashed at night. Dax and me broke up at night.

I died at night.

Whiro has a lot to answer for.

I'm happy to let that particular god stay being a guy.

We sat among our pōhutukawa, listening to lily-white Trish's rap, as the God of Darkness did his thing. And I did my thing. I put the two hits on the ground between us. One resting on a big old pōhutukawa root by Trish, one by me. The glass pipe I'd bought for an extra twenty between them. Trish looked at the drugs.

'We don't need this, girl,' she said. 'We don't need this stuff to be happy.'

I knew what she was saying. Both of us worked like mules to get past the drugs. To leave them behind. But somehow, knowing that we'd defeated rock, that we'd beaten it once and we could beat it again, that made it all okay. For me anyway.

And actually, right then, I needed it. More than oxygen.

'I'm gonna have a taste,' I told her, picking her hit up and putting it back in my pocket. 'You're right. You don't need this, Trish. I forbid you.'

After months sober, I flicked the lighter. Heated the pipe. Breathed deep.

They reckon there's nothing like the first time. The first taste. They're wrong.

I felt big god hands gently scoop me up. They lifted me high over the barbed wire and lowered me slowly into the candy-striped pool. The water exactly the right temperature, clear and perfect. Gentle bubbles rose up to welcome me, cloaking my shins, my thighs, my belly button, my torso, rising over my chin, my eyes.

And I was gone. Lost in the wonder.

Whiro-te-tipua has a House of Death.

A lightless, deep cave.

All evil things reside there.

In my experience, evil and wonder are quite hard to tell apart.

It wasn't drugs that killed me.

In case you're wondering.

It was a person.

5

A STAR FOR OUR STAR

In the photo, Paige is smiling.

She's wearing a slightly bonkers orange wig, backlit by a strong stage light, making the curls absolutely pop, the colour of a carotene-enhanced vitamin supplement. At a small cash-strapped school like Tātā Bay College the budget for the end-of-year production didn't run to professional hairpieces or costumes, and it could have all ended up looking a bit embarrassing, a low-rent retelling of a slightly cheesy, very American story of a little girl and her dog who hold fast to hope, against all odds. But cast in the lead role of Annie, Paige committed completely. She threw herself in at the deep end, and Hana remembered how, as she watched that end-of-year performance, Paige's sweet voice and her confidence and charm meant that she completely forgave the cheap wig and found herself dragged unexpectedly into the emotion of the story.

'You remember the dog in the show?' Paige's father asks Hana. 'It was her dog. Levi. Every performance, the dog trots out onto the stage. The whole audience goes nuts. Our girl's singing her heart out, hitting all those big notes. The dog just stands there doing what dogs do. It wags its tail. It drools. And it gets all the cheers. Drove me crazy.'

The picture of Paige is blown-up, mounted in a big white frame and hung on the wall opposite the front door. It's the first thing anyone sees when they walk into the house. Hana gets that. Losing a child is something that irrevocably changes any family's life, and is made all the more difficult when the loss is the result of an awful act of violence. Having that loss meet people the moment they arrive can get the difficult conversations out of the way. An easy and natural invitation for those entering the house to embrace the parents, to give sympathy, to acknowledge and empathize, and then to move on past the picture, and allow the conversation to move on from the past.

'She spent hours with Levi, every night, out on the back lawn,' Paige's mum tells her. 'For weeks before the show. She had the soundtrack playing on her Walkman, getting Levi to keep his eyes on her as she sang. She'd sing all the big numbers. Give the dog treats. So when Levi got on stage with her, he wasn't going to start howling or turn around and stare at the audience.'

After Hana had brought the unwelcome news of another death in the dunes, Paige's parents had immediately reached for each other's hands. They've stayed like that the whole time since, frozen beside their daughter's photo. Hana knows grieving couples can handle the aftermath of tragedy very differently. Going through the unspeakable, the unimaginable, the unbearable. Losing a child. It can forge a relationship like iron in the hottest furnace. Or it can be the start of a long, slow drift apart: two people who aren't sure how to cry together, who learn to hold their grief somewhere inside and only live it when they are alone in the shower or sitting solitary in the car on the drive to work. Struggling to share their pain with each other. Then not even trying. The solitary grieving eventually spreading out through the relationship, choking it like an invasive weed chokes a lawn. Not sharing grief, then not sharing laughter, then not sharing a bed.

'After it happened,' Paige's dad says, his voice unsteady. 'After we lost her. Levi spent a week not moving from Paige's bed. He wouldn't move away from the smell of her, on her pillows. We had to put a water bowl and food on the bed. He drank the water. But he wouldn't eat. We thought we were going to have to take him to the vet, have him force-fed. Then one morning,

Levi climbed down. He walked out into the backyard. And that was that.'

'He came back out into the world,' Paige's mum adds. 'He decided it was time to move on.' Their words trail away. Their hands clasp tighter still. Hana knows what is left unspoken in the silence.

Paige's parents have survived. But they have never moved on from their daughter's death, not in the way Levi was able to, and they never will.

'The man that did it,' Paige's dad finally says, his voice hard with anger. 'If Levi had been with her that night. If she'd taken him running. Levi would have gone for the guy. He would've taken him apart before he let that bastard touch a hair on her head. I don't wish ill on anyone. But there's karma in how he died.'

Paige's mother moves closer to her husband in the cramped hallway. In Paige's photo there's a silver bracelet around her wrist, far more delicate and subtle than the wig. An interlocked chain, with a small star hanging from it.

'We gave her that bracelet before the first performance,' she says. 'A star for our star. When they found her, the bracelet was gone. We searched the dunes a hundred times. Never found it. It was the last present we ever gave her.'

Hana knows they won't cry in front of her. They won't burden her with that.

But they will cry together when she's gone.

Driving away from the house, Hana thinks about Paige's death. She wasn't friends with Paige, particularly – they both ran with their own crowds – but Hana and her parents dropped off food for the other girl's family in the hours after she disappeared. The whole town formed search and rescue teams, and within a day a group of locals found the disturbed area of sand in the dunes.

Hana remembers watching the police investigation from afar; all those cops on the beach, some in uniforms, some in plainclothes. Doing their jobs efficiently, silently, methodically. The police team was almost all men, mostly white. It was a pivotal moment. None of them looked like her. Why? The first murmur of an idea had formed.

'I could do that.'

The cops determined that Paige had been strangled and they got to the murderer quickly. A man with a history of convictions for violence. Hana tries to remember the name. A Māori guy, not local, but someone who had ended up in the area after walking away from the gang he was affiliated with. She remembers when the case went to trial, the guy offered no defence. But he apologized to the family and the community.

The report in the papers said he cried during the apology.

Less than a year later he died in prison.

Hana pulls into the small Tātā Bay dairy,* picking up milk and bread, like she always does; an order for her and an order for her dad.

As she pays for her shopping, the bell rings. Another customer enters. The woman behind the counter, an Indian immigrant, noticeably stiffens. Hana looks towards the door. It's someone she's seen in passing: a Pākehā guy with not much height, five seven on a good day, a bit taller in the big boots he always wears. A full beard. Cut-off denim shirt, even in winter, that showcases two arms of inelegant tattoos – FTW, skulls and daggers. And a lot of attitude. Hana knows him as Erwin Rendall; her dad talked about him turning up in town a few years earlier, intimidating locals, generally being a pain in the arse.

Hana watches as Rendall grabs an armful of groceries and walks out without paying. The dairy owner stays behind the till, a protective hand keeping her daughter behind her. She catches Hana's eye.

'It's all right,' the owner says. 'It doesn't matter.'

Hana can see this has happened before; the woman isn't going to do anything. She is completely intimidated. Hana isn't. She grabs her purchases and hurries out the door.

'Excuse me.'

---

* Local convenience store.

Rendall's behind the wheel of his big Mark III Zephyr, a noisy gas-guzzler, ready to drive off. Hana barrels straight up to the car, knocks on the driver's window. There are others in the vehicle, three young men, all staring at her.

'Are you paying for that stuff you took?'

Rendall gets out. Leans on the car, a smile on his face. He knows who Hana is.

'The big hero who hunted down the crazy serial killer.' He moves closer, getting in her breathing space, expecting she'll be as intimidated as the dairy owner. 'I guess the sheriff's ridden back into town.'

Hana stands her ground.

'You can afford petrol for this thing, you can afford to pay that family what you owe them. Don't be an arsehole.'

The smile doesn't leave Rendall's face. He takes a $50 note out of his pocket.

'I don't see a badge on you now,' he says.

He tosses the money on the ground at Hana's feet. Without another word he gets back in the car, and with a squeal of tyres the Zephyr drives off, passing the WELCOME TO TĀTĀ BAY sign, heading out of town.

Hana picks up the money and takes it in to the dairy owner.

6

BLOOD MAKES YOU TOUGH

There's a quote stencilled on the wall above the main boxing ring in the gym. It's been there for years, and the big black letters are fading a little.

**BLOOD MAKES YOU TOUGH
SWEAT MAKES YOU STRONG
TEARS MAKE YOU HUMBLE**

The boxing gym is old school. It's been a feature of the community for decades here in Māngere, a noisy, diverse suburb twenty kilometres south of the well-heeled houses of central Auckland. The leather hit zones of the big 90kg hanging punching bags are discoloured and worn, even more than the ceiling-to-floor mirrors, many of which have good-sized cracks running through them. No matter how often you clean, mop and spray a boxing gym, an echo of the past lingers, ingrained in the essence of the place; a faint odour left in the air from all those who have pounded bags and skipped rope and sparred and spilt sweat and blood here.

'So good to see you guys.'

Lorraine Delaney sits on a hard plastic seat in front of the main ring, facing a small group of young men and women. Around the group, there's surprise at the tears forming in Lorraine's eyes. This woman they all knew as a powerhouse, take-no-shit detective senior sergeant. Is she actually about to cry, sitting in front of them?

'I'm sorry. I'm really sorry,' she says. 'I thought this was going to be okay, but . . .'

'What's going on, miss?' one of the young men asks.

Lorraine makes sure her voice is steady before she speaks.

'I've got news about Kiri.'

A few hours after the remains were removed from the dunes, the pathologist advised Jaye and Lorraine that the deceased was most likely a younger woman, perhaps late teens or at most mid-twenties. She confirmed Hana's belief that the remains had been buried relatively recently, within the last five years. There were only a handful of long-term-missing young women in that age group who'd disappeared from the greater Auckland region in recent years. As the files for those cases were pulled, Jaye took Lorraine aside.

'You need to prepare yourself,' he told her. 'It could be Kiri.'

Four years before, a seventeen-year-old Māori woman had disappeared without trace from a car park in central Auckland. Her parents had died in a traffic collision when she was still a baby, and in her mid-teens Kiri Thomas drifted away from her adoptive family and into the city's underworld – drugs and petty crime and sex work. Inevitably, she came to the attention of the cops for theft and possession. She was offered a place in a Youth at Risk programme that Lorraine and a committed team of social workers and dependence counsellors were piloting; a last chance for participants to address their drug use and their offending and avoid entering the justice system.

When Lorraine developed the idea of the programme, the gym owned by her father was always a key part of the equation. Lorraine's dad was a legend in the Māngere boxing community, someone who had supported many young South Aucklanders chasing a dream of strapping on gloves and fighting their way to glory. Over the years, fighters he'd trained had won national titles. Two had competed at the Olympics. The mindset he hammered into his boxers was also ingrained in his daughter, who grew up seeing the big motto on the wall before she could even read the words.

BLOOD MAKES YOU TOUGH

'Tough love' was what many of Lorraine's colleagues called her approach. But it was just Lorraine putting into action the things she'd learned at her father's side from when she'd first been brought into the gym in a baby basket. For almost all of the young people, the programme had real results.

Then Kiri Thomas disappeared.

The funding for the programme was nearly at an end; with tightening budgets, no amount of determination could secure the money to keep going. Then, after the awfulness of Kiri going missing without trace, the air went out of the balloon. The programme was disbanded. The mysterious disappearance of the bright young woman affected a lot of people, especially the counsellors and social workers and cops who had worked with her and passionately believed they could help Kiri turn things around.

'I've felt sick in my gut all day,' Lorraine said to Jaye, quietly. 'I think it's her.'

Later on that afternoon, they were at the forensic

odontologist's office when the dental records of the five missing young women were compared to dental radiographs taken of the remains found in the sand dunes. The deceased had small fillings in the upper-right first and second molars, a larger filling in the lower-left first molar. The ondontologist confirmed: it was an exact match to one of the missing girls.

Kiri.

'I can transfer the investigation to another detective,' Jaye told Lorraine as they drove back to the station. 'If it's too close, too difficult.'

But Lorraine was adamant.

'It is close. That's why I have to do this, Jaye. I tried to help her. What happened, happened on my watch. If I can do right by her now, I'm going to do it.'

The former members of the Youth at Risk programme gathered in Lorraine's family's gym are now early to mid-twenties, the age Kiri would have been. Some continue to struggle with drug and alcohol problems, but most have stayed away from the attention of the police and the court system. Some of them are in training, one is at university, others are doing apprenticeships.

The girl who was Kiri's best friend, Trish, has a little boy of her own, who she loves to bits. And there's the young man known as Dax. Kiri's ex-boyfriend. Lorraine keeps a careful eye on Dax and Trish as she speaks, knowing how especially hard this will be for these two.

'You might have heard on the news that remains were found yesterday, buried in sand dunes. A little place called Tātā Bay, two hours down the coast. I'm so sorry. It was Kiri.'

Trish starts to cry, silently, trying not to wake her little boy, asleep in her arms. Around the group, people reach out, take each other's hands. Dax looks straight ahead, not meeting anyone's eye.

'It's four years on,' Lorraine says. 'Back then, you all told us everything you knew. I'm not expecting miracles here. But if there's anything that's happened since, anything you've heard, rumours, whispers. Anything at all. It might feel like it's nothing. But nothing is all we have right now. I want to do better than that for Kiri.'

Dax's fingers grip the hard plastic of his chair. 'Miss. How the fuck did she get out there?'

'I don't know. But I'm going to find out.'

Even though each of them has a lifetime's practice being tough and staunch, everyone is crying now. Surrounded by the raw emotion, Lorraine stops fighting. Tears fall down her cheeks.

'I'm so proud of you. All of you. Where you've got to. I think Kiri would be proud too.'

'Don't.' Dax can't bear it anymore. He stands up. 'Please don't cry. You shouldn't be crying, miss. You gave us all our best shot. You gave Kiri her best shot. What happened isn't on you. What happened was 'cos of me.'

'Shut up, Dax,' Trish says, her boy starting to stir in her arms. Everyone knows what Dax means. Why he blames himself for what happened to Kiri and will do so forever. But Trish isn't having it. 'Some pervert took her and probably raped her and killed her,' she continues. '*We didn't do it*. It's just as much my fault. I didn't stop her doing rock again. We can't carry that shit, not me, not you, none of us. It's not ours to carry.'

No one is even trying to be tough anymore. Lorraine embraces each of the group, holding them, drying eyes, kissing wet cheeks. She gives each of them her card.

'If there's anything you think of, anything you remember, anything that could be important. Call me.'

Dax is the last one Lorraine embraces. He's an employee of her father's gym now. After falling in love with the physical training regimes that Lorraine put them through, he kept working hard on his strength and fitness after the programme was shut down. A few months later he plucked up the courage to ask Lorraine's dad if he was good enough to get a part-time job as a trainer. Within a year Dax was full-time, and he's been working here ever since, a trusted employee, clean and sober.

'I still think of her every day,' he tells Lorraine.

'Me too.'

7

WE COULD HAVE BEEN FRIENDS

'They took a cast of my good leg. Had it modelled in Australia. It's still settling in. Hurt like hell wearing the thing to start off with, but the scars seem to be toughening up. Take a look.'

Outside Addison and PLUS 1's house, Stan rolls up his trouser leg to show them his new artificial limb. Where his leg was amputated, just below the knee, the casing of the new limb is flesh-coloured, with a shiny cylindrical titanium shank below, leading into an ankle joint and a life-like foot.

'It's a high-activity foot. Synthetic. Light and flexible but super strong. Touch it if you want.'

'Thanks for the offer,' Addison says. 'But that's a bit too intimate, Stan.'

'I'm happy just looking, too,' PLUS 1 quickly agrees.

In the last year and a half that Hana was in the CIB, Stan Riordan was her offsider, a junior detective in her team. Over the time they worked together, Addison and Stan would bump into each other when Stan picked Hana up or dropped her off. Stan isn't very much older than Addison, and they developed a feisty, teasing relationship. An irrepressibly cheeky little sister and her too-serious, slightly geeky big brother. Except, for Addison anyway, describing Stan as *slightly* geeky was giving him the benefit of the doubt.

'Only old men wear loafers,' Addison says now, looking at Stan's zip-up shoes, one on his surviving foot, the other on the artificial foot that has been cast to be the exact same size. 'Shame they couldn't give you a style transplant at the same time.'

Stan beams. He's proud of his new limb. Not in the way you might be show-offy about a shiny next-generation iPhone you've saved up for, say, or a new car. It's way more than that. High-activity prostheses are designed to be almost exact replicas of original appendages, with adjustable dynamic engineering intended to get users back as close to full mobility as possible. For Stan, the new foot is a passport to the life he desperately wants back.

'I'll be able to power-walk. Jog. Run. Jump a fence, climb up a rope wall. All the stuff I have to do, to get my badge back. The surgeon said it would be a year before I could even think about running, but me and my physio are going to show her. We'll do it in half the time. I've been working my arse off.'

On Hana's last case as a cop, as she and Stan closed in on the killer they were pursuing, a booby-trapped vehicle had exploded, taking off Stan's lower leg and nearly claiming his life. It had been several painful months of surgery and rehab before he could return to any kind of work. Now he's on desk duties, on the third floor of Auckland Central Police Station. It's going to be a long hard slog, getting back to the condition needed to pass the physical exams to be a detective again.

'Watch,' Stan says.

As Addison takes out her phone and turns on the camera, Stan walks down the street, fifty metres at a brisk gait, concentrating hard on making the limp as unnoticeable as possible. He turns. Clenches his teeth a little, knowing what's coming won't be comfortable. Then he sets off back towards the others, building to a medium-paced jog. He pulls up in front of the house and leans against PLUS 1's car, rubbing his leg.

'The scars get raw. And there's all kinds of muscles that have to remember their jobs. But I'm getting there. I'm gonna get there.'

He pulls a 'look at me' face at Addison's camera as she buttons off the video.

In the photo, Kiri's smile is dazzling. A burst of radiant energy, like the joy and life inside her is too big to be contained and is seeping out around the edges of her beaming smile.

'She's like a bottle of bubbly shaken up and about to pop. I bet she had the best laugh.'

Addison turns the photo, so Stan can see it better.

After the police identified Kiri Thomas as the young woman whose remains she found in the sand dunes, Addison spent hours reading and googling, trying to piece together Kiri's story from the hints in the media about a troubled young woman with dependence issues who was 'known to the police'.

Stan looks through the photos of Kiri that Addison printed out.

'Your mum told me what happened. Must've been tough.'

'You guys see worse every day.'

'Cops know what we're getting when we sign up,' Stan says. 'You were having a quiet picnic with your whānau.* I'm sorry that happened.'

---

* Whānau – family.

'Do they have any idea who did it?' PLUS 1 asks.

'Early days yet.'

'Code for, you're not allowed to tell us?' Addison asks.

'Code for, I'm not on the eighth floor anymore. I sit at a desk, processing search warrants, uploading digital data, doing searches of suspect records. I'm an office assistant with an incredibly expensive leg. Couldn't tell you anything even if I wanted to.'

Stan loosens the bindings of the prosthetic, his wound irritated by the fast jog.

'Lorraine's smart as hell,' he goes on. 'There's a reason they chose her as your mum's replacement. She'll work out who did it. This is personal for her.'

Stan had brought a half dozen pani popo, Samoan coconut cream doughnuts, from a little family bakery near where he gets his bus, the kind of sickly-sweet carbo-bomb he knows Addison and PLUS 1 love. As PLUS 1 takes a bite of theirs, Stan notices that Addison hasn't touched hers.

'Not hungry?' he asks.

In one particular photo, Kiri is wearing a blue-and-white cardigan. Big pāua-shell* buttons, crochet patches on the elbows.

'She was my age. It seems silly. But I feel like we could've been friends.'

---

* Pāua – native New Zealand abalone with a blue-green inner shell.

Addison puts down the photo. Looks at Stan.

'You don't have to do this, you know. Coming around, keeping tabs on me for Mum.'

'I'm not doing it for your mother.' Stan's face is a little red. Addison had forgotten how easy it is to embarrass him. 'Even if you give me a hard time, you and I are mates. I'm looking out for you all on my own.'

Addison wraps her uneaten pani popo in a tissue for Stan. 'For the bus ride home.'

'You can't eat on public transport.'

'Wear your police ID. They'll leave you alone.'

Stan tightens his prosthetic, for the walk to the bus stop.

'I'm gonna need some help with driving lessons,' he says. 'Get myself back behind the wheel, once I've got the foot more sussed.'

'If you're happy with practicing in the shittiest car in Auckland, I got your back,' PLUS 1 says, grinning.

Stan looks again at the photo lying in front of Addison, of Kiri in the blue-and-white cardigan.

'Sure you're okay, bro?' he asks her.

'I'm okay. You okay bro?'

Stan nods. *Yeah. I'm okay.*

He hugs them both and heads out the door.

There's a street not far from her house where Addison goes hunting for vintage clothing. There are three thrift shops in a row. Mostly it's the usual fare: beaten-up jeans, army ex-surplus coats, woollen hats. Cheap and cheerful garments looking for a good home. Ninety per cent of the time there's nothing you'd ever want to put on and post on Insta, unless you were being really ironic. But occasionally Addison finds a treasure; a designer-label jacket or a piece of jewellery that she just knows will look amazing, shining in the spotlights as she bounds around the stage.

In her dream, the shop doors are all closed and locked.

She pauses at one. In the window, a blue-and-white cardigan. Pāua-shell buttons. Patches on the elbows.

Addison keeps walking.

At the end of the street, a couple of hundred metres further on from the shops, there's an intersection with traffic lights. Addison can see someone standing on the pavement. Very still. Staring straight ahead. Waiting there for the red man to turn green. From this distance, Addison can't see the face. But she knows exactly who it is.

Ahead at the intersection, the rest of the world seems to be in fast motion. Cars and bikes and vans and buses zip past Kiri where she is standing, waiting for the lights to turn. Addison keeps walking, but there's no hurry; she somehow knows the red man isn't going to turn green. As the world keeps moving past in sped-up time, Addison reaches the intersection.

She stands there, next to Kiri.

Kiri doesn't notice Addison, or if she does, she doesn't show any sign. She looks straight ahead at the red man. Waiting for him to turn green.

But he doesn't, so Kiri stands there.

Waiting.

Unable to cross.

Addison wakes.

She's in PLUS 1's bed, where she crashed after they came back from having a cheap tofu laksa with a bunch of friends. PLUS 1 is watching her.

'You were breathing funny. Making those little noises like when you're concentrating hard on painting your toenails. What were you dreaming about?'

'The girl. Kiri.'

Addison rubs sleep from her eyes. Between them, their puppy Boca is flat on her back, paws splayed wide; the kind of sleeping pose you can only do when you completely love and trust those you are with.

'How is she?' Addison asks, rubbing the puppy's tummy.

'She hasn't peed so far. I think she's better.'

'Good girl.'

Addison gets up. Kisses PLUS 1 on their head.

'Love you babe,' she says.

Back in her room, Addison lies on her bed. The

photo of Kiri in her cardigan is Blu-tacked to the wall. Addison looks at her smile. A bottle of bubbly ready to pop.

So full of joy it's hard to keep in.

Waiting at the lights for the red man to go green, Kiri wasn't smiling.

Addison keeps her bedside lamp on.

She falls asleep looking at Kiri's face.

8

BESPOKE

Like they say, there's lots of ways to pluck a duck. At least, I think they say that.

Someone, somewhere, must've said it at least once.

There's lots of ways to fall off a bike. Lots of ways to slip and tumble down a mountain. Lots of ways to get caught in the current and find yourself swept downstream towards the vicious rocks. We get to the place we end up in our own unique ways. There's not a template. It's not one size fits all. I saw this sign in a fancy tailor's window once: 'Bespoke Clothing'. I googled it. It means 'Made for a single particular customer.'

It's a good word. I like that word. How I got where I got is bespoke.

My story is not an abuse story.

Don't get me wrong. Most people who end up

where me and Dax and Trish ended up – where all our mates ended up – for most of our kind, abuse is the alpha and omega. That was Trish's story. Her fucking dad, Jesus. Breaks my heart, and I'd break his neck if I had the chance. It was Dax's story for sure, pretty much everyone in his life did their best to fuck him up. It stuns me endlessly that he didn't end up more of a mess than he is. He's a survivor, Dax. Someone who lives that thing on the sign in the boxing gym.

Blood made Dax tough.

Dax could be an atua maybe. The god of finding a way to get by when the world keeps tossing crap at you. He'd also be the god of cheating shitheads. Two conflicting ideas can be true at the same time. It's called being human. But my story isn't Dax's story. It's not Trish's story.

It's not an abuse story. It's the opposite.

I grew up in a warm stable home. A mum and a dad who loved me. It's just, they weren't my mum and dad. My parents died in a crash when I was a little baby. The car seat that saved my life was the most expensive thing my real parents had bought in years. When I was told about the car seat, it just made me feel like I knew them so well, loved them so much, missed them like hell, even though I never knew them at all. Afterwards, after I got lucky and was saved by the baby seat my parents couldn't afford but bought anyway, I got lucky again. I was welcomed in by the perfect adoptive parents. I was cared for. Loved. Most people would count their lucky stars.

Seems I'm not most people.

There's a certain age where every kid becomes a nightmare. Even the cherubs and the baby saints. Count me in. I hit the speed-bump years, my early teens, and I hit that speed-bump hard. I got airborne, and I never found my way back to solid tarmac. I started pushing the boundaries. Then I pushed the boundaries more. And more. I made it into my own personal art form. It was like I was testing these people who loved me. Blood is thicker than water, right? I wanted to know if that was true. Could people who weren't my real parents truly love me like my real parents? The people who chose to love me, chose to take me into their lives – at the end of the day, I wasn't their blood. I had a brain-worm burrowing around in my skull, and it kept asking the question: how could these people with their DNA so different to mine ever love me like the two dead people who spent all that money they didn't have on a really good car seat?

It became my mission. Getting an A in English or scoring a try for girls' rugby – that stuff's easy when you've got a good brain and legs as strong as a pōhutukawa. Testing the strength of my adoptive family's love – that was the challenge I set myself. It was like those stress tests they do on iron foundation beams before they use them in the construction of a skyscraper, to make sure the building doesn't come tumbling down. That's what I was doing. Stress testing their love for me.

How much could I do before they didn't love me anymore?

What would it take to kill their love?

I was a nightmare, and looking in the rear-view mirror, I feel like a piece of shit. But it's a scientific fact that being a teenager is physiologically and psychologically pretty much exactly the same as having alien blood injected into your spinal fluid, and anyone who survives adolescence deserves a medal.

As you know, I didn't get a medal.

And I wasn't around long enough to realize that my adoptive family did love me.

They loved me like hell.

I ended up finding my way to another kind of belonging. I made a new family, on the streets. I found Dax. He was a dick, but he was endearing. And I found a replacement for my adoptive family's love.

Rock.

With a hit of rock, there's no puzzles, nothing to question. Nothing to unpick. No reason to ask if blood is thicker than water. No reason to ask anything.

RETURN TO BLOOD

No brain-worm. Rock is uncomplicated. Rock is simple.

No questions asked. Made just for you, ma'am. Bespoke.

9

HE DIDN'T DO IT

The area in front of the meeting house, the ātea, is paved with cobblestones, and Hana has had her eye on the weeds flourishing between them for quite a while. It's the place on the marae where visitors are formally welcomed, and she is determined to get the area looking shiny and new. She makes her way along the rows of carefully laid stones with a backpack weed sprayer. There's something soothing in the rhythm. Pumping the handle to build pressure, pulling the trigger, following one row of joins between the neatly arranged cobbles. Coming back along the next parallel line, then the next. Repetitive. Patterned. Predictable.

Kind of the opposite of what Hana's world used to be.

Hana's gift as a cop was to look at the situation in

front of her, to see the pattern, then to go further. To say, okay. That's what I'm seeing. That's the obvious. Those are the facts. But what else is going on here? What else could be going on? What am I not seeing? Or, more accurately, what more could I see, that I am not seeing now, if I just find the right way to look?

She got that from her dad. Eru taught her to draw, something they would do together. He showed her how to hold the pencil lightly between her fingers, the way she does to this day; so lightly that when she draws, the action of the pencil meeting the page is more floating than pushing. When you hold the pencil like that, Eru told Hana, it's at least as much about the subconscious flexes of the hand as about the conscious decisions you are making. It's instinct as much as planning. A direct line between what your eyes are seeing and what your hand is drawing, almost unmediated by front-of-brain thought.

Eru would tell Hana, when you're drawing something, start with the surface. Then go further. If you're drawing the ocean, try and feel what lies beneath. The anger and power on a wild day, like the days Tātā Bay gets so often. Or the stillness and warmth of the water on a day of summer calm.

'That's what you want to draw, bub.'

Same with drawing a person. The skin, the hair, the colour of the eyes, the bone structure. They're the facts you're presented with. But there's always more than the facts. To truly draw a person, you have to look deeper. See what they are feeling, the things they are telling you with the set of their eyes or the tightness of their lips, the things they are hiding, what they are trying so hard not to tell you. That's what a real drawing is, Eru taught her. It's not describing the facts. It's revealing the truth.

As a detective, Hana would always carry a compact artist's sketchbook and a good pencil. She'd make sketches of crime scenes. Forensic photos record moments, facts. Hana wanted to capture what a photo can never record. What it feels like to be there, after the fact of an offence; walking into a place where something terrible happened, where lives were instantly and catastrophically changed. Trying to intuit what it felt like for the offender, standing where you are standing now, the moment after whatever happened, happened. Searching for that feeling. And letting the lightly held pencil turn it into an image that tells more than any photo ever could.

She'd look for the things lurking below the surface, just off the edge of her vision. She'd search the periphery. She wouldn't follow the straight lines.

But back here, on her home ground, going up and down the perfectly even rows of carefully laid cobblestones with the sprayer, Hana has to admit, there's something easy and simple and satisfying about just following the straight lines.

Hana finishes spraying between the final rows of stones. She looks up to see Eru, leaning against the car. He's been there for a while, in front of the wharekai,* and she's not completely sure why. She rinses out the weed sprayer and packs the equipment away in the storage room. When she comes back to the car, Eru is staring at the red-painted beams of the dining hall.

'What's up, Dad?'

For a moment Eru's face is lost. Then he's back there with Hana.

'When we were doing the renovations on the wharekai, he used to come down. Tama Hall.' With the discovery of Kiri's body, Eru is mulling over old memories from twenty-one years earlier.

He knew Tama Hall, the man convicted of killing Paige Meadows. Tama was Māori but this wasn't his home area, and as an outsider from another tribe he wasn't a big presence on the marae. But when they were doing the renovations, he would turn up, pick up a paint brush or a hammer, lend a hand. Eru got to know him as a good neighbour, pitching in and doing what needed doing.

'He had a past,' Eru says. 'He didn't hide it.'

He couldn't really. Tama's history was written all over him. Literally. His former affiliations tattooed on his chest, the gang symbol on his neck. But the more

---

* Wharekai – dining hall.

Eru spent time with him, the more he came to believe the guy with the tattoos had truly turned his life around. He was living clean. He'd taken up the Bible. They shared a beer the night they put the final licks of paint on the wharekai. Eru talked about his time in the army. Tama talked about his days in the gang. Two very different stories. But in many ways the same.

'After a beer or two, Tama got quite emotional. Told me we weren't that different. We both made decisions. Joined up, wore the uniform. Only, Tama came to realize that the fight he fought wasn't any kind of good fight. It was just a fight.'

Tama Hall told Hana's dad about a showdown in an escalating turf war with another gang where the softball bats came out, the chains and broken bottles. That night, Tama hurt someone, badly. After he got out of jail, he made a choice. He walked away from the gang.

'I went to see Tama in prison. After he confessed.'

This takes Hana by surprise. It's something he never told her at the time.

'I offered to be a character witness at his sentencing,' Eru continues.

He looks up towards the skies above the wharekai. There's red in the clouds, the red you only get out on the wild west-coast beaches at sunset after a perfectly still day. The way his eyes are searching, Hana knows he's not really looking at the clouds. He's looking beyond. Finding a memory, the same way he used to go somewhere else when he was drawing something from deep in his past, maybe a remembered house in a village in Vietnam, or Hana when she was a black-eyed baby.

'He sat there, Tama. This silver-haired guy in orange overalls. After I offered to speak for him, he didn't say a word for the longest time. Probably just a minute or two, but it felt like an hour. I could see, me offering to support him, it shifted the ground under his feet for a moment. Like he was coming to a decision.'

'What did he say?'

Hana watches a sadness come over her dad's face.

'He looked at the floor the whole time we were in the visiting room. It was as though, if he looked at me, it would be too much, and he might change his mind about something. Finally, he just said, "I don't need anyone's pity. I don't need no one's forgiveness, but God's. Don't come back here again." And he asked the corrections guy to take him back to his cell.'

A car pulls into the parking area out by the road, the first of the locals coming for the community meeting that night, called after the identification of the bones found in the dunes. As the new arrivals get out of the car and head for the meeting house, Eru looks at Hana. He speaks quietly. But with absolute certainty.

'I never believed it. Never will. Tama didn't kill that girl. He didn't do it.'

'It happened four years ago. That's a long time, we know. Tātā Bay is a small town. No CCTV, no traffic lights for fifty kilometres where someone might have driven through a red light and set off a camera. None of the resources we could access in the city. Our biggest resource is everyone in this wharenui.'*

DSS Lorraine Delaney is standing at the front of the meeting house, Jaye behind her. In Tātā Bay, the marae is the stand-in for a town hall, a function that marae fulfil in many small towns across the country. The detectives have called this meeting to keep the community apprised of developments, and to ask for help in the investigation. The wharenui is packed, a couple of hundred people lining the benches and sitting on mattresses on the floor.

An image of one of the last photos taken of Kiri is projected onto a screen.

Hana looks up at it, as flyers with the same picture are distributed to the crowd. She met Kiri, once; Lorraine invited Hana to one of the group's sessions, to talk about her career. At lunch Kiri sat beside Hana. She spoke quietly about her passion for writing; she loved words and wanted to one day find a way to turn that into a career, maybe in the media, or writing books or poetry. Hana remembered the young woman's smile, her confidence – or at least her show of confidence.

---

* Wharenui – meeting house.

'You look like the photos of my real mum,' Kiri said quietly to Hana at the end of the day, as Hana was leaving.

At the front of the wharenui, Lorraine continues. 'Four years is a while ago, but there's a point of reference we hope might be useful. The night Kiri was abducted, it was a test match between the All Blacks and Springboks. The ABs gave the Boks a thumping. Pretty sure you remember.'

Nods and smiles. Most people remember. The All Blacks and the Springboks are the names for the respective rugby sides of New Zealand and South Africa; there's an intense historic rivalry between the two great southern-hemisphere teams, and test matches are a big deal in rugby-mad New Zealand. The game in question stands out in many people's minds. The All Blacks ran rampant, scoring seven tries to none, an absolute thrashing with South Africa left scoreless and humiliated at the final whistle.

'Think back to that night. The big game. Who you watched it with, where you watched it. Did you notice anything when you were driving home after? Or maybe looking out your window late at night? If you saw anything we should know about, anything at all, we want to hear.'

Jaye finishes passing out the flyers with contact numbers for Lorraine and the Auckland CIB. He leaves a pile of extras for locals to take, to pass on to anyone who was unable to attend. Hana knows Lorraine and her team have a big job on their hands. There's a critical window after someone has witnessed a significant event, say a car crash or an assault, when memories are most reliable. A few days at most, when their recollections are least likely to be contaminated and are therefore most useful for an investigation. After that, the human mind has a way of replaying, changing, evolving the memory, being swayed by outside influences like other people's accounts or media reports. The longer after the fact, the more unlikely that anything will be meaningfully retained.

But the cops have to try.

'Maybe you saw a strange car driving through town,' Jaye says. 'An unfamiliar face glimpsed through a windscreen. Someone behaving oddly that Saturday night. It could well be a man who is responsible. There's no way we can know if Kiri was sexually assaulted. But with a disappearance of a young woman her age, statistically, a sexually motivated offence is likely.'

'Kiri made mistakes,' Lorraine says, as the meeting draws to a close. 'Drugs, petty crime, the things you've heard about in the media. But the people writing those stories never met her. They didn't know the Kiri I knew. A beautiful young woman with a huge heart. Bright, full of joy. Someone who should have had the chance to repair, to heal, to restart. To live the life she deserved.'

Lorraine looks around the faces in the meeting house. 'Please. Help us find who did this to Kiri.'

Afterwards, before he and Lorraine make the two-hour drive back to the city, Jaye takes a moment with Hana. It's a request, it's personal and it's difficult.

'Marissa wants you to come to our next counselling session.'

Hana wasn't expecting this.

Her mind returns unwillingly to the moment, half a year earlier. She and Jaye, both recovering their breath. Lying together in Hana's bed. The first time they'd been intimate since they'd broken up so many years before. A mistake, a moment of weakness and unchecked impulse, a terrible decision made at a terrible moment, in the midst of a rapidly escalating serial murder investigation, in the wake of seeing their daughter Addison admitted to hospital after an overdose of party pills, MDMA. In Hana's bedroom, despair and pain turned into something that exploded their personal worlds in a way that won't ever be fully healed. There were reasons that moment happened. But for Hana those reasons aren't so much explanations as excuses, and she is never going to excuse herself. In the aftermath, Jaye's partner Marissa told Jaye to leave. Now he is renting an apartment near the police station. They've been going to relationship counselling, seeing if things can be repaired.

'Our counsellors say we've reached a point where there's only one way forward. You, me, Marissa. All of us in one room. We face what happened. I hate to ask. It's going to be awful,' he says.

'Tell me when. I'll be there.'

As Hana drives him home from the marae, Eru looks out the windscreen of the car at the passing houses. Hana remembers when her dad would automatically jump behind the steering wheel at night, even when Hana had been driving for a few years, insisting he'd never even had a dent in thirty years of driving, that experience was everything, especially on a dark night on country roads. But Hana has noticed that since she's returned to Tātā Bay, Eru seems happy to let her drive.

As they pass through the middle of the small town, she imagines another car driving along this route, four years earlier, late at night, the streets empty. On that night, the night of the big rugby game, there's a girl in the car. The driver isn't taking her home. She's been bound by her hands and feet. She is either dead already, or terrified and about to die, and the driver is taking her to a place she's never been, a place of cold black sands and wind-swept dunes.

A place she isn't going to return from.

A place where, twenty-one years ago, another dead girl was buried.

Hana looks again at her dad. She thinks back to that afternoon when Eru was reliving the memory of the man who'd confessed to murdering Paige Meadows and burying her body in a shallow grave in the sand dunes.

'He didn't do it,' Eru had said.

Hana trusts her father's instincts as much as her own. If her dad is right, if the man who confessed to killing Paige was in fact innocent, then why did he confess? And if it was a false confession, then along with the question of what happened to Kiri Thomas, there remains another unsolved mystery.

Who killed Paige Meadows?

10

THE CARAVAN ON MOUNTAIN ROAD

The recliner chair in the sitting room of Hana's dad's place is looking the worse for wear.

The pattern is faded, tufts of stuffing are coming out along one of the side seams. As Hana cooks dinner for them, her dad snoozes in the chair, his bushman's hat down over his eyes. It was Hana's mum's chair. When she passed, it became the chair Eru would always end up in at the end of the day. Hana knows she's never going to get him to throw it out and buy something tidier and more comfortable. And when he passes too, she's pretty sure she won't want to get rid of that chair either.

She puts the plates on the table. Eru is mid-snore

as she gently shakes him. He blinks, lost in time for a moment.

'Is it time to pick up the kids?'

'Dad, it's seven o'clock at night. We'll see them in the morning.'

As Eru gathers himself, Hana serves the food. It's a goulash, how Addison makes it. The paprika and chili from a Hungarian recipe, but with thick chunks of eggplant instead of beef. Hana's dad's cholesterol isn't great and she's trying to wean him off his meat-seven-nights-a-week diet. As she finishes filling their plates, there's a knock. Hana opens the door to find a woman her age on the doorstep.

'It's Hana, I think? I'm Chloe Purchas.' The woman adjusts the pale-blue scarf covering her hair. Ill at ease. 'I'm from Eternity Farm. We were at school together.'

Hana remembers Chloe from when they were both at the local high school, but only from a distance. Eternity Farm is a conservative religious collective on the outskirts of Tātā Bay, a handful of Christian families who run a dairy farm and grow vegetables and berry fruit. Nothing particularly cultish or weird, as far as Hana was ever aware. But the Eternity members had some specific rules. The girls all had to wear a head scarf. Every Friday the boys had their hair shaved GI-Joe short. And beyond the unavoidable necessary interactions at school,

Eternity students were discouraged from talking to non-Eternity kids.

Hana had noticed Chloe earlier, standing at the back of the meeting house while Lorraine spoke. 'You were at the marae,' she says, smiling warmly. She knows it's a big deal for Chloe, speaking with someone outside her faith, and she can see there's something the woman wants to say. 'Would you like to come inside?'

Chloe shakes her head and Hana realizes her mistake.

'I'm sorry. The rules of your church.'

Chloe looks towards her car. In the back seat, there are two girls, maybe ten or twelve years old, the same light-blue scarves around their heads. They are staring through the open rear window, not sure what their mum is doing at a stranger's house.

'Girls,' Chloe calls to them. 'Do your homework please. I won't be long.'

As her daughters start in on their schoolbooks, Chloe lowers her voice.

'At the meeting, the policewoman asked if anyone had seen any strange faces. Especially men.' She pauses, seemingly unsure how to continue, or if what she has to say is even relevant. 'This isn't about that poor girl they found a couple of nights ago. It's about something that happened when we were at school. Those detectives from Auckland – I don't want to waste their time. But you used to be with the police. Maybe you can tell me if it's important.'

'It's okay. You can talk freely.'

Hana touches Chloe's hand, to reassure her. Chloe instantly stiffens, and Hana takes her hand away. From the kitchen, Eru calls out, 'Does your friend want to join us? There's lots of kai.'*

'You get started, Dad. Won't be long.'

Chloe steps a little closer to Hana.

'At school, I was always sporty. I loved hockey and I was good, really good. I asked for permission from the Eternity elders to play in the school hockey team. Kids from Eternity aren't allowed to be in the choir or go on school camps. But my dad saw how much it meant to me. He managed to talk the other elders into letting me play. It was after practice one evening. We'd gone on a bit late. I was cycling home ...'

'What happened?'

'A man came out from the dunes. He was strange. We don't have alcohol on the farm, but I'd seen drunk people before. His eyes seemed drunk. But he wasn't wobbly like when someone's been drinking.'

Chloe trails off, and Hana prompts her gently to continue.

'Did he hurt you?'

'I think he wanted to. No. I'm sure he did. I could see

---

* Kai – food.

it in his eyes. He ran after me. I rode faster. He tried to grab me, so I swung at him with the hockey stick, hit him in the head. He fell. I rode back to the farm as fast as I could.'

'Did you tell anyone?'

Chloe's eyes fall. She shakes her head no.

'If I'd said anything, I wouldn't have been allowed to play hockey. The elders wouldn't have let me do anything ever again. I hit him hard. He was bleeding, a big cut over his eye. I hoped that would teach him a lesson, and that he wouldn't try the same thing again. I have daughters now. I wish I'd said something. I really wish I had.'

'I'm sorry you had to go through that alone.' Hana means it. There's no judgement or blame. 'How old were you, Chloe?'

'It was when I was in Year 13. I'd just turned seventeen.' A frown settles on her face. Hana can see, this has haunted her. 'It happened the year Paige Meadows was killed. A few weeks before. At most, a month.'

Hana's instincts kick in. 'The man who killed Paige. Tama Hall – Māori guy, tattooed, would have been late fifties. Was it him?'

'The man who chased me was early twenties. If that. More a boy than a man. He was Pākehā.'

'You're sure?'

Chloe's voice is firm. 'He wasn't the man they arrested.'

'I know it was a long time ago. But can you remember the way he looked?' Hana asks. 'Anything about his face?'

'It was the longest twenty seconds of my life. I'm not ever going to forget.'

A car passes. Chloe shuffles nervously. Even now, as an adult and a mother and a minister of her church, she risks the disapproval and censure of her fellow Eternity members if she is seen here.

'I know you need to go. But if I can keep you just five minutes more?' Hana grabs a sketchpad from the hallway table, and a good pencil.

'I need you to describe everything you remember about the man.'

Mountain Road runs up from the low-lying main street of Tātā Bay, climbing the foothills of the maunga* that towers above the surrounding area. Hana follows the road as it grows steadily narrower, until it's one lane. She pulls in outside the Mountain Road Holiday Park. A welcoming enough name, if you were to read it on an accommodation booking site, and it's in a beautiful location, nestled among tall rainforest trees that climb the steep slopes of the maunga. But the holiday park

---

* Maunga – mountain.

has seen better days, and those better days might not even be of this century. Most of the rental caravans are boarded up, the shower block desperately needs to be painted and repairs to the kitchen facilities are long overdue.

Hana turns off the engine. She opens her sketchbook to the drawing she'd made following Chloe's description of the man who tried to assault her when she was a teenager. Her recollection had been detailed and precise, the resulting sketch resembling a kind of DIY identikit; a portrait of a young man with bushy eyebrows, intense eyes and unkempt blond hair. Looking at the image, searching her memories from that time, there's nothing familiar about this face for Hana. Like Chloe, she's sure this person didn't go to their high school.

'You didn't see him any other time?' Hana had asked, as they'd stood on the doorstep together the night before. 'In town, at the shops?'

'We weren't allowed to go to the shops. That's the elders' job.'

But Chloe thought she had seen him once more, a few weeks after the terrifying moment near the dunes. The Eternity bus was driving the whole community to a prayer meeting at a church in a neighbouring town.

'We were passing that caravan park, up on Mountain Road. I think I saw him, coming out of a caravan. I didn't want to look. I thought I was going to be sick. I'm sure it was him.'

By this point, in the car, Chloe's daughters were getting restless. Before she left, she looked at the image Hana had drawn for a long minute. The face from twenty-one years before. Hana saw a shudder move through her.

'That's him. That's the man,' she said.

Now Hana takes the sketchbook from her car and heads down to the holiday park's office. The owners are a couple in their seventies who have run the park for thirty years. They're apologetic about the state of repair of the place, assuming Hana is there to rent a caravan.

'People prefer to be down by the beach these days,' the wife says. Deirdre has a bright, open face. Her husband Billy is a few years older, angular, silver-haired and equally apologetic.

'We're hoping for an offer,' he adds. From the resigned look he gives his wife, Hana has the distinct feeling that neither of them is expecting developers with fat chequebooks to come knocking any time soon.

'I'm not actually looking to stay', Hana assures them. 'I'm wondering if I can pick your brains.' She shows them the drawing. 'This might be a bit left-field, but I think this man might have stayed in one of your caravans. It would have been twenty-one years ago.'

As her husband retrieves his reading glasses, Deirdre studies the sketch.

'That's a long time ago. But there's something familiar ... what do you think, dear?'

She hands Billy the drawing. A glimmer of recognition comes to his eyes.

'Is it that boy? You remember, the one who watched those videos all day long. It's him, isn't it?'

And now Deirdre places him.

'Yes. Gary something? No ... Gordon. His name was Gordon. What was the surname?'

She turns back to Hana.

'I keep all our records, way back from when we first bought the place. Billy laughs at me. "Pedantic." But you never know when you might be asked.'

As Deirdre digs through her records, her husband looks again at the image, remembering.

'Must have been in his early twenties,' he says. 'Didn't work. He was on some kind of sickness allowance. The caravan rental was paid directly from his benefit. Funny boy. He'd stay locked inside for days at a time. While I was doing the gardening around the caravans, I'd hear him playing his VHS tapes. Seemed to be all *Friday the 13th*, Halloween-type films.'

'Here we go,' Deirdre says. 'He was here for nearly six months.'

She puts the records she's found down on the counter in front of Hana.

'Gordon John Weeks.'

Billy nods, that's the name.

'He was a loner. The only person he ever spent any

time with was the older bloke in the house up the way. He seemed to look out for the boy.'

Billy takes Hana to the door of the office, pointing to a rusted section of roof that is just visible at the crest of a hill.

'Does the man still live there?' Hana asks. 'Maybe he'll know where to find this Gordon Weeks.'

Deirdre smiles, apologetic again. 'You're not going to have any luck talking to him, love. He's dead.'

'Died in prison, a few years ago now,' her husband says. 'Māori chap. The one who killed that girl.'

The house on the crest of the hill hasn't been lived in since Tama Hall went to prison.

As Hana makes her way from room to room, it's clear this place was never a prize. Now it's all but derelict. What wallpaper remains is stained, with graffiti everywhere. Cheap cans of pre-mixed rum and coke and broken beer bottles lie around from where teenagers have come to party. She carefully opens a door that's just barely hanging on to its broken hinges. The room was once a bedroom, but whatever furniture used to be there has long gone, stolen or smashed or rotted with the damp coming from the rusted-out iron roof.

The couple told Hana before she left that they

remembered that the chap with the tattoos would come down to the caravan park from time to time.

'He'd knock on the door until Weeks finally came out,' Deirdre said. 'He'd take the boy up to his house, get some food in him.'

Billy remembered seeing Tama and the boy working in the gardens of Tama's house.

'Like he was trying to get him grounded. Get him out into the sunshine. Away from those bloody movies.'

Picking her way back through the house, Hana feels a floorboard nearly give way beneath her. She closes the front door as she leaves, but it's a pointless formality. The locks are long since rusted through.

In her car, she gets out her sketchbook. Turns the pages. There are notes she's made of what her dad told her about Tama Hall, the things Chloe said the night before about the man who tried to assault her, and now the things Deirdre and Billy remember about the man who rented their caravan. And the identikit of the person Hana now knows is Gordon John Weeks.

Looking at the sketchbook, Hana can't help the feeling of familiarity. It might as well be one of her notebooks from when she was a cop.

At the caravan park, Deirdre had found the date the rental payments for the caravan were cancelled. Hana checks it against her other notes, making a timeline. Chloe from Eternity Farm fought off a man who fitted

Weeks' description. Less than a month later, Paige Meadows was murdered and buried in a shallow grave in the sand dunes. Tama Hall confessed to the killing the day after the body was found.

Then two days after Tama was arrested, Gordon John Weeks handed back the keys to the caravan and disappeared from Tātā Bay.

11

WE'LL LOOK INTO IT

Hana's still getting used to the pace, or lack thereof, of her new life in Tātā Bay.

No screaming sirens at night. No calls at three o'clock in the morning to attend cold, sad murder scenes. No 'seven days a week, twenty-four hours a day if the case demands it'. But there are the other differences too. No decent coffee a two-minute stroll down the road. Nowhere to get really good handmade pasta, the one true extravagance in her old life. And, as with much of rural New Zealand, there are bugger-all paying jobs in Tātā Bay.

'The storm took off three sheets of roofing iron, right above my bedroom.'

Hana is with a young mum named Sandra, in a small house at the end of a cul-de-sac. The house sits at the cul-de-sac's highest point, and when an unusually strong early spring storm hit this pocket of West Auckland, the narrow street became a wind tunnel. Hana has an ongoing arrangement with an Auckland private investigator, an ex-cop named Sebastian Kang. When Seb has his hands full and needs an experienced investigator to work on a job, he gives Hana a call, and she heads back to the city and dosses down in the spare room of her house. It keeps her in touch with the ongoing curiosity that is Addison's life and it earns her a few bucks. The job Seb flicked Hana's way this time is a water damage investigation claim. 'Private Investigator' might sound like a thrilling career, but it's not like the movies. Checking the validity of claims for insurance companies is nine tenths of the day-to-day work. The kind of stuff Hana can do in her sleep.

'My ex had my two boys that night. Thank God. My youngest has trouble sleeping anyway, since the break-up. Never really feels safe without his dad here. If he'd woken up to half the roof coming off, I don't know if he'd ever sleep properly again.'

Sandra is house-proud – the gardens and the home itself are tidy and well kept – and while it's clear this solo mum doesn't have the resources to afford many luxuries, Hana gets the feeling that whatever spare cash she has is spent on her kids. But as Sandra takes Hana through the house, showing the effects of the water damage, Hana can sense a slight tension in her. It might just be the discomfort of a stranger in her home ...

Or there might be another reason.

Hana looks through the list of items on the claim, her eyes falling on one in particular. 'Got the time?' she asks casually.

Sandra pulls her phone from her pocket. 'Just after 2:30. I need to pick up the boys in a minute.'

'That's an iPhone, right?' Hana says, looking at the phone in Sandra's hand. 'The make and model of the one that got water damaged. That you threw away?'

Sandra's flushed cheeks and frightened eyes answer the question for her.

Hana can see that Sandra isn't a habitual fraudster, nothing of the kind. This is probably the first time she's tried anything like it. Her guess is that an opportunity presented itself, a way for Sandra to get an extra phone for one of her boys maybe. The phone she's claiming for isn't even the latest model. This is a slightly bumbling attempt, by a young mum who is only just making ends meet, to try and get a half-step ahead.

Hana puts the claim forms back on Sandra's kitchen table.

'Why don't I leave these with you. Might want to double-check the paperwork. You maybe made a couple of typos. I'll be back later in the week to pick them up.'

The fish taco restaurant is a cheap-eats place among a strip of noisy, cool young bars in central Auckland. Hana opens the plain brown envelope sitting in front of her, looks at the wad of notes inside.

'This is two days' pay. For three hours' work. That's just silly, Seb.'

'It's half what I'm being paid by the insurance company, and I'm too busy to do it myself. Shut up and eat your tacos.'

Seb Kang came through the police ranks three graduation classes after Hana, Jaye and Lorraine. He's of Korean descent, but was raised in Auckland after his parents moved here when he was still a baby to take up positions as pastors of a Korean Presbyterian church on the city's North Shore. Located just a few parallels of latitude below the southern edge of Asia, Auckland has a steadily growing immigrant Asian population, making up a quarter of the city's population in the last census. Seb was brought up to be fluent in Korean, his parents sending him to Mandarin classes for good measure, and with his easy but determined manner as an investigator, he was quickly identified as an asset to the police force in a city with a rapidly changing demographic.

Seb was based in the North Shore policing district, and Hana only occasionally crossed paths with him at work; they got to know each other properly in the ocean. As the waters warm up in the summer months, a series of events are held in Auckland Harbour: long-distance deep-water swims from one side to another, or from different inner-harbour islands in towards the shore. Thousands of Aucklanders take part. The race briefing always features the same message: 'We can't be responsible for what lies beneath the surface of the harbour. There have been no recorded shark attacks in the history of our races, or of Auckland Harbour, but there's always a first time.'

The races were Hana's replacement for the much wilder swims she used to do off the black sand beaches of Tātā Bay, and over five or six swim seasons she'd bump into Seb at various events, getting to a point of familiarity where they'd warm up together, share Vaseline and training tips, line up for the deep-water starts side by side. A tall guy with a big reach and great technique, Seb would finish most races five or ten minutes before Hana.

The last swim of the season is always the longest; 4.5 kilometres from the volcanic cone of Rangitoto Island, in the middle of the harbour, back to the mainland. Before one race a few years ago, Hana noticed that Seb was unusually quiet on the ferry that takes swimmers out to the start line at the island's main wharf. Forty-five minutes after the starting hooter, halfway back to shore, she saw him treading water, gasping for air. He was having trouble getting his breathing in rhythm, and Hana trod water next to him, not prepared to leave him behind. Seb tried a couple of times to get started again, Hana following, but he'd get 100 metres and have to stop. When he pulled up a fourth time, Hana thought she could see, behind his goggles, what looked like tears in his eyes.

'Neither of us is going to get a personal best today,' she told him. The water was warm, a gentle swell. 'Let's float for a bit. Enjoy the sunshine. Take our own time getting back to shore.'

She could sense his gratitude. And she had a feeling there was something going on that was bigger than bilateral breathing. Floating a mile offshore, with the rest of the field well gone, Hana asked if something was wrong. Seb took off his goggles. Wiped salt water out of his eyes. He told Hana what had happened a couple of weeks before.

He'd answered a welfare check in an apartment building, a mum and young child. The husband was overseas on business, and he'd been calling for his little girl's second birthday but hadn't been able to get an answer. Seb had the building manager open the flat. The mum and the little girl had been dead for more than a day. It emerged later that the mother had been suffering depression since the birth of the child. She'd felt isolated and alone, her husband constantly travelling for work. She'd refused medication, telling her GP she didn't want chemicals in her body. She'd ordered a specially decorated birthday cake featuring a My Little Pony, her daughter's favourite character. The cake had been cut, two candles blown out, two pieces eaten. Then the mum had used the same knife to cut first her child's throat, then her own.

Floating out in the water, Seb told Hana that he'd come across a lot of things on the job. Car crashes, the aftermaths of gang shootouts, a body discovered a week after an overdose. But something about that day ... A young mother, her arms wrapped around the child she'd just killed. Birthday candles blown out. He hadn't slept since. Panic attacks. Like that day, being out in the water, not able to breathe properly on a swim he'd done every year for ten years. He hadn't been able to talk to anyone at work, he'd said. Nor to his parents, who'd wanted him to follow them into the ministry, and would have just seen it as confirmation he'd made the wrong career decision.

They swam slowly back to shore together. After their talk Seb had been able to get his rhythm back. They were the last out of the water. As they were drying off, Seb said he felt he had to make a decision. Stay or go. Hana understood what he was asking her. The job is tough, uniquely tough. But how do you know when it's too much? Do you walk away from your career because you've seen something no one should ever have to see? When do you know it's time to leave?

Hana told him every cop faces the question sooner or later. There's only one answer.

'When you know, you know,' she said.

A week after the swim, Seb handed in his notice. He started up a private investigation company a few months later, and when he heard that Hana had retired from the CIB in the wake of her traumatic final case, he immediately texted her.

when you know you know. if you want to talk, i'm here

Another text followed a minute later.

plus if you need work i have more than i can handle

Now, as she eats her fish tacos, Hana tells Seb about the event at the little house in the cul-de-sac in West Auckland, how the young mum Sandra was trying it on, but only in a small way.

'No reason to take it back to the insurance company. I hope you agree.'

He does.

She takes out half the payment, slides the envelope back across the table to Seb with half what he is offering her still inside.

'Seriously,' she says. 'It's too much, Sebastian.'

'It's only my parents and you who call me that.'

'Sorry.'

'Don't be. I like it.'

'Something else,' Hana says. 'I've got a question.'

She takes out the drawing she made of the man she

now knows as Gordon John Weeks. She explains the perplexing information she's found out from Chloe and the owners of the caravan park.

'It's historic,' she says. 'It's not even a cold case – it's a murder that was solved when I was a teenager. I knew Paige. We weren't friends or anything. But I knew her. And now, a girl who was at school with us says this guy chased her, not long before Paige died.'

'What's the question?'

'Another killing, years later, same place, a girl the same age.'

'If you're asking, do I think your antenna should be pinging?' Seb shrugs. 'Maybe. Maybe not. But that's not the point. Whatever your or my antenna think, there's nothing we can do about it. We're not cops anymore. You've got a name for this guy. Approximate age. A description. Hand it on to the people whose job it is to follow up.'

Hana nods, making the decision to go and see Lorraine and Jaye with the information she's discovered before heading back to Tātā Bay.

As they finish their tacos, Seb slides the envelope back into her pocket, with the remainder of the fee inside.

'You want the work? You take what I pay. Deal?'

Hana smiles.

'Deal.'

A small, round, grey plastic button. The number eight etched into it, backlit by a tiny LED.

Hana stands in the elevator, finger poised.

Staring at the button for the eighth floor.

Before she retired from the cops, before Hana came down in this same elevator and walked out the front door of Auckland Central Police Station for the last time, away from her career, she would have pushed this button several thousand times. Automatic. No thought required.

It's different now.

Even if it's only for a few minutes, getting back into this elevator means going back to a world she chose to leave behind.

Finally, Hana pushes the button.

In a conference room on the eighth floor, Jaye and Lorraine sit on one side of a big shiny-topped table, Hana on the other. The sketch she made of Gordon John Weeks from Chloe's description lies between them, along with the timeline she has constructed, linking the attempted attack on Chloe and the murder of Paige Meadows less than a month later.

'I'd forgotten what it's like when you get the bit

between your teeth. Impressive,' Lorraine says. 'I'm just not completely sure what it is you think you have here.'

'Neither am I,' says Hana, and it's the truth. She looks at Jaye. 'You know my dad. He has a hell of an instinct when it comes to people. He knew Tama Hall, and it always stuck in his craw. Dad's certain he didn't kill Paige. Tama confessed. But we all know false confessions happen.'

Hana gathers up her materials and hands them over to Lorraine, the identikit on top of the pile.

'This guy Weeks was never looked at for Paige's murder,' she says. 'I think he should have been. Especially now there's been another killing, in similar circumstances.'

Lorraine takes photocopies of Hana's materials.

'We'll look into it,' she says.

Hana has said this too many times to remember. *We'll look into it.* The fob-off every cop gives to busybodies, nosy neighbours. And it's fair enough; this isn't Hana's investigation. She's got time on her hands. The most exciting things in her life are teaching teenagers to drive and doing dog-work for insurance companies. Maybe she's pulling at threads that aren't actually connected to anything; maybe she's just trying to get back a little taste of the buzz and thrill of the chase she used to get every day when she pushed the button with the little eight on it.

'Any progress with Kiri?' Hana asks as the elevator arrives.

Lorraine gives her a kiss on the cheek. 'Talk soon, mate.'

Before she leaves the station, Hana stops in at the third floor. As soon as Stan sees her, his face lights up. 'Hey, sarge!'

'Hey, detective.'

It's playful, self-deprecating. Neither of them are detectives anymore.

'My daughter tells me you've been showing off your new toy,' Hana says, looking at Stan's artificial leg. 'Glad it's going well. But you're not taking things too fast?'

'Got a moment? I can give you a demo out in the car park.' Hana has to smile at the familiar puppy-dog look on Stan's face.

She glances around the floor. It's open plan, but the nearest of Stan's co-workers are standing by the printer, deep in conversation as it churns.

'I need a favour,' she says, quietly.

She hands Stan a piece of paper, with a vehicle registration on it. After the confrontation with the guy Rendall at the dairy in Tātā Bay, she took down his licence plate number.

'There's been burgs* in our area, car conversions. Anything you can find in the system about this guy, it could be a help.'

'Boss, I'm assuming you don't want Jaye to know about this?'

'I'm not your boss. And yes, that would be preferable.'

Stan tucks the piece of paper discreetly into his to-do pile. As Hana leaves, she pauses at the elevator.

'We worked together for over a year. You never once bought pani popo for me.'

Stan grins. 'You never asked.'

Ferns and towering native trees. Rich, dark volcanic soil. Herbs and wetland grasses.

Hana's garden was always the place she would retreat to after a shit day getting nowhere on a case, or on a day when she'd witnessed some of the darker things that humans are capable of and really didn't want to speak to another person for a few hours. She's glad to see that Addison and PLUS 1 have done their best to look after the place, even if neither is the natural gardener she is. And she tries to overlook the fact that the rescue puppy, Boca, currently bouncing around the

---

* Burgs – slang for burglaries.

lawn, has been digging holes in the grass and shredding a few of the smaller ferns with her new teeth.

Addison comes out from the house to retrieve Boca. 'Soup's ready, Mum.'

Addison likes the change in roles since her mother has become the guest in the house; making food for Hana, carefully laying out a towel and a little soap on the bed in the spare room when she comes to stay. She watches her mum inspect her precious garden.

'I know why you're checking behind your kawakawa.* We're not growing dope there.'

As Addison heads in to serve up the soup, Hana has to smile.

Her daughter knows her so well.

Over dinner, Hana can feel something eating at Addison. She isn't surprised when, well after midnight, she wakes to the spare room door quietly opening, and Addison looking in.

'You okay, love?'

'The girl. Kiri.'

Hana signals to her daughter, *come in*. She makes room on the bed and Addison lies down beside her.

---

* Kawakawa – small native New Zealand tree, the leaves used traditionally and today for medicinal purposes.

'In all the photos, she looks so young, so bursting with life. I can't stop thinking about her. It's awful, Mum. Tied up. Murdered. Lying there, alone in the cold sands.'

Hana takes Addison in her arms.

She kisses her daughter on the shiny baldness of her head.

They fall asleep together.

12

ONLY FOR DAX

When the Earth Mother and the Sky Father were pushed apart by their unruly offspring, one of the niggly kids, upset at the break-up of the family, completely lost it. Tāwhirimātea, God of the Weather and Winds, ripped his eyes from their sockets, crushed them up into tiny bits and tossed the pieces into the heavens, where they became Matariki, a sacred constellation.

Our ancestors used those smashed-up pieces of a god's eyes in the sky to navigate when they sailed their waka* across the oceans, to find their way to Aotearoa.† The shining shards of godly retinas and pupils became their GPS, their Google Maps.

---

* Waka – canoes.
† Aotearoa – New Zealand; literally 'the land of the long white cloud'.

Addiction doesn't have Google Maps. There's no broken-up eyes in the sky laying a path for you to follow. You're stumbling blind, like the god with the empty sockets.

Some people do rock once, just one hit on the pipe, and that's that. No turning back, the train is running, off to the races. Day and night it's the only thing they can think of. They live and die for the next inhale. It's not rock, for them. It's their lifeblood.

Others can use once a week; look forward all week to a grand Saturday night and keep it at that. They don't have a single twitch the other six days, no obsessive thoughts, no staring into space thinking about scoring.

I could take it or leave it. Don't get me wrong, I loved the feeling. Looooved the feeling.

But what I truly loved was the clarity. Like mist rising out of a valley, so you can see the trees clearly, at last. My brain is a messy place full of questions and anxiety, and rock made all that stuff blow away for a few hours. When I'd had a taste, I didn't want to turn up the music or drive fast or dance, like other people. All I wanted to do was grab a piece of paper, sharpen a pencil. Write. The rest of the time, the words and thoughts and phrases swirling around in my brain felt like beautiful soup, and it would take days or weeks to pull them into some kind of order, and even then, they were never really, exactly right.

When I was using, the jumble got straight.

Form appeared from the void. It was like those old videos of abandoned skyscrapers being dynamited and falling to a random heap on the ground, only played in reverse. The rubble pulls itself together, rises from the ground, becomes perfect and whole.

Drugs cleared my head. Pulled the pieces into place. But they weren't what I *needed*.

No question, I was an addict. But my addiction wasn't to rock, it was to a boy with kind eyes and a stupid name.

I was stronger than the drugs. Even after Dax turned into the God of Fuckheads and had sex with a stranger and I lost the plot and used his $100 to buy a couple of bags. Even then, I knew what I was doing. I was band-aiding the pain. I was using rock so I didn't lose my mind and put a bread knife into Dax's head or drive Trish's car off the Harbour Bridge. I'd got sober once; I'd get sober again. I had plans. I was going to be well known. People would read the things I wrote. They'd buy my books, queue for me to sign them. If that didn't work out, I'd go to uni and become a teacher, help beautiful young humans find their beautiful young voices, help them find themselves.

I'd have my shit together by then.

I'd fall asleep every night entwined with someone who loved me. And one day we'd have an unruly little creature lying between us, pushing at us with her or his niggly little heels, and we'd hold tight, and the kid wouldn't push us apart, and we'd all lie wrapped in each other's arms, and it would be warm, and it would be good.

That was where I'd navigate my waka to, eventually. Because I was using drugs. They weren't using me.

The real addicts?

The guys whose salaries paid my salary, the ones I took money from to pay the rent – to pay for food, to pay for rock – the guys who would hire me by the half hour. They're the junkies. Their addiction, they won't ever get over. I feel sorry for them. They're the weak ones.

So you know, I never actually fucked them. Once you have a guy ready to go, they're a pushover. You lay down the law. I'll get handsy with you and that's all. Take it or leave it. They always take it.

They're gonna ask for more, but what they're asking, I wasn't giving.

Sex was for Dax. After that day in the boxing gym, the day Dax and I held each other for the first time. After he cried in my arms, and we rode around the city all night. That was me gone. No turning back, off to the races.

Only for Dax.

But then Dax broke me in two.

So here we are.

13

I'M OKAY

When PLUS 1 was in intermediate school, age ten or so, they had long hair. PLUS 1 did competitive diving back then, bold as hell, always was and always will be, never had to think twice about plummeting head-first off the 10-metre platform or doing a double somersault from the lower board. And they were good, reaching a ranking in the Auckland region in their very first year diving. They'd keep their mane of hair tied up for the dives, but it was their greatest kick to undo it as they climbed out of the pool after the final dive, flick it back over their shoulders, let it fall, wet and jet-black and heavy, tumbling down below their bum.

People would gasp.

Then, in the first year of high school, looking in the

mirror became a different experience. It's not right to say that 'something changed'. That's not true. PLUS 1 has always felt the same person inside. What shifted was their perception of their outer being. The hedge of hair that was such a source of pride started to feel like a pair of shoes that didn't quite fit properly anymore, or, more accurately, that maybe weren't ever actually the right shoes for PLUS 1. They got a job making ice creams at the local dairy on the weekends, saved up, and went to an Ethiopian hairdresser who transformed their long Goddess hair into shorter, tighter, perfectly oiled dreads. After four hours of intense pain from the stripping and scraping and back-combing, PLUS 1 looked in the mirror and smiled.

'Yep. That's me.'

Soon after, the pronouns and the name started to feel like the old hair: shoes that didn't fit properly anymore, or never really did. 'She' became 'they'. There were a few tense months of back and forth, when their family had to work hard to catch up to where their child well and truly was already. Their father struggled for ages with the chosen name.

'PLUS 1? What does that even mean?'

'It's saying I'm what I always was, Dad. Only more.'

Finally, their mum and dad agreed to support their underaged child in legally changing their name. The dead name was left behind.

What never changed for PLUS 1: the music.

PLUS 1 doesn't *have* a love of music. It's *in* them. It's in their fingernails, in their spinal fluid, in their teeth. They eat, drink and sleep music. When PLUS 1 and Addison found each other in music class at high school, they knew immediately they were a team. Addison had the words, the charisma, the hunger for the spotlight; PLUS 1 had the musical training, starting from when they were two years old and able to climb up and start picking out notes on the family piano. They both had the passion to create, to move, to use music to make people look at the world in new ways. To make people think.

Tonight, onstage in Sailor Bar, the regular Thursday night residency they've had for the last six months, it's like every other Thursday.

Except it's not.

PLUS 1 is at their turntable. Addison is out front, ruling the stage like a bald-headed Cleopatra. They're filling the place most Thursdays now, and the audience is loving every moment, as usual. But twice tonight, Addison has missed her cues or tripped over her verses. As she bounces across the stage, she's wearing a cardigan she found in a vintage shop a couple of days before. Blue and white. When she'd brought it home, PLUS 1 saw it was almost the same as the one Kiri was wearing in one of the photos Addison had printed out.

Ever since Addison found the dead girl's bones in

the sand dunes, it seems to PLUS 1, she has started to drift away.

From her music. From her world. From PLUS 1.

'I'm not sure what's happening,' PLUS 1 says to Addison.

It's late, a couple of hours after the show, and they are back at their house. A few weeks after Hana moved to Tātā Bay and they officially took over her place, PLUS 1 found an old cast-iron kitchen sink thrown out on the side of the road; it was ancient and dinged up, but they knew it would make a perfect fire pit for their backyard. It took forever to drag the big heavy thing home, and it's become a nightly ritual to haul out the old couch that sits on the back porch, burn branches or fallen fern fronds in the sink, and sit and stare into the flames.

PLUS 1 has never avoided tricky conversations. Life's too short not to say what you think.

'You're an obsessive,' PLUS 1 says, lighting a joint. 'Both of us, that's who we are. I get that something happened to you, something really big. You found her in the dunes.'

Addison picks up a piece of wood, throws it into the fire. Sparks fly up like a big handful of burning red glitter tossed up into the night.

'You've had so much big stuff going on, Addison. You've been through a hell of a lot. I'm worried.'

PLUS 1 hands her the joint and Addison plays with it between her fingers, not really feeling like taking a drag. She knows exactly what PLUS 1 is talking about. Hana's last big case before she quit the cops got very close to home. The killer who Hana was pursuing was someone Addison knew, a charismatic lecturer at her university named Poata Raki. They'd admired each other and shared many similar views about politics and activism. Even as Hana was closing in on Raki, Addison was in contact with him. Then she was there at the end, when Hana finally had her gun on him; Raki took his own life in front of her.

It had been awful, terrifying.

Jaye and Hana had organized professional support for their daughter, but counselling isn't for everyone. Addison attended a few sessions, finally telling her parents that she was okay, that something terrible had happened, but she wasn't going to let that take over her world, stop her from living her life, make her live in fear and trauma. 'We're our own counsellors,' she told her parents, meaning that her friends and her family and her music were the ways she dealt with problems, big and small.

'After everything else,' PLUS 1 continues, 'finding Kiri in the sand dunes. Cops are trained to deal with that kind of thing, it belongs in your mum and dad's world. Us normals aren't meant to deal with stuff like that.'

'You seriously define you and me as "normals"?' Addison says, laughing, trying to tease PLUS 1 out of the headspace they're in.

PLUS 1 remains serious. 'Missing an intro. It's no biggie – you're the queen. But with the dreams ... If it was me, I'd be scared going to sleep.'

'I've always had dreams,' Addison says. 'Not trippy ones like when you're high. My dreams are like you're walking in the actual world, not in dream-time. From when I was a little kid. Nothing seismic. Not like, dreams that predicted things. But I don't know how else to put it ... They were real.'

She picks a thread from the worn arm of the couch. 'I had this cat with one ear. I called her One-Ear.'

'You do better with lyrics than animal names.'

'I hope so,' Addison says, grinning. 'One night I dreamed One-Ear was nuzzling me. Licking my face. This really sad look in his eyes. Like he was saying goodbye or something. Then he turned and walked away. I woke up and Mum was sitting on my bed. In tears. One-Ear had been hit by a car.'

'I'm sorry.'

'I was six. I'm coming out the other side.' Addison rests her head on PLUS 1's shoulder. 'Kiri and me. Our worlds collided in the sand dunes. Of all the people on earth who could've found her, it was me. We did karakia for her. Dreaming about her doesn't freak me out, no more than the dream about One-Ear. It feels okay. Normal.'

Addison hands the joint back, unsmoked. 'Thanks for worrying about me, babe. But you don't need to. I'm okay.'

They sit in silence on the couch, as the flames burn lower in the cast-iron sink.

14

THE BEEKEEPER

A constant buzzing fills the air. Worker bees come and go from the seven beehives along the fence line at the far end of the property.

'Our smallest hive – there's probably forty thousand bees.' The man moves from one beehive to the next, checking the frames that are nearly ready to have their honey harvested. 'The one down the end, the green and white boxes? Maybe seventy thousand. That's a bigger population than most towns in New Zealand.'

He's not wearing any protective gear, just blue latex gloves so the oils from his skin don't taint the honey. As they watch him taking the top off a beehive, Jaye and Lorraine keep a careful distance.

'Don't you get stung?' Jaye asks, watching a bee

crawling up the man's neck, then picking its way lazily across his beard.

'The secret is, don't annoy them. Don't twitch or try and swipe them away. Don't give them a fright when they land on you. Most times, they'll be fine.'

The man has a slowness to the way he talks and the way he moves. Careful, considered. Jaye notices that he even blinks in an unhurried way. Probably a good way to be when you deal a lot with bees.

'They might land on you, have a little walk around, a bit of a sniff. They'll get bored soon enough, go back to their jobs. Very focused, bees. Strong work ethic.'

The drawing Hana made of Gordon John Weeks is surprisingly accurate. It's twenty-one years after the incident with the young woman from Eternity Farm, and he's in his early forties now. But he still has the same bushy eyebrows that Chloe described, the intense eyes. The unkempt blond hair is receding a little, and there are flecks of grey at his temples and in his beard. But the likeness to Hana's drawing is very clear.

'Working with the bees is good for the men here.' Weeks uses a well-worn long-bladed uncapping knife to scrape the wax seal off one tray, revealing the thick mound of honey underneath. 'They like to get involved. They help me with harvesting, preparing the honey. You should see their faces when family come to visit, and they can give them jars of honey that they've gathered themselves.'

When Hana came to the eighth floor and handed over the drawing she'd made of Weeks, it was an awkward situation for both Lorraine and Jaye. The homemade identikit, the information Hana had gathered from enquiries with the holiday park owners about the guy who had lived in the caravan in Tātā Bay for a few months. It was getting messy. Hana wasn't a cop, and this was blurring the lines. But information is information, and there was enough in what Hana had found for Lorraine and Jaye to follow up.

Lorraine tracked Weeks to where he works as a caretaker at a transitional home, a church-funded halfway house where inmates are released when they are first paroled from prison. He's employed to look after the grounds, do maintenance on the rooms and the buildings and facilities. And then there's his passion. The beehives, and the things he believes the social organization of the bees can teach the residents of the transitional home.

'There's an order to a hive,' Weeks says as he slides the tray back into the box. 'Everyone has a role. Everyone works for the greater good. Everyone is there to protect the centre of their universe, the queen. I talk about this with the men. The role of all these bees – to protect the woman at the heart of the place. The Bible means bugger-all to these guys. But the power of bees is a thing they can take onboard. A swarm that can turn angry and violent if treated badly. But treat them with care and respect, and they produce something life-giving. When these men go back to the real world, that's something to hold on to. The idea that their job is not to harm, but to protect.'

Weeks holds out the honey-laden blade of the uncapping knife to Lorraine and Jaye. Both take some honey on their fingertips.

'It's good,' Lorraine says, licking the drips.

Gordon John Weeks carefully scrapes the rest of the honey from the knife into a jar. He turns to look at the cops. The same slowness of movement and speech.

'Is this something to do with Tama Hall? Is that why you're here?'

When Lorraine and Jaye had introduced themselves as police, saying they had questions about his time in Tātā Bay, Weeks had taken them down to the beehives to talk, away from where the residents of the home could hear.

'Breaks my heart what happened,' he says. 'I was going through a rough patch. Trying to get my meds right. You know. Up and down. Something I've struggled with for a long time.'

Jaye connects the dots. The slight slowness in Weeks' speech and movement is likely a result of his medication.

'Tama looked after me. But I didn't see what was going on for him.'

'His cancer?' Lorraine asks.

'That was one battle. But it wasn't the only one Tama was fighting.'

Weeks carefully puts a finger to his cheek, where a bee has made its way. It climbs up onto his fingertip and he eases it onto the side of the hive, near the entryway, so it can make its way back into the community.

'Tama said to me, afterwards. After what he did to the girl. He said he knew he couldn't beat the disease eating his body. But he thought he'd beaten the darkness inside. He thought he'd left it behind. Maybe the cancer made him too weak to fight that darkness. I still don't understand. I wish I'd seen. I wish I'd been able to help him.'

Weeks looks towards the buildings of the halfway house.

'Tama is why I ended up working here. He knew about the place, he'd been a resident here when he was first paroled. He didn't want me to be on my own. After he was arrested, Tama told me this would be solid ground for me. The people that run this place were looking for a caretaker. They helped me find a flat nearby. I've worked here ever since.'

'Do you know this girl?' Lorraine takes out a photo of Kiri from her bag and hands it to him.

'She's been in the papers the last few days,' Weeks says.

'Her name's Kiri Thomas,' Lorraine continues. 'She went missing in September four years ago.'

'The news said it was the night of the big All Blacks win,' Weeks says.

'Do you remember where you were that night?' Jaye is careful to keep his tone conversational. But Weeks immediately understands the insinuation, what's left unsaid, why two senior detectives have turned up here asking questions.

'Seriously? I lived in Tātā Bay for a few months, years ago. I knew the guy who killed that other poor girl way back then. And that gives you reason to question me about this?'

'We're talking to people with connections to the area. It's standard procedure,' Lorraine says, firmly. 'But there is something else. We've had a report about you behaving strangely when you were in Tātā Bay. Frightening a young woman, shortly before Paige Meadows was murdered.'

Weeks blinks, even more slowly than usual. Thinking back. A deep sigh. He reaches into the little backpack that he keeps his beekeeping gear in. Pulls out three different bottles of medications, shows them to the cops.

'When I was in Tātā Bay, I was struggling. I'd been given meds, but the doctors couldn't get the doses right. Then I'd forget what I was meant to take, when to take it. When I got here, they took me to a good doctor. She got everything straight for me. But back then, things could get jumbled.'

Weeks puts the pill bottles back in his backpack.

He pulls off the blue latex gloves and slips them in his jeans pocket.

'The young woman who said she saw me. I can't remember anything like that. I can only think I was having some kind of episode. I'd get confused sometimes. I was probably trying to ask her for help. I definitely wasn't going to hurt her. I'm so sorry I frightened her.'

He looks at the picture of Kiri again. 'I remember the All Blacks game. Seven tries to none, right?' Lorraine nods, *that's the one.*

'My mate Paulie and me used to go to Point Marlon RSA* to watch footie, just down the road. They have a ramp, one of the only places Paulie can get his wheelchair in. We watched the match there. It was a hell of a game.'

'Can your friend confirm this?' Lorraine asks.

'Paulie passed away last year. The same damn disease that put him in a wheelchair.'

Weeks blinks again. He looks towards the door of the main building, where a couple of the residents have become aware of the intense conversation out by the beehives and are watching. He lowers his voice.

'I'm a good worker. I'm part of a community. I try to help these men, and being here helps me. I knew

---

* RSA – Returned Services Association, a social club for war veterans and the general public.

someone years ago who hurt a girl. He was a good person who did a very bad thing. He paid the price. He set me straight. He found this place for me. I'm not sure why any of that leads you here.'

Weeks hands the photo of Kiri Thomas back to Lorraine.

'I wish I could help,' he says. 'But I don't know anything about her.'

Driving away from the halfway house, Jaye asks Lorraine to slow as they pass the nearby Point Marlon RSA. The wheelchair-accessible ramp leads up from the sidewalk. Signs on the outside welcome members and visitors to enjoy affordable meals and live sports on the big screens.

With the serious crimes that the CIB deals with – rape, serious assault, murder – many of them are solved within hours. In the majority of cases, charges will be laid within days. Violence that happens in a rage or from desperation or depravity tends to be messy. Trails are left behind. It's actually very hard to get away with serious crime, once the offending is on the police's radar. For those who know what to look for, the answers come quickly. That's with most cases.

Then there are the outliers.

Kiri's case is four years old. When she first went

missing, the police invested hundreds of hours of investigative time. They followed up with people from her world, in the drug trade, other sex workers, clients. The CIB was motivated. Lorraine ensured the investigation was as thorough as possible. It was a tough day on the eighth floor when Jaye had to pass on the news that no more resources could be expended on a search that had produced no results.

No cop wants an unsolved case on their hands, especially a homicide. They at last have Kiri's remains. But this is a very cold case. The chances of finding out what happened to Kiri Thomas, and who hurt her, have grown smaller with every passing year.

In the car, Lorraine and Jaye are silent as they head back to Central Station.

15

A MOMENT IN TIME

A police tangihanga* for a cop who has died on the job is a big deal. Police are trained to be even and calm, to do their work unemotionally, with clear heads and clear eyes. When the force comes out to farewell a colleague who has died doing their job, those expectations go out the window.

Marissa's husband Tony was one of the thirty or so officers killed in the line of duty in the history of the New Zealand police to date. A leader of the Armed Offenders Squad, the AOS, he'd been in an hours-long stand-off with an armed hostage taker who had barricaded himself inside a downtown department store. A member of the public in the store who was in contact

---

* Tangihanga – funeral rites.

on a cellphone reported that the gunman was becoming irrational; the situation was unravelling and he was threatening that he was going to start killing hostages.

Tony made a decision. The squad had spotted a tea room window that could be breached in the back of the store. He and three other officers were to break in through that window and draw the gunman's attention, while others in his squad would blow open the locked front doors and toss in stun grenades and smoke canisters. There was a chance that innocent lives might be lost, but Tony believed that without intervention, casualties were a certainty.

He led the way, refusing to allow those under his command to go before him, but as he pushed his way through the window he realized the gap was too small for an officer in full protective gear. He had to remove his helmet and outer body armour before dropping to the floor of the tea room, but by then the offender had been drawn by the sound of the glass breaking. Before Tony's team could join him, the hostage taker shot Tony in the face with both barrels of his sawn-off shotgun.

The gunman never got a chance to reload the weapon. The other officers brought him down, firing through the window. Because of Tony's courage, the only deaths were his and that of the man who murdered him.

Hana will never forget the moment, at the end of

the service to farewell Tony, as his casket was carried out from the cathedral. Several hundred cops in full dress uniform had formed a guard of honour, and as the casket approached the hearse, in complete silence and in perfect unison, they all ripped off their police jackets.

A guttural scream, as one, 'Kia mau!'*

The members of the New Zealand police force launched into a haka, the traditional Māori challenge and gesture of deep respect. Eyes roll, tongues protrude, thighs and chests are slapped. It's explosive, visceral. Hana joined the haka; so did Jaye. Policewomen and men, Māori, Pākehā, Pacific Islanders, Asian, another dozen ethnicities and origins. Many weeping and trembling even as they screamed the words, no one attempting to hide the intensity of their sorrow.

After the final words of the haka, complete silence. Only broken by the gasping of air into hundreds of burning lungs. And the sound of Marissa and Tony's two young daughters, Vita and Sammie, sobbing at the sheer emotion. Hana remembers Marissa holding her girls tightly, not giving in to the urge to weep, to let go. Staying tall and strong at the head of the casket, for her children. And for Tony.

Later, at the hākari,† Hana was in the bathroom

---

* 'Hold fast'.
† Hākari – feast after a significant occasion.

when Marissa came in. She had stayed dry-eyed throughout the two hours of the service and the cremation of Tony's body. But alone for the first time that day, her children outside in the care of Tony's mother, she fell apart, collapsing into Hana's arms.

Hana locked the bathroom door and held Marissa until she'd cried herself silent.

Jaye was Tony's best friend. He stood side by side with Marissa through the service, and within a couple of years of Tony's death, they had moved in together. Their shared grief over the loss of the man they both loved had united them in a deep and profound way.

Until what happened six months ago. In Hana's bedroom.

The relationship counselling team that Marissa and Jaye are seeing are a wife and husband themselves, Virginia and Arthur. In their practice they walk the walk, modelling the kinds of communication skills they want their clients to adopt. Each listens attentively to the other, never interrupting, always waiting a moment or two after the end of their spouse's thoughts, leaving open a gap where a lingering thought might bubble free, if allowed the space.

'Thank you for being here, Hana.' Virginia has calm eyes, her hair cut in a neat bob. 'We recognize the generosity of spirit it took for you to agree to this.'

It's the first time since Marissa asked Jaye to leave that she and Hana have been in the same room. The chairs are arranged in a semi-circle around a solid granite coffee table holding a jug of water and, Hana notices, a bowl of peanut M&M's. Marissa stares at the bowl of candy, avoiding any eye contact, her hands clasped tight, her breathing shallow. Hana takes her cue from this very clear body language; a hug of greeting isn't going to be welcome.

As she sits down, Arthur outlines the process they will follow.

'Jaye will speak first. Then you, Marissa. So that you both can talk about the work we've done so far. And the reasons we invited Hana, and why it is so important that she is here.'

As Arthur speaks, Marissa eases back into her chair. Her breathing relaxes. Her eyes rise from the multi-coloured M&M's, towards Hana. The two women hold each other's gaze. Hana is taken aback to see that there seems to be no anger in Marissa's face.

In his chair, Jaye shifts his weight, clears his throat. But before he can utter even a word, Marissa interjects.

'You know what, Jaye?' she says, her eyes still on Hana. 'No offence, but please don't talk. I don't need to hear what you have to say.'

A glance shoots between the two counsellors as they

silently try to work out which one of them should intercede. Marissa doesn't give them the opportunity to decide.

'Virginia, Arthur. Can you take Jaye and go somewhere, please,' she says. 'Get a coffee, or a gin. Whatever.'

'There's a reason therapeutic sessions need to follow a defined structure, Marissa—' Virginia attempts, but Marissa ignores her.

'I didn't realize until you sat down,' she continues, talking directly to Hana, as if no one else is in the room. 'This isn't about anyone else. This is about you and me. We're the ones who need to sort this out.'

All eyes turn to Hana.

'Okay then,' she says.

Arthur is about to chime in, to try to wrestle them all back to the agreed therapeutic process, but Marissa cuts him off.

'Arthur, for fuck's sake, hear what I'm saying. *Go*.'

The others head for the door. Arthur trails reluctantly after them.

'Shut the door behind you,' Marissa says.

He complies, the established counsellor–client dynamic now completely turned on its head.

Marissa and Hana are left looking at each other across the M&M's. A long uncertain silence.

Finally, Marissa speaks.

'I loved you. Because of who you are. Because I love

the two people who love you most. Your daughter, and Jaye. I still love you, somewhere down inside.'

This is quietly spoken, surprisingly intimate. Walking into this room, Hana wasn't sure what to expect. It certainly wasn't this.

'When you held me in the bathroom, after Tony died. Two women can't share that, then pretend what was between them doesn't exist. I hope one day I'll be able to kiss you hello or goodbye again. Hug you, hold you. And do it with love. But I can't do that today.'

Marissa takes a tissue from the box beside the M&M's, wipes her eyes.

'How can I?' she continues. 'When I don't know if what is between you and Jaye will always be there. An inch below the surface, waiting to come back. One day. One day, when you're hurt or vulnerable or sad. Or he is. And that will be the day that Jaye's gone for good.'

Marissa finishes talking. To her surprise, Hana feels wetness on her own cheek. Marissa takes another tissue from the box and hands it to her. Hana knows there are answers Marissa needs and she is the only one who can give them.

'I fell in love with Jaye when I was a child. When I had no idea who I really was or what I really wanted. Jaye and I, we made something extraordinary together. Addison. Because of our child, I will never not love him. That's something you can't ask of me. But she was the reason the universe put us together, for a moment in time. Then the moment passed. Because of Addison, Jaye and I will always be connected. But we are much better people apart.'

Hana takes a few deep breaths. Marissa stays silent.

'I can't undo what happened. It was wrong and unforgiveable. It will never happen again. I have no right to ask you to believe me. But it's the truth.'

The only sound is the quiet ticking of the clock on the wall above Marissa's head. Both women sit in silence. The second hand sweeps a full two circuits before Marissa stands. Hana stands too, as Marissa comes to the other side of the table and stops, face to face with her.

'I can forgive you. I will forgive you. I do forgive you. But I can never forget.'

'I know that.'

'I see you,' Marissa says quietly. 'All that is so good and extraordinary in you. And all the harm you can do. I see it. I hope you see it too.'

Marissa puts her arms around Hana.

They hold each other.

Marissa and Hana emerge into the waiting room. The counsellors and Jaye look up, expectant, with no idea what has transpired behind the closed door of the counselling room.

'I'm going home now. See you next week,' Marissa tells them.

'Would you like to share what happened with the rest of us?' Arthur asks.

'Not right now,' Marissa says firmly. She turns to Hana. 'Shall we meet for a drink next time you're in Auckland?'

'I'd like that.'

To everyone's surprise, Marissa kisses Hana on the cheek, and heads out the door.

Outside on the street, as Marissa gets into her car, Jaye catches up with Hana. 'That went ... well?' he asks, tentatively.

'I don't want to speak for Marissa. Why don't you ask her.'

Watching the car drive away, Hana lowers her voice. With the session over, there's something else she needs to talk to Jaye about.

'Look, Jaye. I know my place. I know I'm a civilian now, and I'm not asking for privileged information. But if there's anything you can tell me about developments with Gordon John Weeks, I'd appreciate it.'

When he answers, it looks like it's against his better judgement. 'The night Kiri disappeared, Weeks was at the Point Marlon RSA, watching the All Blacks test.'

'What about the earlier murder? Paige Meadows, twenty-one years ago?'

Jaye rubs the back of his neck, irritation in his voice. 'I understand why this has got under your skin. But all this, because your dad had a soft spot for the guy who confessed to murder?'

He catches himself, softens his tone.

'Listen, I've got to head off.'

He turns towards his car, then looks back at her, genuine gratitude in his eyes.

'Thanks for giving my marriage a fighting chance,' he says, before walking away.

Before she leaves the city, Hana makes a stop. Stan texted earlier that he had something for her. When he heads out from the front door of the station to where she is waiting across the road in her car, she can see he's noticeably favouring his artificial leg.

'Your guy with the ugly tattoos,' Stan says, after he's climbed into the passenger seat and closed the door. 'He has a history of convictions. Theft, assault, burglary. His longest stretch was nine years in Waikeria* for importation and dealing, after a big undercover bust. The last few years, he's kept his slate clean.'

---

* Waikeria prison, one of the largest in New Zealand.

'I guarantee Rendall didn't clean up his act,' Hana says. 'He just got smart.'

'I talked to some local cops who've had dealings with him and the gang. He recruits vulnerable wannabes. Gets them to do his dirty work. If things go wrong, they take the fall.'

Stan hasn't come with a file for her, and Hana knows why. Duplicating police information and passing it on would be a crime, and the end of any hope Stan has of winning back the right to do the job he loves.

'Thanks, Stan. I really owe you one'.

'One more thing. His name is on the property records of an industrial warehouse in a little town an hour from you. Kaikākāriki Junction. He bought it two years ago. Cash sale.'

Both of them know, if a property is bought for cash, the money is rarely earned legitimately. Hana watches as Stan rubs his leg where it meets the artificial limb.

'You looked a bit ginger, crossing the road.'

'Bloody thing. Might've been pushing myself a bit hard.' Stan trails away as he looks back towards Central Station. 'I can't be a desk jockey, boss. I'm not made for it', he says quietly. 'I'm gonna make it back.'

Hana squeezes his arm gently. 'If anyone can, it's you.'

When Stan looks at her, she is surprised by the emotion in his face. 'I heard you, you know.'

Hana isn't sure what he means at first.

'In the police helicopter,' he says. 'I heard you talking to me.'

After the explosion that cost Stan his lower leg, Hana was at his side on the emergency chopper rushing him to life-saving surgery, talking to him through the whole of the fifteen-minute journey that felt to her like fifteen hours.

'I was unconscious. But I heard you. I heard you saying, "You're not dying on me. I'm not gonna fucking let you." Your voice was like one of those orange rings they throw at someone who's fallen off a boat. Thank you, boss.'

Some relationships are forever stuck in time. Hana's connection with Stan will always be that of the senior officer and the bright young newbie she took under her wing and mentored. He's always going to call her 'boss', and she'll always like it. But it's more than that. There's a lot of unspoken love between these two. All the more so after what they've been through, together.

As Stan crosses the road back to Central Station, Hana drives away.

The irony doesn't escape her.

Stan is doing everything he possibly can to get his badge back and fight his way up to the eighth floor again. While Hana took her badge off. And walked away from the building forever.

16

THE GYM

'Left, left. Left jab, left jab, now right. Keep it going. One more minute.'

Addison is sweating hard, concentrating hard.

There's so much to think about: the position of her feet, keeping her stance elastic. Trying not to dwell on the uncomfortable moistness of the inside of the boxing gloves she's been loaned, and how many people might have sweated in them before her. What did the guy say? The force of each jab should start in the strong muscles of the legs and glutes, go up through the torso and the shoulder. Gives you so much more firepower than swinging from the elbow.

'Bring the weight of your whole body to the punch.'

She's breathing hard, but she's not out of breath. Addison inherited her mum's strong, muscular body, and her fitness. They compared their resting heart rates one time using Hana's running watch: Hana's was low 40s; Addison's was 51, a very decent level of cardiovascular fitness. Which was no surprise. On stage, Addison is in constant motion, bouncing from one side to the other, stalking, the rhythm of her rapping reflected in the rhythm of her movement. To keep match-fit for performances she runs circuits up and down a local peak near the house, looking out over their inner-city suburb, and does sit-ups and squats. Hana always tried to talk Addison into coming running with her, but Addison likes to keep her exercise solitary. And actually, that's what Hana prefers too.

'Left, left, left, and right. Take a breather. How you feeling?'

'Doesn't this place have aircon?' Addison says.

'Good to sweat out the toxins,' the trainer replies with a grin. 'You're a natural. But you gotta work on your upper body strength. Twenty push-ups. I'll do them with you.'

Addison finds herself on the canvas of the training ring, perspiring her way through a series of triceps-burning push-ups with the personal trainer she'd booked a session with.

Kiri's boyfriend. Dax.

That morning, a few hours earlier, Addison was on Facebook, following an interconnected maze of threads linking the people Kiri knew, her friendship groups. She found one particular photo of Kiri in a group of people her age, all of them with a certain staunchness, a bit of a shared 'don't fuck with me' vibe. Kiri was looking into the camera, with the familiar smile that never seemed to leave her face.

Addison noticed something else.

A guy in the photo, beside Kiri. Red hair. A distinctive nose. Good-looking and not good-looking at the same time. In the photo, Kiri and the guy were standing closer than the others in the group. When she zoomed in, Addison realized they were holding hands.

Huh. Kiri had a guy.

When it was time to leave for their political studies lecture, Addison told PLUS 1 she was feeling a bit under the weather and wouldn't make it.

'Take notes for me, babe?'

After their conversation in front of the kitchen-sink fire, Addison had taken down the pictures she'd printed of Kiri. She didn't want PLUS 1 to worry about her or feel uncomfortable. But she didn't stop thinking about Kiri. And when she found the Facebook photo of her holding hands with the guy, she couldn't help herself. She looked through the tags on the image, saw the name of the boxing gym where it was taken. When

PLUS 1 left for uni, Addison headed down the motorway towards the gym in Māngere.

She walked in the door, stopped in her tracks. The person behind the counter was the same guy from the photo. Surely it couldn't be this easy, hunting someone down! Maybe her mum's job wasn't actually that hard. Or perhaps, along with the low heart-rate, Addison had also inherited some of Hana's investigative skills.

For a moment, she hesitated. The night before, PLUS 1 hadn't used words like 'weird' or 'fucked-up' to describe Addison's obsession with Kiri, but they hadn't needed to. A momentary encounter with the remains of a young, murdered girl had affected her in ways that made no logical sense. But she couldn't help it. Their paths had collided in the dunes, and the growing sense Addison had of somehow being drawn into the dead girl's orbit just wasn't going away.

She walked up to the counter.

She asked Dax for an introductory session.

It's the last set of sparring and upper-body exercises, thank God. Addison is red-faced, sweat dripping onto the canvas floor of the ring, doing the final set of push-ups.

'I feel so gross,' she manages to get out. 'I must smell like a pig.'

'You're in a boxing gym. If it helps, you're almost definitely the least disgusting person here.'

'That makes me feel so much better.'

Beneath the hand-painted sign about blood and sweat and tears, Dax studies Addison's face. 'This whole session I've been trying to figure it out.'

'What?'

'I know you. Never been to see you perform or anything. But I've seen posts of you onstage, I've heard a couple of your tracks. You're good.'

'Thanks.' Addison finishes her push-ups. Despite every inch of her aching, the session was way more fun than she would ever have thought. It was strange to enjoy what was basically legalized grievous bodily harm, but there was something in the steady, repeated pattern of the jab-jab-punch, something about the slap of her sweaty leather gloves against the punching pad, the rhythmic nature of boxing, that seemed like it could be meditative, reflective. She could see herself growing to like it. But it wasn't just the physicality of the workout. She was instantly drawn to Dax. His sweet nature, encouraging without being pushy; a quiet voice and smiling eyes that made Addison feel at ease and unembarrassed when she mixed up her lefts with her rights, a spatial dyslexia she'd had her whole life.

But as comfortable as she feels with him, she still hasn't broached the reason she's actually come to see him. The longer the pretence continues, the weirder it will be when she finally asks about Kiri.

'Live round here?' Dax asks, as Addison pays for the lesson with a fifty-dollar note.

'Central city. I drove down.'

'Long way to come. Not like there's not a dozen hipster boxing gyms in town you could go to.'

Addison pockets her wallet. It's now or never.

'You knew Kiri, right?' she asks, trying to sound casual, offhand.

A sudden guardedness seems to come to Dax, like a boxer's defensive stance.

'What is this?' he asks, his eyes burning. 'You wanna turn Kiri into a song? That why you came all this way?' He hands back Addison's cash. 'I don't want your money. Fuck off, vampire. Go get rich and famous off of someone else.' Dax turns his back on her, heads for the smoko room.* Conversation over.

She calls after him, trying not to sound as panicky as she feels. 'I found her.'

Dax turns and stares at her. 'What did you say?'

'It was me who found her. In the dunes.'

'That's such a fucked-up thing to lie about.'

'I'm not lying.'

Addison is shaky, but she can't stop now.

'I can't explain why I came looking for you,' she

---

* Smoko room – staff tea room.

says. 'She was around the same age as me. I keep thinking, that could've been one of my friends. Or me.'

In Dax's face, the guarded look retreats a little.

'Can we talk?' Addison asks. 'Just for a few minutes?'

The boxing gym is built on top of a scrub-covered slope rising above the train tracks that run beside the motorway between the city and the sprawling suburbs of South Auckland. Out the back of it are big piles of equipment waiting to be repaired: heavy hanging bags with splits in the aged leather and weights that have been chipped over the years and are in need of a bit of touch-up paint. Dax sits on a broken treadmill that's long since rusted out.

'This gym. It's what turned things around, for me and Kiri both. But really, it was Lorraine.'

'My mum's a cop. Well, she used to be. She knows Lorraine.'

Dax pulls a vape from his pocket. Turns it over in his fingers. 'This is the strongest thing I've done in four years,' he says, 'apart from the occasional jay. If you'd told me when I was seventeen, vaping was gonna be my only bad habit, I'd have laughed at you.'

Below, on the motorway, the morning rush hour is well over, but there's a line of trucks hauling containers south, commuter buses heading the other way, into the city.

'We'd both got into some pretty intense stuff,' Dax continues. 'We had charges pending in the youth court. Drugs, petty theft to pay for the drugs. Lorraine offered us places on the programme. A way to stop being locked up. But it became a whole lot more than that.'

Dax offers Addison the vape.

'I don't.'

'Weed?'

'Sometimes. Not great for my voice, onstage. But awesome for the anxiety.'

'MDMA?'

'I like it. But I feel like I could like it too much. Once in a blue moon.'

'Rock ... ?'

'I'm not a fucking idiot.'

'Good. Stay being a not-fucking-idiot.'

He takes a long puff on the vape.

'The cops and the social workers. They weren't all love-and-tenderness. The opposite. Lorraine was ... I dunno. Not a mum. Not really anything like a mum. But if any of us had mums like her, maybe we wouldn't have got to where we got to. Once you've been using long enough, you figure out how to game every system, you know? How to bullshit everybody. How to twist people round your finger, get them to believe whatever you want them to believe. Lorraine's not like that. Feed her a line of bullshit, she'll be onto you before you've finished the sentence. Tell you to your face, stop talking shit.'

Below, a commuter train pulls into the station at the bottom of the slope. A group of teenagers get out, hoodies and big sneakers, laughing and hooting and pushing each other.

'Lorraine took us on these long mountain runs through the Waitākere Ranges, out west. Out in the forest, the sounds of birds everywhere. Running until your body and lungs ached, throwing yourself into a freezing-cold mountain stream afterwards, tasting the water and smelling the air. Stuff none of us had ever experienced. Lorraine says the best way to attack addiction is to replace one physical extreme, the drugs, with another. Run till you drop. Kayak across the harbour. Weights and boxing bags. She got that from her dad. Blood makes you tough. Sweat makes you strong.'

'It worked?'

'Not for everyone. For me, shit yeah. And it worked for Kiri. I got off drugs and cheap booze. Kiri got straight.'

Dax pauses. A long silence. After this, Addison suspects, the story gets more difficult.

'I found a cardigan in a secondhand shop,' she says gently. 'It's a bit like what she was wearing in one of the photos.'

'The blue-and-white one? With the patches and big buttons?'

'The one I found doesn't have the patches. But yeah. Nearly the same.'

There's something Addison really wants to ask. She takes the plunge.

'The stories in the news said she was smart. Funny. Strong. But she'd started using again. Why?'

Below, on the motorway, the sound of sirens approaching. A row of emergency vehicles passes, lights flashing. Looks like something very bad has happened somewhere further down the motorway. As the flashing red and blue lights and the screaming sirens disappear into the distance, Dax gets to his feet. He pockets the vape, avoiding Addison's eyes. She's hit a nerve.

'I've got another client.'

'I'm sorry if I upset you,' she says, but it's too late. The wall has gone up. The defensive stance that seems to come so naturally to him.

'She's been found,' he says. 'Thank Christ. Now Lorraine can work out who did it to her.'

Addison watches as Dax heads back into the gym.

17

SEAFOAM GREEN

Green-coloured eyes actually have no colour.

It's weird. But it's science. It's about the amount of melanin in the iris. If your eyes are brown, it means you've got heaps of melanin. A genetic fifty-to-one longshot like me, with green eyes, has none of the stuff. With no melanin to hit, the light refracts in my eyes, giving the appearance of green. Same thing as with how the sky, which is no colour at all, looks blue.

The absence of my real parents defines me. The absence of melanin defines my eyes.

Defined my eyes?

Let's stick with present tense.

What does it matter that, when I look at my eyes, they're not actually green? What does it matter that what I see isn't really there? If you see it, why not commit? Make your own reality. My eyes are green. The shade of green changes. In bright sunlight, they're seafoam green. It's my favourite colour. It took me ages to find spray paint that's the same shade. When I found the right one, I got a box of a dozen cans so I wouldn't run out. When we're bored, Trish and I take a couple of spray cans of seafoam green and paint pictures on toilet walls or bus stops. Because public toilets and bus stops are the ugliest places in civilization, and we think people should have nice things to look at.

You're welcome.

You already know the Armageddon story, how Dax and me broke up. But I never told the creation story. How we got together.

I like this story better.

In the Youth at Risk group, they did this thing with us at the gym, 'confrontation sessions'. They paired us up and we had to roleplay, one of us playing the other's addiction. They told us to physicalize beating the drugs. We put on boxing gloves. It was intense and physical as hell, shoving each other around.

Sounds like bullshit. But lots of things that actually work sound like bullshit. Until you commit. I was paired up with Dax. They talked about taking the pain and damage we were doing to ourselves and letting it out through the boxing gloves. I don't know, maybe I was in a particularly emotional mood that day, but it just made so much sense I wanted to scream. When it was my turn I punched Dax, punched and punched, so fucking hard his lip bled. I stopped punching. I tried to hug him and I saw the tears in his eyes that he was trying to hide but he couldn't hide. And I realized, him almost-crying had zero to do with getting a split lip a few moments prior, but had everything to do with pretty much every other minute of his last seventeen years.

He finally let me hold him and we both cried. Everyone was staring. One of the social workers sent all the others home and sat with us and told us that it felt like something important had just happened.

Shit yeah, something had happened.

Outside the gym, it was a bit awkward. But also, it wasn't. We both knew tectonic plates had realigned; the axis had shifted. Dax started up his shitty old scooter. I got on the back. We rode the streets. The sun went down; the streetlights came out. We rode and rode for hours. Not even talking. We didn't need to talk. We didn't need words to say how we were feeling. Sitting on his scooter, the rattling going through our bones and the fumes from the rusty exhaust pipe going through our hair, my hands around his little muscley waist, just being together, riding the back alleys and cutting across parks and going the wrong way down one-lane streets. In perfect silence. We were talking. We were telling each other how we felt.

But neither of us said a word.

We got to the Domain. This huge park near the museum, hundreds of hectares of playing fields and duck ponds. The big irrigation sprinklers were out, throwing great rooster plumes of water high into the air, the lights of passing cars and street lamps refracting through the arcing spray to form magical prisms floating above us.

Red, orange, yellow, green, blue, indigo, violet.

Uenuku, the God of the Rainbow, riding their celestial moped above our heads.

Dax was trying to dodge the walls of water flumes, but being a crap rider, as well as a complete dick, he was misjudging and getting us drenched. Both of us soaking wet and laughing like fools.

The gas ran out.

We got off the scooter. His lip had stopped bleeding. Standing there surrounded by rainbows and water arcs. In the movies you'd kiss. We didn't kiss. Didn't need to. We both knew how we felt, and what was going to happen. I told Dax I'd meet him back at his place. I'd been writing something in my head the whole time we were riding, and for once it was coming together sweet, without needing a hit. I had to get the words down. Dax pushed his scooter home. I went to this rocky cliff face near the base of the Harbour Bridge. I got one of my spray cans from where I kept my stash in among the bushes. And I wrote the poem. This wasn't for public consumption, not like the pictures Trish and I did on bus stops and toilet walls. This was just for me. At the base of the rock, hidden behind the bushes, I started spraying the poem that had formed in my head riding on Dax's scooter.

I wrote the words small and delicate and pretty. Like the things I was feeling.

When I ran out of words, I sat looking at the poem until the battery on my phone ran out. I knew it wasn't finished. There was a beginning and a middle. But no end yet.

I figured I'd work the ending out.

I went to Dax's place. He'd left the door open. I found his room and climbed under his sheets. He stirred. Turned his face towards me. I kissed him on that nose that was quite a bit bigger than necessary. Then I kissed him on his split lip.

In another kind of story this might be the end. And it would be warm, and it would be good.

But clearly, good endings aren't my strong point.

18

JUST BE HERE

Hana's car is parked on the street out the front of Tātā Bay's now defunct movie theatre. She had her first kiss there. Actually, more like a failed kiss. The boy who'd invited her to see *Footloose* was captain of the high school rugby team. A year older than Hana. A nice guy and crazy good-looking. Hana liked him well enough. But with him being captain and crazy good-looking, there was a fair amount of expectation and entitlement, which wasn't nearly so attractive to her. She remembers at a certain point in the movie, he moved the big bag of popcorn that was sitting between them and set it down on the floor. 'Casually' put his arm around the back of her seat. It took another few minutes for the arm to actually make contact with her shoulder. Then the pace quickened, like the pace of

Kevin Bacon's dance sequences on-screen. She felt the hand on her shoulder draw her in his direction, gently at first, then a little more forcefully. His free hand pushed her hair back from her face, before moving down, cupping her chin, turning her head towards his. She remembers his smile, a look of absolute confidence that she recognized from when he would line up the rugby ball for a shot at goal; four steps backwards, one small step right. On the rugby field, the ball would always go over the bar. Seeing that look, Hana felt a sudden pang of irritation. He closed his eyes, pressed his lips against hers. Hana didn't respond. Didn't move away or make a fuss. But she sure as hell didn't move towards him or press her lips back against his.

Sensing the lack of response, because how could he not, the captain of the first fifteen opened his eyes. This wasn't how it usually went.

'What's up?'

'I'm watching the movie.'

Hana turned back to the screen.

After the end credits, the captain went to a party with his teammates, and Hana went home.

The irony was, she'd thought a lot about what it would be like to kiss him. Or any boy. She'd even looked at a few of the senior girls, wondering if kissing a girl's lips might feel different to kissing a boy's. She didn't have any experience of either, and she was feeling like it was high time to find out. But that look of certainty – just like when he'd take the four steps back, one step sideways, facing the goalposts, knowing without a doubt the ball was going to go over – made her rethink.

She could wait.

When *Ghostbusters* was on the next weekend, the captain of the first fifteen didn't ask Hana to go with him. She was just fine with that. A few years later a fire destroyed the projection room, though the theatre had been running at a loss anyway. The place has been boarded up ever since, like quite a few of the other shops in the small town, and now, if they want to go to the movies, kids have to drive 35 kilometres to the nearest cinema.

'Seat belt on. Check your mirrors. Start the engine. Indicate. Take the handbrake off.'

Now, outside the abandoned movie theatre, Tīmoti is behind the steering wheel of Hana's car. He'd missed quite a few of the training sessions with Hana and her dad, but at last he'd turned up. With even more attitude than usual. Hana had told him they were going to have a practical lesson out on the roads, like he was going to have to do in a few weeks' time when he sat the actual test. Tīmoti's basketball boots tap the floor of the car. A familiar, irritated, I-got-somewhere-else-I-wanna-be look on his face.

'I checked the mirrors. Twice.'

'Do it again. Just like you're gonna do on the day.'

'I just wanna drive.'

'Uh-huh. That's why we're doing this. So you can get your driver's licence, so you'll be able to drive for work out of Tātā Bay, or go to the city and have a good time, whatever. You get that licence, you have options.'

Sitting in the hot car next to him, Hana smells the slightly sweet, slightly acidic tang of someone who's drunk too much the night before. The sound of an engine makes them both look towards the end of the street. Hana recognizes the approaching vehicle, a Mark III Zephyr, and she knows the driver: Erwin Rendall, the guy she'd confronted outside the dairy. As he drives past, arm hanging out the window, heavily adorned with the unlovely tattoos, he stares in through her windscreen, taking in Tīmoti and Hana. Hana sees the look that passes between Rendall and Tīmoti; she sees Tīmoti's eyebrows rise in greeting. Rendall turns his stare on her. A sneer on his face. Then there's the rev of his engine, and a squeal of tyres as he accelerates away down the main street.

'You know that guy?' Hana asks.

No answer. In the small hot car, she can sense the rising tension in her cousin's teenage son. Tīmoti's fingers drum the steering wheel, an opposing rhythm to his boots. Hana's had enough.

'You're sitting your test in less than three weeks' time, Tīmoti. You don't get a licence, you're going to be pulled over eventually; you'll get fined, you'll be on the cops' radars, you'll be pulled up every time they see you. The fines will get bigger, eventually they'll take the car. You'll end up in court. Which bit of that do you want to happen?'

'I just wanna drive,' he says again. Staring straight ahead.

'Then we both want the same thing. Go through the list. Seat belt on. Check the mirrors. Just do it, please.'

A long, silent moment. Then Tīmoti takes the keys out of the ignition. Opens the door. Gets out.

'Tīmoti, stop acting like a child.'

'You're treating me like a child.'

'I'm trying to help you.'

'You think you know what I need. Did you ever ask me? You or matua? Anyone?'

Hana wasn't expecting any of this. Tīmoti is grasping the car keys so hard his knuckles are white.

'No one ever asked if I wanted this. Going to work on some farm, or cutting down trees, whatever shitty job you think I need a licence to get. You just reckon you know what's best for me.'

It's more words than Hana has ever heard him speak at one time, and she's struggling to find answers to his questions. Because it's true, neither she nor Eru asked Tīmoti if he wanted to take part in the training. Eru persuaded his mother to sign him up. It was all decided by everyone except him.

'I'm not dumb,' he says.

'No one thinks you are. Please, let's take the heat out of this. Get back in the car.'

'Fuck this. And fuck you.'

Tīmoti throws the keys at Hana; she has to dodge to avoid getting hit in the side of her head.

He turns and walks away down the main street.

Hana sits in her car, staring at the picture she drew of Gordon John Weeks.

After Tīmoti had stormed off, she'd driven back to the marae, alone. Opening her glovebox and taking out the picture, she couldn't help experiencing an unwelcome feeling of impotence. If Kiri Thomas was Hana's case, no matter how faint the scent she was following, she'd chase it until there was absolutely nothing left to pursue. But she's not a cop anymore. The sense of frustration gives her the same sick taste in her mouth as watching Tīmoti walk away. If he was her child, she'd know the strings to pull, how to cajole him back behind the wheel, to go through the damn checklist, to give him the best chance possible to get a driver's licence.

But Tīmoti isn't her son. Just like the investigation into the murder in the Tātā Bay dunes isn't her case.

As Hana folds up the identikit, her cousin pulls into the marae car park, ready to pick Tīmoti up. Hana gets out to meet Eyes. Knowing this isn't going to be easy.

'He's not here.'

'What do you mean? Where is he?'

'I don't know. We were in the middle of the lesson. I asked him to do the things he'd have to do for the driving test. He got out and walked away.'

Eyes fixes her cousin with a look Hana has come to know so well, like she doesn't belong here, doesn't understand how it works in Tātā Bay and never will.

'My son doesn't like being ordered around. He doesn't like being talked down to.'

'I don't believe I was doing either,' Hana says, wondering even as she says it if she maybe had been a little hard on Tīmoti.

'Yeah? Seems to me like you talk down to pretty much everyone round here.'

Hana takes a few beats, not wanting to reply with the same energy that's being sent her way. *One potato, two potato, three potato.*

'He's a good kid,' she says at last. 'I'm not saying he's not. And maybe he's got a point. He feels we all pushed him into this thing. But I've got to be honest, I think something else is up.'

For a moment, a glimpse of vulnerability in her cousin's face. Like there's something eating at her, something Eyes really needs to talk about. Hana presses on.

'Has something changed? Is Tīmoti hanging out

with new people? Is he drinking?' she asks, remembering the sickly-sweet smell in the car.

There's a scar on Eyes' forehead, from when they were kids, riding their old hand-me-down bikes down a hillside. Eyes was always the boldest, always the one who would be the first to jump off the bridge into the river, always the one who'd go hardest and fastest, pushing the limits. That time, riding way too fast down the hillside pitted with uneven sheep tracks, her bike hit a big hole. She fell off at speed, landing face first, opening up a big cut above her eyebrow, blood everywhere. Hana gave her cousin her sweater to stop the blood, pushed her wrecked bike back home for her. It was the closest she'd ever seen Eyes to crying. But she didn't, even with a cut that needed six stitches. Eyes is the definition of staunch. Too proud to ever shed a tear. At least, not in front of anyone else.

'Maybe drugs?' Hana is tentative as she asks the question. It's a big thing to suggest to any mum. 'I'm sorry,' she presses on. 'I just have to ask. Have you noticed? Do you think there's something wrong?'

Eyes looks like she did after she fell off her bike. Teetering on the edge of letting go, sitting down and weeping. But she holds it back. Just. The fleeting glimpse of vulnerability in her face hardens into something more familiar.

'Wow. Thirty years on and you're still telling tales.'
Hana's lips tighten. She knows exactly what Eyes

means. Eyes and Hana are the same age and, growing up, their two households spilled over into each other, Hana regularly sleeping over at Eyes' family's house or vice versa. When they hit their early teens, Eyes physically matured before Hana. And she got interested in guys earlier. When Eyes stayed over one Saturday night, she tried to persuade Hana to sneak out with her to a party; a bunch of older boys had asked them both to come. Hana was too much of a rule-follower to climb out the window with her cousin. Eyes went anyway. Upset and worried when she didn't come back at the time she'd said she would, Hana finally woke up her dad. Eru put her in the car, and they went and extracted a furious and humiliated Eyes from the party. That was the start of a bitter rupture between the two cousins, that only deepened when Hana joined the cops and left Tātā Bay.

'It's not just you who knows how to raise a kid,' Eyes says.

'I'm not trying to piss you off.'

'Well, you are.'

'I'm sorry,' Hana says. 'I just want to help Tīmoti.'

'Nuh. You want to pass judgement. On me, on all of us. You love it.'

Eyes heads back to her car. She pauses at the open door.

'Don't know why you even bothered coming back,' she says.

Standing on the paving stones of the forecourt as Eyes' car drives away, there's a sick feeling in Hana's gut. She turns to see Eru coming towards her from the meeting house.

'You heard that?' she asks.

Eru nods, *yeah*. He heard.

He takes Hana by the arm. Leads her into the carved wooden meeting house. They slip off their shoes at the door; it's cool and quiet inside after the harsh sunlight out in the forecourt, the polished floors smooth under Hana's feet. There are stacks of wooden benches around the walls of the wharenui. Eru lifts one into the middle of the floor. He takes off his battered bushman's hat and takes a seat, indicating for Hana to join him. In silence they sit, surrounded by the beautiful carvings and weavings that line the walls of the house. The designs that tell the legends of their tribe, of their ancestors, the journeys across the oceans to Aotearoa, the stories of the exploits of their people in the centuries they have lived in the area.

'You okay?'

'I'm fine, Dad.'

But Hana can't hide it; the confrontations with Eyes and Tīmoti have thrown her.

'See that up there? Your nanny wove that,' Eru says.

There's a woven flax panel on the far wall of the meeting house. It's beautiful and delicate, representing the waves of the oceans that lie beyond the Tātā Bay dunes. Eru smiles at his daughter.

'I love that you're home. Everything you're doing. The drivers' licence programme. Growing the tree seedlings in your back yard to plant around the marae. Getting the marae ātea spick and span so we can stand proud and face our guests as they arrive.'

Eru's fingers entwine with Hana's as they look up at the weaving of the ocean waves.

'You are woven into the walls of this house, e kō.* You're in the soil of this marae. Don't worry what that cousin of yours says. It's not a popularity contest. This is your home. You don't have to keep trying so hard. You don't have anything to prove. Just be here.'

His fingers squeeze hers. Loving. Gentle. Then he stands and heads for the door.

'Close the door when you leave, eh. I'll make kai tonight.'

Among the carvings and weavings, Hana stays on the seat for a long while. Outside, the sun sets and shadows fall.

She sits. Comfortable.

Just being there.

---

* E kō – daughter.

It's dark when Hana closes the carved doors of the wharenui and gets back into her car. Sitting behind the wheel, she looks once more at the sketch that she drew. She screws it up, ready to throw it away and move on, to accept the inevitable, that there's no scent left to follow and in any case she's in no position to follow it. But a thought makes her stop.

She reaches for her phone. Googles a phone number in Auckland. Dials.

'Good evening, Point Marlon Returned Serviceman's Association.'

'This is going to sound like a funny question,' Hana says. 'Do you keep your sign-in records for visitors?'

On the other end of the line, the man asks, 'What's this about? And who is this calling please?'

For a moment Hana considers giving her name as Detective Senior Sergeant Westerman, which would have been true six months earlier, but would now be committing the offence of imitating a police officer.

'My name's Hana Westerman.'

This unexpectedly achieves the same goal. The man at reception recognizes her name, from her final case, which he followed avidly.

'You do good service for your country,' he says, warmly. 'You're welcome here any time. How can I help?'

'I'm interested in your records from the sixteenth of September four years ago. The night of the rugby test, All Blacks versus the Springboks, seven tries to none.

I'm hoping there's a way to confirm the patrons who were there that night, watching the game.'

'Everyone has to sign in when they come in the door. And we keep the sign-in books. Got shelves of the things. But we don't have anything for that date.'

'Could I ask you to just look?'

'No point. There's nothing.'

'How do you know?' Hana asks.

'We were closed. We were having the new restaurant and bar put in,' the man says.

Hana's spine straightens against the back of the driver's seat. 'Are you sure?'

'We closed late August. Reopened first week of October.'

Hana hangs up, takes the sketch that she'd scrunched up, straightens and smooths it out.

She stares at the face she drew on the page.

19

ROGUE

'To get this straight. You're running a parallel investigation to the cops?'

'I'm trying to work out what's going on.'

'And Jaye would be all good with that?'

Hana and Sebastian Kang are in a coffee shop, the identikit picture sitting on the table between them. The office of Seb's investigation company is a small converted upstairs apartment on K Road, the seedy, exhilarating, noisy and colourful one-mile stretch of vape shops and cafés and vintage clothing stores in the beating heart of Auckland. There's an unspoken rule that to work or play on K Road you should be tattooed, intriguingly pierced and preferably vegan. Seb is none of the above. But he loves the energy and the flavour of the place, and the café downstairs from his office has become his ersatz meeting room.

'I'm not running an investigation,' Hana insists. 'I've talked to a few people, made some calls. My daughter found the girl's bones. I'm invested.'

Seb picks up the sketch, noticing something Hana has written on the reverse. A street name and flat number.

'You found out where he lives?' he asks.

Hana sips her coffee. No response. Which answers Seb's question.

'How'd you get this address? Companies register? Social media?'

'He doesn't own a company and he's not on socials.'

'Meaning, you searched both.'

'Of course I did. I found his address in the electoral rolls.'

'No offence, but this is getting obsessive,' Seb says.

'No offence taken.'

'Where are you going with this, Hana?'

'Two girls go missing, both bodies end up in the same sand dunes. Weeks was in Tātā Bay, behaving suspiciously, when the first girl disappeared. He lives in the same part of Auckland where Kiri was taken.'

'That same part of Auckland is home to maybe 200,000 people.'

'He lied about where he was, the night she disappeared.'

'Tell Lorraine and Jaye about the guy's false alibi. Then let it go. This isn't your job anymore.'

Hana looks at Seb for a long moment.

'If you were me, that's what you'd do?'

'Yes,' he says, emphatic.

She takes the identikit, folds it up and returns it to her bag.

'Seriously, Hana. What are you thinking of doing?'

'I'm going to take your advice. Let Jaye and Lorraine know. Let it go. It's not my job.'

Hana walks out of the coffee shop and gets into her car.

Seb watches her drive away. From the way she looked at him, he's pretty sure that Hana isn't about to leave this alone.

An hour later, Hana's car is parked across the road from the address Seb saw on the back of the identikit drawing. The flat where Gordon John Weeks lives is a small downstairs apartment. When she pulled in, she could see movement inside. Years of time-consuming surveillance jobs when she was a junior detective have given Hana patience and an iron bladder. Before she heads home to Tātā Bay, she's going to see what she can see. Maybe get a glimpse of the guy who's set alarm bells ringing for her. Get a feel for him as flesh and blood, not as a sketch on a piece of art paper.

The truth is, Hana's not at all sure what she's waiting for.

When she was a kid, she heard discussions on the marae about 'muru'. Muru is the concept of natural law, justice in a traditional Māori sense. Back in the day, if a boy stole a kumara* from another tribe, he would be brought back to the pā† he stole it from. The two sides would have a hui‡ about the appropriate way to rebalance what had been done. It could be in the form of payment of other goods or services; it could be symbolic, for instance the cutting of the boy's hair; or it could be punitive, a physical punishment. There's an unavoidable tension between traditional Māori ideas of justice and the British common law system that was introduced when New Zealand was colonized; like the grasses and trees and animals and settlers who took over the land, the new judicial system took root and inevitably overwhelmed what was there before. Instead of discussion and mutually arrived-at agreements between aggrieved parties, law books and statutes inherited from the other side of the world determined how justice was

---

* Kumara – sweet potato.

† Pā – village, community.

‡ Hui – a meeting for the purposes of discussion between two sides.

meted out. It became institutionalized, laid out in leather-bound tomes, enforced and adjudicated upon by police and lawyers and judges, people with absolutely no knowledge of or relationship to those who were actually affected.

Waiting outside the apartment, Hana thinks about the girl in the orange wig on the stage in the Tātā Bay College Hall. There was an investigation, a confession, a trial, a verdict. Someone was locked away for the crime. In the eyes of the legal system, justice was done, and was seen to be done. But with everything Hana has since learned about the murder, she is starting to fear that true justice has not been served for Paige, or her family. Nor for the man who went to prison for the murder and died there: Tama Hall.

Hana sees movement in the flat. A window being locked; someone drawing the curtains. Weeks getting ready to head to work, perhaps. The front entrance is obscured by a staircase leading to the apartments on the upper floor, but a few moments later she hears the sound of the door opening, then being locked.

Gordon John Weeks walks out towards the street. His workbag in his hands.

Hana watches him without watching him, the way a cop learns to do. Peripheral vision. Her head directed straight at the phone in her hand, pretending to tap out a text. From the corner of her eye, she follows him as he unlocks his car. When he's behind the steering wheel, she turns her head just enough to look directly at him, only for a moment. Though she's never actually set eyes on him before, she recognizes him immediately. The same bushy eyebrows she'd visualized from the description Chloe had given, the blond hair flecked with grey now, but the same intense eyes.

She turns her head back to her phone screen, hearing his car engine start. Adjusting her rear-view mirror, she watches the car pull into the reflection, tracking it as it heads down the street, turns the corner.

Then he's gone.

Her eyes go back to the apartment.

The empty apartment.

The sensible thing would be to start the engine. Drive back to her house by the dunes. Take the advice Seb gave her. Let it go. Ignore the things she has discovered about the beekeeper who lived in Tātā Bay for a few months twenty-one years ago. Just as the CIB and the justice system will almost certainly ignore him. With an official verdict long since delivered and filed, Hana is confident there will be no appetite to dig into the weeds again, to vigorously explore whether Gordon John Weeks had a role in Paige's death, or in Kiri's murder nearly two decades later.

Unless something shifts.

Hana takes her keys from the ignition, slips her phone into her pocket and grabs the door handle, ready to get out and walk across the road to the empty apartment. But before she can, the passenger door opens.

Seb slides into the other seat. 'For fuck's sake, Hana.'

'You followed me?'

'I saw the look on your face. You're a dog with a bone. Anyway, I didn't follow you, I came to the address you wrote on the back of the picture. And here you are.'

'You've been *watching* me?'

'Same as you were watching Weeks.'

'I'm not actually your employee, Sebastian. You're not my boss—'

'I'm your friend. I'm shitting myself that you're about to take the law into your own hands. Break in. See if you can find anything solid that's going to make Lorraine and Jaye pay attention.'

'You don't know that.'

'Yes, I do. It's what I'd do. Except I'd lose my investigator's licence.'

Seb sighs. He pulls something out of his pocket. A skeleton key.

'You don't have a licence to lose,' he says.

He presses the key into Hana's hand. His eyes on hers.

'I'll wait. Get in and out of there in ten minutes. Preferably five.'

Inside the downstairs flat, to Hana's considerable relief, she finds there's no alarm. The apartment is small, shadowy, silent. Everything is tidy, meticulously so. The person who lives here craves order. In the little kitchenette area, there's a board on the wall with the shapes of various kitchen accessories outlined and the corresponding items hanging in their assigned places: fish slice, potato masher, soup ladle. A row of knives are displayed, going from small through progressively bigger blades, ending with a large butcher's knife.

On a shelf beneath the knives, a row of pill containers. Hana scans the labels. Antidepressants, mood stabilizers, anticonvulsants. Beside the meds, several packs of individual-serve mānuka honey health drinks, the packaging indicating the heavy little bottles were manufactured in Taiwan.

The sound of a vehicle pulling up outside. Hana curses under her breath, *shit*. Did Weeks just go out to fetch something from the shops? Has he come back? She hurries to the window, easing the curtain open a centimetre. It's a courier van, dropping a package off at a neighbouring house. As she watches the van pull away again her heart is racing, and not just because of the legal consequences of breaking and entering. If her hunch is right, she is in the home of a man who has killed once.

Perhaps, twice.

She heads on through the small, connected rooms of the flat, moving quicker now. There's a desktop computer. A large TV. A pile of DVDs tidily stacked beside it, the hand-written labels identifying them as recordings of the gospel sessions of a local televangelist, a self-proclaimed bishop with a large following based in his sprawling, ornate quasi-cathedral in South Auckland. Whatever else has happened in Gordon John Weeks' life, it seems he has at least moved on from the violent VHS films he watched in the small caravan in Tātā Bay.

The last room in the flat is the small bedroom. Like the rest of the apartment, it's ordered, impeccable. The single bed is made with the kind of creases you see in hospitals. There's a pinboard on the wall opposite, with one item pinned to it. A memorial order of service, the first line of Psalm 23 on the front, written in te reo Māori.

Ko Ihowā tōku hepara, e kore ahau e hapa.*

Hana carefully eases open the leaflet, looking at the inscription inside. It's from a burial service that took place several years ago. The funeral of Tama Hall.

The floor under the bed is empty, and as spotless as the rest of the room. Hana opens the wardrobe. Neatly laundered clothes on the hangers. At the back, shoes. Nothing else of note. She is about to shut the door when she sees it.

A floorboard at the back of the wardrobe doesn't quite line up with the others.

---

* 'The Lord is my shepherd, I shall not want.'

Like one row of paving stones slightly out of alignment on the marae ātea.

Hana opens the door fully, kneeling down. She carefully touches the floorboard. It moves. It's not nailed in place. She eases it out using her fingernails.

There, in a recess in the floor, a box. She removes the lid.

Inside, a bracelet.

Hana inhales sharply.

She's seen this bracelet before.

She pulls her phone from her pocket, and even as she's lining up a photo of the bracelet, it rings, making her gasp, the buzzing seeming far too loud in the complete silence of the flat.

'Sebastian?'

'Get out of there.'

In Hana's car, Seb is watching a vehicle heading down the street towards the flat. The car that left only a few minutes before. Gordon John Weeks behind the wheel.

'Get out. *Now*.'

Hearing the urgency in Seb's voice, Hana doesn't ask why.

His keys are colour-coded. The keys for the front door and the individual rooms of the transitional house have a red plastic ring. The key for the padlock on the shed out back of the transitional house that holds his beekeeping equipment and the cleaning supplies has a yellow ring. His car key is white, the same as his car.

Gordon John Weeks slides the blue key into the front door of the flat. He heads in.

As the door closes behind him, there's movement in the shadows beneath the stairs leading to the upstairs flats. Hana slips out. In the half minute it took for Weeks to find a parking space, she slid the lid back on the box and replaced the floorboard. She closed the wardrobe carefully, knowing how ordered Weeks keeps his world, then she hurried out the front door, pulling it closed behind her, and concealed herself.

She walks quickly across the road, one eye on the door of the flat, and slides into the driver's side of her car. 'Jesus,' she exhales.

'Yeah,' Seb says, watching the flat.

'You think he saw me?'

'I'm sure he didn't.'

Hana takes out her phone. She opens the gallery. She shows Seb the photo she took of the bracelet in the box hidden under the floorboards. An interlocked chain, with a small star hanging from it.

'The bracelet belongs to Paige Meadows. The girl who was murdered when I was in school.'

The last gift Paige's parents ever gave her.

A star for their star.

20

THINGS KEPT, TO REMEMBER

2 eggs
10 tbspns of flour
32 cooked mussels
3 tbspns finely sliced spring onions
2 tbspns finely sliced mint
2 tbspns finely sliced coriander or parsley
1 tsp chopped garlic
½ cup grated courgette

A half mile's walk south along the beach from Eru's house, there's a headland that juts out into the ocean, forming a natural surf break on the incoming tide. When the conditions are right, surfers will drive from Auckland city to catch waves. Another 200 metres further on, a sprawling rock shelf emerges when the tide recedes, and when Hana was small, the rough pitted moonscape was like a glorious technicolour playground: natural bowls in the rock filled with iridescent blue starfish, rust-coloured algae splattered across the shelf like paint tossed from an abstract artist's brush, strands of yellow and green and red seaweed like roughly plaited pigtails left behind by some rainbow-coloured mermaid who lingered too long and got snagged as the tide pulled her out.

All around the rock shelf, small living forests of mussels.

Four times the size of the black- or blue-shelled mussels Europeans and Australians are familiar with, indigenous, green-lipped mussels look like they're artificially manufactured in a lab with hormones and growth-inducers. They're not.

When Hana was a kid, one of her favourite things was going as a family down to the rock shelf, when the outgoing tide coincided with the setting of the sun. Her dad would get waist deep in the water, finding the mature mussels and pulling them off, while Hana collected them in a plastic shopping bag. On the beach her mum would gather driftwood and start a big fire. Every half dozen mussels he harvested, her dad would crack open the next one and eat it raw. He said it was tradition, the old way to eat kai moana.* Hana knew that was a big fat fib, that Eru just loved raw mussels and when it came to seafood (actually, most food), he had the patience and willpower of a toddler. The sight of her dad biting into the still-living flesh, salty juices dripping down his bare chest, made her scream.

'Dad! You're such a greedy pig!'

He'd oink in reply.

She'd laugh till she cried.

Afterwards, as darkness fell, her mum would put the mussels on the embers of the fire until the shells opened, Hana would chop up the flesh and add it to the courgette batter they'd made earlier that day, and they'd cook the fritters in an old cast-iron camping frypan. Full to bursting, Hana would lie back on her mum's lap, looking up into the Heavens and trying to work out which constellation was Orion and which was the Southern Cross. Most times she'd fall asleep as happy as she can ever remember being, and Eru would carry her in his arms all the way home.

A few weeks after her mum passed, Hana found a lined exercise book like a schoolchild might use in the back of the pantry. It was both a joyous and a melancholy thing for her, looking at her mother's neat, meticulous handwriting, the preciseness of

---

* Kai moana – seafood.

her tried-and-proven recipes laid out in the perfectly formed letters. Her mother had been a nurse when she met Eru, but she retrained as a teacher when they married and moved to Tātā Bay. She was a hungry reader with an avid interest in international politics and social justice, and a passion for magical realist writing from South America. She loved cooking not because that was her role in the house – it wasn't. Eru would cook at least as often as her. But when she did cook, she took to the task with the same focus as when she read, or when she debated socialism with friends over a sherry at night, or when she taught kids at the local school who were struggling in the lead-up to school certificate exams.

The handwritten book of recipes was a treasure.

A thing kept, to remember.

'I got the recipe from Mum's book,' Hana says.

At the little wooden table beside the kitchen area, Eru reaches out towards the pile of mussel and courgette fritters. Hana slaps him away.

'Don't you dare use your bare hands.'

'It's the old way,' Eru says, grinning, using his bare hands.

Hana opens a bottle of prosecco she'd bought in Auckland. Eru makes short work of his first fritter and starts on a second, making her glad she didn't halve the recipe as she'd considered.

'Mum's fritters. Bubbly. What's the occasion?'

'Keep up, Dad.'

It takes him a moment to scroll through the possibilities. His eyes go to the calendar hanging near the stove. He realizes what date it is.

'Oh. Oh gosh. Completely fell off my radar.'

Hana hands him his glass. Takes her own.

'I feel terrible, forgetting.'

'Shush. It's fine. You remember now.'

She clinks her glass against his.

'Happy birthday, Mum,' she says.

Eru raises his glass to toast the photo of Hana's mother above the piano.

'Hari huritau, e ipo.'*

Between 1989 and 1992, Ivan Milat killed five women and two men in a rural area of New South Wales, Australia, in a three-year binge of nightmarish brutality that became known as the Backpacker Murders. Milat would pick up hitchhikers on the Hume Highway and, instead of dropping them off further down the road as promised, he took them to the remote Belanglo State Forest. As well as being prolific, the murders were torturous and, over time, escalatingly perverse. One of his victims was completely decapitated. Another had been used as

---

* 'Happy birthday, my darling.'

target practice, with ten bullets found in their ruined head.

When police finally closed in on Milat, he had long since disposed of the weapons and vehicles he'd used in the killings. There was zero hard evidence linking him to his crimes.

Until the cops ripped apart his house.

The FBI calls items taken from a crime scene, or from the victims of a crime, 'souvenirs' or 'trophies'. In their definition, a souvenir is something the offender uses as a fantasy or fetish item, to revisit the circumstances of the crime and the death of the victim. A trophy is something held as a proof of ability, a tribute to assure the killer of his own self-worth (almost without exception the killer is a 'him'), like a big game hunter keeps an elephant tusk.

Things kept, to remember.

In Ivan Milat's house, secreted away in spaces in the ceiling and hidden in gaps between the walls, the police found sleeping bags, shirts, a camping stove, water bottles. Other items he'd taken from the murder victims had been gifted to his friends and family members. The items were positively identified as belonging to the dead backpackers, proving his guilt beyond doubt, and Milat was jailed for the rest of his life.

'There's a shoebox in his wardrobe. He keeps the bracelet there.'

'How did you take this photo?'

Earlier that day, after Hana had found the bracelet and taken the slightly out-of-focus photo, she knew she finally had the kind of conclusive evidence that could shift things. She went straight to Central Police Station. As she rode the elevator up, as the adrenaline faded, she had a feeling the conversation on the eighth floor wasn't going to be a comfortable one. She was right.

'How did you take this photo?' Lorraine asked again. 'Were you invited into his house?'

'The bracelet belonged to Paige Meadows. I'm confident that her parents will confirm it when we show them the picture.'

Seeing the look that shoots between Lorraine and Jaye, Hana instantly regretted her choice of the collective 'we'. She hurried on.

'Four years ago, when Kiri Thomas went missing, the Point Marlon RSA was closed for renovations. The alibi he gave you was a lie.'

'You need to answer the question.' Jaye didn't even attempt to hide his impatience. 'Did Weeks ask you into his flat? Did he willingly show you the shoebox and its contents?'

'Of course not.'

'Christ, Hana. What am I meant to do with this?' Lorraine's voice was harsh with frustration.

Hana looked out through the glass walls of Jaye's office, into the open area of the eighth floor. On the other side of the CIB area was the office that had been hers until six months earlier, now occupied by Lorraine. If the office were still Hana's, she'd be doing exactly what Lorraine and Jaye were doing. She'd ask the same questions, she'd try to work out what the presence of a dead girl's bracelet in the flat meant. And, if the information had been obtained in a manner that meant it could actually be used evidentially or to secure a search warrant.

'Here's what I think happened twenty-one years ago,' Hana said, quickly. 'Tama Hall took this troubled kid from the caravan park under his wing. He gave him things to do in his garden and around the house, tried to get the boy's feet back on the ground. But he couldn't lock him in his caravan and throw away the key. One night, Weeks went roaming, he acted out on the things he saw in the slasher porn movies he watched endlessly. And he killed Paige.'

Hana knew she wasn't answering their questions, she could see she was pissing them off. But right now, she didn't care.

'Tama knew he was dying. He was a big-hearted man, he wanted to believe Weeks made a one-off mistake. He wanted to give the boy a second chance. So, he confessed to the crime.'

She opened the email app on her phone, sent them

the photo she'd taken of the bracelet under the floorboards in Weeks' wardrobe.

'This is a textbook killer's trophy. Weeks kept the bracelet, to relive what he'd done. Over the years those same urges started to build again. Two decades later, he killed a second time. The same kind of victim, young, teenage, female. The same dumping ground.'

'Nothing you've given us is usable. Right now, there's one charge that we can lay,' Jaye said. 'The offence of breaking and entering, committed by an ex-cop gone rogue.'

He held open the door of his office, avoiding eye contact as Hana headed out. Lorraine walked with her to the elevator, pressed the call button.

'Remember what old man Maley used to say?' she asked quietly, and Hana knew what she meant.

When they were at Police College, Ross Maley was a senior cop with thousands of hours on the clock, an occasional tutor for their classes in procedure, a man who was exponentially more a pragmatist than a rule-follower. Lorraine and Hana were drawn to his approach. Jaye not so much. More than once Maley had told their class, 'Better to do what needs doing and apologize later, than ask for permission and be told no.'

The elevator doors opened and Lorraine stood back.

'Thank you. Now please,' she said, firmly. 'Leave this alone and let us do our job.'

Eru isn't a big drinker, never has been. But Hana knew what she was doing when she picked the semi-sweet prosecco in the little bottle store near Central Police Station, after the meeting with Lorraine and Jaye. Her father's taste buds haven't evolved much since he was ten years old. If it's sweet and bubbly, as much like lemonade as possible, he'll enjoy a glass.

After the kai to celebrate her mum's birthday, and a glass of the prosecco that was a bit too sweet for Hana, but that Eru oohed and aahed over like the $15 bubbly was Dom Perignon, he opens the lid of the piano. He plays the song that he and his wife used to play at family gatherings, Eru at the piano keys, Hana's mum singing in her gorgeous soprano.

> *Smile the while you kiss me sad adieu,*
> *When the clouds roll by I'll come to you,*
> *Then the skies will seem more blue,*
> *Down in lovers lane with you.*

Hana's eyes shine as she listens to his gravelly baritone.

> *And wedding bells will ring so merrily,*
> *Every tear will be a memory,*
> *So wait and pray each night for me,*
> *Till we meet again.*

Eru's face is full of joy and love as he holds the final note. There's a lump in Hana's throat.

'That was so beautiful, Dad.'

'When your māmā sang, it was beautiful. I'm just the sidekick who won't ever fit her shoes,' Eru laughs.

'You're the sunniest human I ever met. I don't think I've ever seen you cry.'

It's true. Even when they were burying Hana's mum, Eru was sombre, devastated. Of course he was. But he never cried.

'You know me, love. I'm the glass-half-full kind.'

Eru closes the keyboard, gets up from the piano stool, kisses Hana on the top of her head.

'You take what you're given. You muddle on through. And you keep smiling.'

Eru heads to bed. Hana pours the remains of the prosecco into her glass. She heads out to the deck overlooking the ocean. In the distance, moonlight falls on the sand dunes. Hana sips the bubbly, reflective. She's done all she can to unravel the twisted threads of what really happened to Paige, and whether those threads connect to Kiri Thomas.

Now, it's out of her hands.

The volume on the big-screen TV is up loud.

On the screen, one of the many DVDs is playing, the

self-proclaimed bishop quoting scripture to his born-again flock. Gordon John Weeks hears the words. He sees the images of the bishop, his moist sweatiness as he walks the stage exhorting his audience to follow scripture, to love thy neighbour and to tithe generously to support the good works of the Church. But the bishop's utterances are making little sense to Weeks.

He paces his small rooms. Back and forth. Forth and back.

The same route the woman walked, when she was in his house.

If you live in a place on your own for almost two decades, when you keep it just as you like it to be, you become part of it, it becomes part of you. Every inch, every corner, every odour becomes familiar, particular.

The day before, after he'd turned around halfway to work, remembering that he'd left behind the tools he'd need that day to fix a broken window latch at the halfway house, Weeks knew something was amiss the instant he opened the front door and came into the flat. Something had changed. He couldn't put his finger on it at first. The slightest hint of an unfamiliar odour in the still air.

A pleasant enough smell. Not a fragrance. Deodorant. That's what it was. Deodorant.

But it wasn't *his* deodorant.

He went from room to room. The olfactory nodes in the nostrils and the back of the tongue are quick to desensitize, and what he thought he'd smelled when he'd first come into his flat was fading fast. Perhaps it was just in his head. He'd been so upset by the two cops coming to his work a few days before. The stress. The tension. Maybe he was imagining things.

Then he looked at the pinboard near his bed.

Tama's order of service.

No one else would have noticed that it wasn't lined up, neat and tidy, like the hospital creases on his bed. Exact. The way he liked it. The way he needed it.

It was out of line. Only a tiny bit, maybe 10 millimetres askew.

But it *was* out of line.

Someone had been here. Moments before.

He hurried to the window. Looking out carefully through a gap in the curtain, he spotted two people in a car across the road. The woman behind the steering wheel looked somehow familiar. He waited, watching, as a tall Asian-looking guy got out and went to another vehicle parked further down the road. The woman started her car, glancing back towards his flat for a moment. Looking through the sliver of a gap, Weeks knew he couldn't be seen by the driver.

But he could see her.

He stared at her face for the time it took for her to pull out from where she was parked and drive away. It was only a few seconds, but it was enough for him to be quite certain.

He recognized the woman driving the car, the woman who had been in his house.
He couldn't remember where or when.
But he'd seen her face before.

21

THREE DAYS TO GO

When you're in a car crash, they reckon the world slows down.

It's not that you're given extra time by whichever atua is in charge of accidents; you're not given more wiggle room to correct whatever went wrong, to change direction, to swerve out of the way of the oncoming truck. What's gonna happen is gonna happen. The ticket's already clipped; the die's been cast. It's just that what's happening happens in slow-mo.

Which makes me think: did time slow down for my real mum and dad, when they crashed, when I was saved by the fancy car seat that they couldn't afford but bought anyway?

Time didn't slow down when I drove the car into

Dax's scooter. If anything, it was the other way round. It all sped up.

I'd done a couple of jobs that night, got some cash. I'd got me and Trish some Japanese takeaway, a bit of a splash-out, sashimi don. We were in her McDonalds-paid-for car. I was driving.

It was like the car found its own way to Dax's street.

Or maybe it was like a Ouija board, where it's not actually a voice from beyond talking to you. With the Ouija board, they say it's your subconscious subtly twitching the muscles in your hand, so you get the message you want, from the person you want it from.

I didn't want to see Dax, that's for sure, not after what he'd done. Didn't want to see him ever again. That's what I told myself.

A thing I'd like to have done: get him in the boxing ring again at the gym in Māngere. I would've taken off the gloves, used my bare knuckles. He'd have got more than a split lip. God of Fuckheads.

Anyway. There we were, me and Trish, at the end of the street, where the car had found its way. Engine running. Sitting behind the steering wheel, looking at Dax's scooter, parked outside his place.

A feeling grew in my stomach, like seismic tremors along a fault line.

Rūaumoko, God of Earthquakes.

And tattoos.

It was suddenly so clear to me what would happen

next. Rūaumoko moved within me. From my gut, straight down to the accelerator pedal. I put my foot down.

'The fuck are you doing?'

'Watch.'

By the time I hit the scooter, the car was flying. The scooter broke in two, which was poetic given Dax had broken me in two just a few days earlier. One wheel went one way, and the other went the other, and as I hit the brakes hard to avoid colliding with the cars in the street, something went flying up in the air directly above the bonnet of our car: the mudguard with the spraypainted words *The Gods of Auckland*. In the glow of the streetlight the mudguard turned one time, two times, three times then *smash*! It landed on the concrete pavement.

Disintegrated.

Like the rest of his shitty old scooter. Like me and Dax.

The front door flew open; Dax flew out. He looked at the car, the street, his scooter rent asunder. I've never seen him like that. He came to the car door, pulled me out, pushed me up against the wall.

'You're crazy, bro. I see you again, I'm gonna fucking kill you.'

With Dax's hands pinning my shoulders to the wall, his eyes looking like they were gonna pop out like how you pop fresh peas out of a pod: *that's* when time stood still. I saw in his wild peapod eyes everything I loved. Everything I hated. Everything we had. Everything that was gone. He wasn't scary. He was two years old. A frightened bubba stumbling round the playpen. Like all of us.

'Get back in the fucking car! Please.'

'Shut up, Trish.'

Now that things were in slow-mo, I saw everything with dazzling clarity. It made me so sad. So fucking angry at the same time. I couldn't work out what the hell I was meant to feel or what I was meant to say or what I was meant to think.

Instead, I just did.

I headbutted Dax, right on his nose. It wasn't a hard target to hit.

Dax fell to his knees, way more blood than seemed feasible erupting out of his nose, spraying all over the shattered pieces of metal that used to say *The Gods of Auckland*.

I got back behind the steering wheel. We drove away.

That was Wednesday night.

Three days to go.

22

THE UNFINISHED POEM

On stage, Addison and PLUS 1 are a matching pair of mind readers.

Addison out front, PLUS 1 the engine room behind her, bent over their turntables. They work the crowd, completely in sync, anticipating each other's every move; if Addison decides to freestyle new lyrics, PLUS 1 is all over it, building the tempo or pulling it back, laying the runway for Addison to take off from. If PLUS 1 decides to change the beat in the moment, Addison anticipates the drop almost before PLUS 1 has even done it.

They're like twins who finish each other's sentences. Normally.

But they're not finishing each other's sentences tonight.

There's a big gaping disconnect, a gulf between them. PLUS 1 feels it; Addison feels it. Even as she's onstage, mic in hand, rapping and smiling and in perpetual motion, being the Addison everyone's come to see, she herself knows she's only half there. Half of her is elsewhere. All night she's been a beat behind or a little off-key. She took down the photos of Kiri from her room, because she knows how PLUS 1 is feeling. But her own gnawing feeling hasn't gone away, the sense of connection to someone she doesn't even know.

She's had the dream again. Every night.

Kiri waiting for the red man to turn green. But he never does. And she can't cross the road.

It's the last number of their set, 'Brown and Screaming', their big song that's doing very decent numbers on Spotify and SoundCloud and getting interest from a good-sized music label. It's their song, their signature. Addison and PLUS 1 have played it a thousand times; they could do it in their sleep. But tonight, Addison completely misses the cue for the chorus. PLUS 1 takes the beat around a second time, covering for her. If anyone in the audience noticed, they're not showing it. Addison shoots PLUS 1 an apologetic look. Her eyes return to the audience, to one particular person at the back of the crowd. A latecomer who's just arrived.

It's someone PLUS 1 doesn't recognize. But Addison does.

A guy with red hair and a nose like a Roman sculpture.

Bzzzt bzzzt bzzzt.

The intermittent buzzing from the faulty security light in the alley out back of Sailor Bar is a pain. The filament has been threatening to blow ever since PLUS 1 and Addison got the regular Thursday night gig. After the shows, loading the turntables and gear into PLUS 1's car, it's always kind of grim. The alley is full of crates of empty bottles, piles of old boxes, an overflowing dumpster waiting to be collected. It's a weekly reminder that you might be rising up the ranks in the local music scene, you might have a growing band of loyal followers, but don't get big-headed. You're still loading your own gear into a crappy old car, in a place that smells of urine and looks like a location scout has chosen it for a movie scene where someone gets mugged or murdered.

The ginger with the big nose is waiting in the alley after the show.

'PLUS 1, this is Dax. Dax, PLUS 1. PLUS 1 is my flatmate.'

There are a lot of words Addison could have chosen to describe PLUS 1: my bestie, my oldest mate; one time Addison called PLUS 1 'the Yin to my Yang'.

PLUS 1 wrote that down in the back of one of their university notebooks. It was sweet. Poetic. One of the nicest things anyone had ever said.

In comparison, 'my flatmate' is a brush-off, PLUS 1 thinks. It stings a little.

And who's this guy Dax?

'Hey,' Dax says, eyebrows raised towards PLUS 1 in a polite but less-than-interested greeting, before turning back to Addison. 'Wanna go for a ride?'

Under the flickering light of the security lamp, PLUS 1 is taken aback by Addison's enthusiastic smile.

'Sure! Sounds good,' she replies.

'My car's on the street. I'll wait.'

PLUS 1 watches the stranger head away down the alley.

Bzzzt bzzzt bzzzt.

'How do you two know each other?'

'He's a friend.'

PLUS 1 slides their turntables into the boot of the car, trying to sound casual and unconcerned. It's not particularly successful.

'You never mentioned someone called Dax.'

Addison hears the tone in their voice. She thinks about explaining. But it's a lot. PLUS 1 is already worried about her obsession with Kiri. Addison revealing that she hunted down Kiri's ex-boyfriend won't land well.

'He's a friend. I'll see you at home.'

'We were getting kebabs.'

'Tomorrow night.'

'What the hell? What's going on?'

'Jesus, PLUS 1,' Addison snaps. 'The fuck? We don't own each other.'

PLUS 1 looks like they've been electrocuted, and Addison instantly regrets it, but it's already too late. The words are in the ether.

'He's just a friend. Okay? There's nothing to worry about.'

She gives PLUS 1 a hug.

'Don't wait up, babe. Love you,' Addison says.

PLUS 1 watches as she buttons up her blue-and-white cardigan and hurries down the alley to where the guy's car is waiting.

The music on Dax's stereo is loud. As he drives through the midnight streets, Addison remembers how the conversation outside the gym closed down like a door slamming shut; she feels like Dax is one of those sea anemones in the rock pools below her grandpa Eru's place, the ones that shrivel up closed when you get too close. She could see the pain he'd been carrying for four years for Kiri. She pushed too hard, wanting answers to all the questions she had about the young woman, hoping the person who knew her better than anyone else might pull back the curtain, tell her the kinds of things you don't get from a newspaper article.

Like the yellow and blue tentacles of an anemone, Dax closed up.

'Nice car.'

'Used to have a scooter.'

'What happened to it?'

'It died.'

There's a narrow winding road along the downtown Auckland waterfront that follows a boardwalk, passing marinas full of moored yachts, heading under the raw, exposed metal beams of the bridge. Addison read one time that the Harbour Bridge was designed as a temporary structure, to last fifty years or so, to be replaced by something bigger and grander. It's been standing nearly seventy years now. If you get underneath it, you can see stuff that looks unsettlingly like rust. Whenever Addison drives over the bridge, or whenever she's on this road under it, she unconsciously holds her breath. Wondering if this is the day the bridge decides it's too tired and old and needs a lie-down. One time Hana noticed she was holding her breath going over the bridge. Addison explained this particular anxiety. Hana smiled.

'The Eiffel Tower was only meant to stand for a couple of years. I think we're okay.'

Addison still holds her breath. Every time.

Dax pulls into a parking area a couple of hundred metres from the base of the bridge, at the bottom of a steep rocky bank. He turns off the engine. The music stops.

'The other day,' he says, in the silence. 'I didn't thank you.'

'What for?'

'Finding her.'

Along the embankment overlooking the water, a few groups are casting fishing lines into the darkness of the ocean. An older Asian couple, a group of Pacific Island men. Other groups are parked up in cars, teenagers smoking and drinking, music playing. More than a few nangs are being inhaled, the little silver nitrous oxide canisters making intermittent metallic pings as they're tossed out of windows onto the tarmac.

'I've spent four years thinking she'll just walk in the door of the gym. That smile on her face. Saying, "just tricks, bro". Deep down I knew I was kidding myself. Now at least we know.'

The headlights of his car are still on.

'You'll run your battery flat.'

'Something I wanna show you.'

Dax opens the door, gets out. His headlights are lighting up a big stand of undergrowth at the base of the rocky bank. Addison follows as he pushes through the scrub.

'Just here,' he says, beckoning.

In the beams, Addison sees writing at the base of the

rock face. Seafoam-green spray paint, forming delicate letters. She reads the words aloud.

> we've forgotten the language of the sky
> our gods get lost
> under the choke of this city's lights
> sometimes
> it's easier to be fucked-up
> to let the streets swallow us whole
> sometimes
> we forget where we're from
> so we make homes out of each other
> the city doesn't have stars
> we can't see our gods
> so we make our own

Addison knows who wrote it. Reading Kiri's words is almost overwhelming, and it takes a moment for her to be able to speak.

'I've been trying to imagine her voice. This is exactly how I thought she'd speak. How she'd think.'

'Outside the gym. You asked what happened with her. What went wrong.'

'I had no right to ask that. It's none of my business.'

'I want to tell you. I happened. I was a kid. She was too. But she was also more grown up than I'll ever be. Her heart was so big. Her feelings were so big. Someone who could write something like that poem. It was scary.'

In the glare of the headlights, the worry lines on Dax's forehead seem much deeper than someone his age should have.

'I thought, she'll get bored of me. She must get bored of me. She was beautiful, you know? I thought, one day, she'll look at me and see the guy with the big nose and the Sideshow Bob hair. A loser guy on a loser scooter. One day she'll tell me it was fun, but it's over. Inevitable. So why not get it out of the way?'

'What did you do?' Addison asks.

'I slept with someone. Just a random girl. I told Kiri. And that was that. I knew how she was wired. I knew she'd walk away. I knew there'd be fireworks, and there were. But I didn't think she'd go back to the drugs. Put herself in danger.'

He looks again at the base of the rock shelf. The poem. 'After Kiri went missing,' he continues, 'Trish told me about what she'd written here. She came and wrote it the first night we were together. I had no idea. I wish I'd seen it, before I did what I did.'

He blinks a couple of times.

'Trish said Kiri could never find the right ending. After I broke us up, she came down here. Spray painted a final line.'

'What was it?' Addison asks.

'She wrote, "It's all fucked."'

Dax lets the bushes go back to where they were, covering the poem from view, making sure council workers or other graffiti artists won't see it and erase the words.

'I scraped that line off. That's not Kiri. That's not how she is. That's not the end of her story.'

Back in the car, the headlights off, they sit staring out at the water. Neither feeling the need for small talk, nor to turn the music back on. A shared sadness. But also, an unexpected ease.

'I don't know how to ask this,' Dax says. 'When you found her, in the sands ...'

He can't finish the question. Addison knows what he's asking.

'She was bones. Just bones. It wasn't scary, you know?' She searches for the right way to describe what she saw. 'It was kind of pure.'

Silence again for a moment.

'I'm glad you used that word.'

Addison realizes Dax is crying.

'Oh hey. Hey.' She reaches out, her hand on his. 'You loved her,' she says. 'You just loved her too much. You were scared. You were fucked-up and human. Like she was. Like all of us.'

She pulls him towards her. He lets himself be held. Addison finds herself crying too, with Dax.

'Hey now. It's okay.'

Hours later.

To the east, over Rangitoto Island, the perfect black volcanic cone that emerged in the middle of Auckland Harbour over six centuries ago, a burning yellow-red sunrise is filling the horizon. The fiery colours reflect off the water into Addison's face. Her eyes slowly open. They've both fallen asleep, her arms still wrapped around Dax.

Their faces close together.

Addison stares at Dax. The intensity of the past couple of days has been coming to a head over the last few hours. Dax opening up to her was moving. Intimate. He stirs. His eyelids flicker open. It takes him a moment to focus, to realize that Addison is there, so close. Face to face. A proximity that usually only lovers experience.

He pushes forward. His lips meet hers.

Addison's fingers wrap around his hand, surprisingly small for a guy. She presses back against him. Giving in to the moment, emotion turning into physicality. Then she pauses. Their lips are touching still. But suddenly, neither of them wants to do more.

'It feels wrong,' Addison says.

'Yeah.'

She kisses him gently, on the forehead. A protective kiss. A kiss that says, *there's not going to be any other kind of kiss.*

He rests against her shoulder.

Both stare out at the harbour, as the sun rises over Auckland city.

23

CLOSING IN

Hana is running. 10.13 kilometres, at speed.

It's still an hour before sunrise. When she lived in the city, her run was through the 24/7 glow of well-lit streets. Here in Tātā Bay, it took her a while to work out a new route. There are only three streetlights over the whole run, so Hana uses a headlamp to light the way. Her trail takes her along the coastal track from her house, cutting inland over farmlands up to a green hilly promontory that looks over the town, then down through deep bush into a valley with a beautiful waterfall, along a narrow gravel road that takes her past the back paddocks of several farms, before winding through the township back to her home.

After a few attempts at reworking the course with her GPS watch, adding a twist or turn here and there, finally Hana had a route that was the right distance. Down to two decimal points.

The 10.13-kilometre thing is weird, she knows.

Addison and Jaye have both said as much, looking at her online running log and seeing the exact same distance at nearly the exact same pace, day after day after day. It's almost impossible to explain to anyone who's not a runner, the sense of solid ground that comes with the routine of running. If Hana did 100 metres more or less than her 10.13 kilometres, it would just feel wrong. If she talked to a professional in the mental health industry, they'd probably come up with a diagnosis. That's their job. But Hana knows unusual doesn't mean abnormal, and there's a lot of other things you could be hooked on that are considerably worse than the compulsion to run 10.13 kilometres pretty much every day of your adult life.

She climbs the steepest part of the run, up the tall hill. The first half dozen times she did this section, crossing the rough ground pocked by cattle and sheep tracks, she took a few stumbles, even falling flat on her face once. Now she knows each dip, each indentation well enough that she can run fluidly, instinctively, the way she likes. And she can think about other things than where her feet should fall.

This morning she's got a lot to think about.

After the driving lessons down at the marae the day before, when Tīmoti was a no-show once again,

Eru made dinner for Hana at his place. He prepared chicken wings marinaded in basil from his garden crushed up into an olive oil paste, and as he was cooking he asked Hana to jump on his computer and fill out an online application to renew his car registration. Her dad had always struggled with entering the credit card details in the right place. Hana used her own credit card, knowing his superannuation was a lot less than her police payout. Logging out of the rego site, she accidentally opened Eru's recent Google history. In his searches over the last year, similar items kept coming up, again and again.

Forgetfulness.

Memory loss.

Early-onset Alzheimer's.

Hana crests the top of the hill. She adjusts her head torch to the brighter beam and starts into the forest, descending the track that follows the small flowing river down into the valley. Looking at the search history, things had suddenly fallen into place. Eru's memory lapses, like waking up in the evening completely blanking out that they'd just been to the meeting at the marae and thinking it was time to go work with the kids on the driving programme. Forgetting her mum's birthday. The sense that he was recently just a step or two slower on the uptake. Her dad hadn't talked to her about what was going on. He hadn't said a word. He's not that kind of man. But she could see that the searches had been increasing in frequency. He was worried.

Hana reaches the bottom of the descent. She pauses, her head torch picking out the waterfall, its cascade tumbling the height of a two-storey house into a rocky pool below. She cups a handful and drinks. It's cold and good. The moon and the beam of her light ripple in the waters.

She feels awful that she hadn't known what was going on with Eru. And that he hasn't been able to tell her. Thinking back, the conversation a few nights earlier about him being a glass-half-full kind of guy takes on a different tone. Even the sunniest person couldn't help but be shaken by the nagging suspicion their mind was failing. Is her dad's optimism something he's desperately clinging to, rather than something he's actually feeling?

Hana continues down from the waterfall and climbs the wooden gate at the bottom of the track, emerging onto a one-lane road. The route from here is the fast bit, mostly downhill, the light-coloured surface of the gravel road glowing under the moonlight. She flicks off her head torch, lengthens her stride. It's the section where she can stretch out and really get her heart rate maxing.

Running fast, she almost misses them.

Voices in the distance. Something in the low, urgent tone of what's being said makes her stop. A couple of hundred metres up a side road there's a series of buildings. Hana knows that this land belongs to a farming family who live several kilometres away on the other side of the big hill. There's a large hay shed and a building next to it where farm vehicles are stored.

A car is on the road. The lights are off, but she recognizes it. Rendall's Mark III Zephyr. There's movement at the gate and at one of the buildings. Several silhouettes in the darkness. Whispered conversations. The sound of chains being cut and crowbars working at locks.

Hana can tell they haven't seen her. She wants to keep it that way.

She silently backtracks to the fence line. She gets flat on the ground, slides under the lowest wire. There's a line of concealing trees running towards the buildings, and she makes her way silently down it. As she gets closer, the silhouettes become more defined. There are three people around the gate and the building. And someone else still in the car.

Hana knows what to do in a confrontation, one on one, even against a bigger guy coming at her with intent. A few months before she left the force, she'd gone with Stan to follow up on information received about an aggravated burglary. The tip-off was vague at best, and the house was in one of the fanciest neighbourhoods in the city. They hadn't felt there was a need for any kind of back-up from a uniformed team, let alone an Armed Offenders Squad. They'd gone in the gate, Hana leading the way. She didn't even get to the front steps before the door flew open and a guy came rushing out at her. They found out later he'd been up for the best part of a week on a motherlode of methamphetamine bought from the proceeds of the hold-up. He was spiralling, and they'd picked the moment of his breaking point to walk into his front yard. It all happened at lightning speed. Hana tried talking him down; he just came at her harder, a machete in his hand. She went into survival mode, the mindset of 'do what you have to do to get home tonight' kicking in, and as he swung the machete, she managed to deflect his hand with one arm and push hard off her rear foot to transfer all the power possible into her other hand, aiming the flat of her palm upwards into his nose. The crunch of breaking cartilage told her it was a direct hit, and even with the chaotic maelstrom of meth-fuelled adrenaline in his system, the blinding white light that comes with a badly shattered nose put the guy down just long enough for Hana to spin him onto his front, and for Stan to come down hard as hell with his knee on the centre of the guy's back, knocking the wind out of him and giving them the seconds needed to get cuffs on.

In a one-on-one confrontation, Hana would be confident against most people. She'd give herself a fighting chance against two assailants. But going up against four guys in a back road in the middle of the night without even an extendable baton? That's a really dumb idea.

She keeps moving silently down the tree line. Fifty metres from the men, she gets out her phone. She eases her way to a gap in the trees where she can see what's going on. They're all wearing gloves; one of them is holding a torch, another is working with bolt-cutters at the heavy chain locking the gate. The door of the shed has been opened, and inside a third man is hotwiring a farm vehicle, a late-model ute* that would be worth a nice chunk of change. Hana dims her screen so there's no glow to be seen. She starts filming. She makes sure she gets footage of each of the men. The one working the bolt-cutters manages to break the chain. He turns to take the tools back to the car. Hana sees who it is.

Tīmoti. Her cousin Eyes' son.

Trying not to think of what she is going to have to do next, now that she knows what Tīmoti is tied up in, Hana lines up a decent shot of the person she knows is the ringleader. She gets Rendall square in her screen. Suddenly, she's startled by a flapping of wings very close to her.

A bush pigeon takes flight from the nearest tree, spooked by her presence.

Rendall turns, looks directly to where the bird flew

---

* Ute – pick-up truck.

from. Staring just a few inches above Hana's head. She stays calm, knowing that in the pitch-black shadows there's no way any of them can see her.

'Gimme that,' Rendall says to Tīmoti. Tīmoti hands over the torch he's holding.

Hana slips through a low gorse bush as silently as she can, the thorns tearing open scratches in her arms. She ignores the sharp pain and pulls herself flat into a shallow ditch behind the scrub. She slips her phone beneath her, hoping this isn't the one moment in Addison's life when she has got up before dawn and decided to give her mother a catch-up call.

Rendall heads towards the stand of trees, cursing under his breath. Hana can't hear exactly what he's saying, but she doesn't need to. It's almost certainly a promise about what's going to happen to anybody he finds in the shadows.

'Hey? Someone there?'

Hana doesn't dare breathe. Hoping the heartbeat she hears in her ears isn't as loud to others as it seems to her. If it all goes wrong, she thinks, will Tīmoti come to her defence? Out of some kind of lingering family loyalty, despite the complete lack of whānau love that seems to be held for Hana by him or his mother? A few years ago, maybe Tīmoti would have done the right thing, giving the woman he used to call Auntie a fighting chance. But now?

Rendall approaches the gap in the trees where Hana

was only moments before. 'Come on, fucker. Make it easy on yourself.'

Peering through gorse branches, Hana glimpses him moving around the trees, the beam of his torch searching the shadows. He's only a few metres away. This close, she can see that the torch is a long weighty thing, and that he's gripping it like a club. She glances around for a fallen branch, a metal pipe. Anything that could be a weapon. There's nothing.

Rendall points the torch down the nearby row of trees. Then around the neighbouring field. A group of dairy cows have gathered, staring. The intense light of the torch reflects off their retinas like white dazzling discs, a discomforting sight. If Rendall took five steps towards the cows, he'd pass the gorse bush. Then all he'd have to do is take a half-turn sideways, and he'd be staring straight at Hana, lying defenceless on the ground.

Rendall stands completely still. Listens. His eyes searching.

'ARRGGGH!'

He explodes with a sudden, angry shout, like someone just knifed him in the back of the leg. Hana flinches. But she holds her nerve. Stays completely still. Completely silent. In the tree above him, another bird takes flight, startled by the furious scream.

The heavy wings flap away into the night.

'Fuck it. Let's get out of here.'

The men, who've wandered up to Rendall by now, return to the shed. In moments the engine of the ute is rumbling. Rendall gives Tīmoti a shove.

'Earn your money, Timmy.'

Hana cautiously raises herself. She starts filming again as Tīmoti climbs behind the steering wheel of the stolen ute and drives it out the gate, following Rendall's vehicle down onto the side road.

Staying low behind the gorse, Hana keeps filming the cars as they accelerate down the gravel road, their headlights killed until they're well away.

Twenty minutes later, she is running back through the pools of sodium yellow beneath the three lonely streetlights on the main street of Tātā Bay. She's about to cut down the coastal path to her place when she sees a row of vehicles at the sand dunes. Police cars, blue and red lights flashing in the darkness. SOCO vehicles. Police tape blocks off a wide swathe of the beach.

There's a uniformed cop at the perimeter of the taped-off area. He recognizes Hana as she approaches.

'Sorry, senior. No one's allowed in there.'

'I understand.'

The constable had been involved in one of Hana's investigations the previous year. She remembers him as being a nice guy, a hard worker, a bit star-stuck whenever Hana talked to him. It's unexpected and touching that he still respectfully addresses her by her former rank. She looks towards the part of the dunes where Addison found Kiri, the area where most of the activity is focused. The young policeman's radio crackles to life. It's Lorraine; she has spotted Hana from where she is overseeing the renewed search. The young cop buttons off the radio and lifts the tape, holding it high for Hana to go under.

'The boss says you can come through.'

Hana follows the row of battery-powered lights set up on sandbagged tripods that line the path up to where Lorraine is waiting. As she approaches, Lorraine stares at the bloodied scratches on Hana's arms.

'What the hell happened to you?'

For a moment Hana considers telling Lorraine about Rendall. But car conversion in a sleepy backwater isn't a high priority for the CIB. And in any case, if Hana turns over the video on her phone, Tīmoti goes to court.

'I took a tumble running.' She wipes away the blood with her shirt. 'Have you found something?'

Lorraine leads Hana a few metres away from where the two dozen or so officers are working. 'I need to make something clear,' she says, and from the tone of her voice Hana knows this is the part where she lays down the law. 'You overstepped. Badly. What you did was completely unacceptable.'

Hana would be lying if she apologized. Whatever is happening here, if it's a result of what she did, breaking into Gordon John Weeks' house and finding the bracelet, she's glad.

'I can't use what you found,' Lorraine says. 'But I can't ignore it.'

In the stark white tungsten light, Hana can see that an inch-by-inch examination of the entire area is taking place. Sand is being carefully lifted, run through sieves of varying mesh sizes. Anything found is being bagged to be sent for testing by ESR* scientists. It's an extensive, painstaking job.

'There's a worst-case scenario here.'

Hana knows exactly what Lorraine means. It's something that's also been lurking at the back of her mind, every day she's run past the dunes since Kiri's bones were found. Two girls died here, well over a decade apart. What if there are other dates on the timeline, as yet unknown? If both killings were at the hands of one person – if Gordon John Weeks killed Paige twenty-one years ago, then Kiri four years ago – could he have murdered more young women in the intervening years? Could there be still more bodies to be found?

That's why the dunes are being searched again, inch by painstaking inch.

---

* ESR – the Institute of Environmental Science and Research, whose scientists work closely with police in crime investigations.

'Thank you for taking this seriously,' Hana says. 'Good luck.'

Lorraine watches as Hana turns and picks her way back down the dune.

Behind her, over the distant line of mountains, dawn is rising.

24

WHAT HAPPENS NOW?

There's always something playing on the Bluetooth speaker at PLUS 1 and Addison's place.

Music is the grammar of their relationship. All the big moments of their shared experience are soundtracked by the music playing at the time, like the first song they composed together in high school music class. Or the exhilarating Indigenous Mexican rap music that PLUS 1 introduced Addison to when they first started hanging out. Neither of them could understand a word the woman was saying, but you didn't need to speak Spanish to feel the pain and anger in her voice. The rapper's name became the name of their puppy. One night they went camping in a coastal park north of the city; they tried to figure out how the hell to put up the tent they'd borrowed but after thirty minutes and most of a bottle of sale-price pinot noir, it all seemed too hard, and they chucked the tent back in the boot of the car. Addison had been listening to Hana's playlists and was going through a bit of a retro thing. They played 'Heart of Glass' and 'California Dreamin'' thirty-odd times that night, falling asleep side by side on the beach in their sleeping bags.

There's no music playing in the house this morning when Dax drops Addison home.

The sun has already been up for hours when she comes in, closing the door behind her. She looks into PLUS 1's room. PLUS 1's eyes are closed, the puppy curled up alongside them with only its too-big paws emerging from the duvet. Addison knows PLUS 1 isn't really asleep. The kind of person her best friend is means they would have been awake all night, worried. And upset. Addison saw the discomfort and confusion in their face the night before, when Dax turned up out of the blue and she headed off with someone who was a complete stranger to PLUS 1, almost a complete stranger to Addison herself. The moment she said it Addison knew her dismissive 'we don't own each other' was petty and hurtful. But by then it was already done.

She sits on the bed. Smooths away a stray dreadlock falling across PLUS 1's cheek.

'I was a bitch last night.'

'Uh-huh.'

'I'm sorry.'

PLUS 1's eyes open. 'I don't want to own you.'

'I shouldn't have said that.'

'I just want to know you're okay.'

There's a framed photo above the bed. PLUS 1 and Addison at the high school ball. They're wearing matching pink pantsuits they found online and had sent from a vintage shop in Budapest. The shipping cost ten times the outfits, but it was worth it. If there'd been crowns given out for Freaks of the Ball they'd have won them. Even at their liberal and open-minded school, the neon-pink pair were the oddest of the oddballs. But they didn't care. They always looked a million bucks, and they were always together. Nothing else mattered.

'I'd love some of your eggs,' Addison says.

PLUS 1's go-to is herby, buttery scrambled eggs.

Dripping with oil and protein, they're the textbook hangover recipe. PLUS 1 makes them with parmesan and basil leaves, and since moving into Hana's place they've started adding some of the native plants in plentiful supply in the garden.

As the eggs cook, Addison tells PLUS 1 about spending the night with Dax. Hearing him tell his story of two confused kids stumbling their way towards each other, then stumbling so awfully apart, and the disastrous aftermath. How maybe none of it would ever have happened if the two of them had just been able to be comfortable in the things they felt for each other, if both had been able to accept the love they were feeling and accept the love of those around them.

She tells PLUS 1 about reading Kiri's unfinished poem.

'I'm glad last night happened,' Addison says. 'It had to happen. Like when my shitty phone plays up and I have to reboot. I went down a rabbit hole after I found Kiri. Now it feels like I can start finding my way back out.'

PLUS 1 brings their plates to the table with some slices of toast. Addison piles a fork with eggs. Devours it. Another forkful.

'Peppery.'

'Your mum's kawakawa.'

'It's good.'

Addison takes another mouthful. It's a natural place for the conversation to end. But there's something she hasn't said, something that is maybe nothing, but that might be something, and either way she knows if it remains unsaid, it could somehow define her relationship with PLUS 1 from here forward. The open book they are to each other – Addison would be closing that book just a little. She doesn't want that.

'I kissed him.'

PLUS 1 spreads butter on a piece of toast. Carefully. Right out to the very edges.

'Nothing else happened.'

'Huh.'

'I wanted to. For a moment, I wanted to be with him. I thought I did. But it wasn't real. It was a moment, then it was gone. Nothing else happened.'

The sound of whining. Boca is at the door, wanting to get out.

'Do you love him?' PLUS 1 asks, quietly. Addison wants to laugh at the idea, even though the shakiness in her friend's voice is the least funny thing she's ever heard.

'Babe. I don't even know him.'

PLUS 1 heads to the door, lets the puppy out. Boca races over to one of the palms and raises one leg to it even though she's a girl, because most of her dog friends in the park are male. Halfway through, she unbalances and falls on her back. It's a bit of a mess.

'You weren't a bitch. We don't own each other.' PLUS 1 turns back to Addison. 'Buying a blue-and-white cardigan the same as hers. Hunting down her boyfriend. Kissing him, wanting to get with him. I think I get it. But I hate it.'

The look on PLUS 1's face breaks Addison's heart.

'Every day I fight to be who I am,' PLUS 1 says. 'But it's like you're fighting to be someone else. Someone you don't even know.'

Addison pushes the remains of her food around the plate. The fresh kawakawa an intense green against the yellow of the egg yolks.

'I feel like shit,' she says quietly.

'All I want is you back. The real you.'

PLUS 1 goes outside to play with their puppy.

He hasn't slept for days.

It was always a problem for him. When he lived in the little caravan on Mountain Road, when his inner chemistry was so erratic, so out of whack, when he was spending days on end watching dark, angry VHS movies about dark, angry, unloved men finding power by overwhelming beautiful young women, Weeks couldn't sleep. His friend helped him. From the moment they first met, the day Weeks walked past Tama's house, Tama greeting him with a cheery 'Kia ora'*, Weeks responding with 'Go fuck yourself'; from that moment when Tama saw all the warning signs of the pain and anger in Weeks, the same pain and anger he'd seen in so many young men in gangs and in prisons; from that day on, Tama looked out for him. Tama did everything he could to help him. He would come, turn off the television, put away the VHS tapes, make

---

* Kia ora – hello.

Weeks go with him back to his home. Tama would get him out in the garden, digging over the kumara, harvesting the kamokamo.* They'd eat together. And Tama would get Weeks to close his eyes. Breathe. Listen to the tūī† in the trees outside. Get him to picture colours, behind his eyes.

Blue, the colour of peace. Yellow, the colour of serenity.

Tama gave Weeks things no one in his life had thought to give him. His mother, with her own mental health and addiction issues, had been completely unable to understand, let alone cope with, his fluctuations between energy and stasis, finally resorting to a leather belt to try and beat him into being a normal kid, the same parenting technique she'd experienced in her own troubled childhood.

Tama was the only thing approaching a real parent Weeks had ever known. When he was with Tama, he felt like he could keep some kind of handle on the spiralling things he was feeling. But then Weeks would go back to his dark little caravan. He'd forget the breathing exercises. He'd forget to imagine the colours of peace and serenity. If he closed his eyes, the colour he'd see was the colour from those movies. Red, the colour of blood. He'd put the VHS back in the player.

---

* Kamokamo – winter squash.

† Tūī – a melodic native songbird.

Watch the young men again, as they regained their self-respect, their power, their dignity. By hurting women. And he'd watch the women in the movies, watch them closely, pause at certain moments. Looking at the fear in their eyes as the things that happened to them happened to them. He'd wonder, how would that be? Having the power to make another human feel fear? To make someone else scream?

What would that feel like?

In all his years on earth he'd never had any kind of strength, agency, power to make anyone feel anything. The more he watched the films, the more the questions turned into something else, less theoretical curiosity, more and more a need for answers that could only be found by doing the things he saw in those dark, angry movies. The more the need to answer those questions grew, the less he slept. The more the chemicals inside him swirled in eddies, the more he felt like a tightrope walker whose rope is being shaken by the hand of someone big and omniscient, the same kind of unstoppable force as his mother's hand bringing down the belt on his thighs, on his back. At some point Weeks began to feel that resistance to an unstoppable force was futile and you just had to give in and tumble off the tightrope and fall and fall and fall, and maybe then you'd find an answer to all those questions.

In his dark, airless apartment, he walks past his untouched medications.

Back and forth.
Forth and back.
He hasn't taken any meds for days. Since the stranger was in his flat. Since everything he'd held so tightly together for so many years started to feel like it was unravelling. What's the fucking point? The big powerful hand is once again shaking the tightrope his whole life is so precariously balanced on. He can't remember when he last ate. He's phoned the transitional house for five days in a row, told them he has a sore throat; he doesn't want to be around the men if he's carrying some kind of virus. He's been playing the DVDs of the bishop and his sermons and appeals for generous tithes, night and day. The bishop's words used to calm Weeks, almost in the way Tama had. Not anymore.

Not since the woman was in his flat.

Knock-knock-knock at the door.

'Go away, leave me alone, I'm watching television,' Weeks shouts out over the booming Jesus talk on the screen. 'GO AWAY!'

Knock-knock-knock, louder. Weeks rushes to the door, ready to tell whatever neighbour is there to complain to fuck off and mind their own business.

It's not a neighbour.

The detective with the blonde hair and the bright red lipstick is standing there. The one who'd come to his work with the male cop, who'd shown him her badge and asked him questions until he made up some story about watching a rugby game, just to send them away.

Now she's back.

Deep down he'd been expecting something like this, since the woman with the sweet-smelling deodorant was in his apartment. He turns down the volume of the television.

'What happens now?' he asks Lorraine.

A DNA swab isn't a pleasant experience.

Lorraine tells Weeks that the sample she's requesting is entirely voluntary. She has no warrant. He is under no obligation to provide the evidence. But she also makes it clear: if the sample is not given voluntarily here in the privacy of his flat then she will have to come to his workplace, get out her badge in front of his employers and the residents at the institution, and ask him to accompany her for further questioning about the disappearance of Kiri Thomas.

'I'd rather do this the comfortable way,' she says. Weeks consents to having his DNA sampled and a uniformed officer begins the process.

What he doesn't know, what the police have no intention of telling him, is that during the most recent examination of the Tātā Bay sand dunes, one of the search team found a blue latex glove under a drift of black sand, near where Kiri's body had been buried. Jaye and Lorraine both recognized it as the same type of glove Weeks used to prevent contamination of the honey from the hives. The glove was taken to ESR for testing, DNA traces were found and immediately it became a priority to obtain a sample of Weeks' DNA for comparison.

After the uniformed cop has taken the swabs, Weeks tells Lorraine that someone has broken into his flat.

'Was it one of you? What are you people trying to do to me?'

'If you have proof that someone has illegally entered your apartment, you need to make a formal complaint. The appropriate measures will be taken to investigate. But I can assure you, no member of the CIB would enter a house without a legally obtained search warrant.'

Lorraine heads out the door; Weeks follows her.

'You've got this wrong, completely wrong,' he says, talking fast. 'I'm a decent hard-working man, I had nothing to do with that girl.' Near panic, he reaches out towards Lorraine's shoulder, trying to get her to listen, but his hand has barely touched her when *whomp*, he finds himself pushed up hard against the wall.

'You want to be charged? Assault on a police officer?'

He sees the unhidden anger in the cop's eyes. And in that moment, it's suddenly completely clear to Weeks.

She thinks I did it. She really thinks I did it. And

she hates me for it. She thinks I killed the Kiri girl. I'm fucked.

Lorraine lets him go.

'I never met her in my life.'

'Then your DNA will prove that.' She closes the door behind her.

Back in the shadows of his apartment, Weeks turns to the television again. The bishop's face silently mouthing words. Words whose power to soothe, to heal, have gone away. Just like the one person in his life who ever gave a shit went away. Left him. Died in a prison hospital.

Weeks scrabbles for a bottle of the Taiwanese mānuka honey. He goes to take the top off, but the damn plastic seals, they're so hard to get your fingernail under, he can't get the thing open. He tries with his teeth, but nothing works – *oh my god oh my god* – and he hurls the heavy little glass bottle, hard, straight at the television. The glass smashes. The image of the bishop erupts into a meteor field of glass splinters, showering his face and arms.

He stands there. Panting. A beaten dog.

He goes to the window. Stares across the street, at the space where the woman's car was after she'd been in his house. She'd looked towards him, not realizing he was there looking back through the sliver in the curtains. The memory is burned into his mind. He can see her now as if she was still right there.

Late thirties. A strong, confident face.
Dark hair, dark eyes. So dark it's hard to know if they are brown or black.
This is her fault. It's her fault.
Something so familiar about her. He knows he's seen that face.
Her fault. All her fault.
He's seen that face before.

25

THE GOD OF WEATHER

The city doesn't have stars. But on a good night you can see the moon. It's the first night of the sickle moon tonight. Saturday. Seven days after Dax told me he did what he did. The sickle moon is going to rise in the wee small hours of the morning. But I'm not going to see it.

Yeah, it's that day.

The day my story ends.

Shit, eh.

Rock makes you powerful. You defeat fear and pain. You defeat your sadness about a boy with a big nose and kind eyes who doesn't love you anymore. You're almighty, like Tāwhirimātea, the God of Weather, boss of the rain and the lightning and the thunder and the clouds. Except for you, the clouds come from the little glass pipe, and you inhale them and hold them inside and exhale and they float up through the pōhutukawa branches and past the flashing lights on the Harbour Bridge, and *up up up* into the void where the sickle moon is about to rise.

We've got a system, Trish and me.

I put up my ad. When the guy texts to rent me for a half hour, a detour on the way home to his darling, perfectly formed wife and his darling, perfectly formed kids, I text him the address of the car park by the candy-coloured swimming pool. The pool is closed after sunset, so there's never anyone around. Trish comes with me and takes the money from the guy, so he can't be a dick and try and take my pay back after he's busted a nut. She writes down the number of his plates, and she makes sure he knows what's what.

'My girl's not back in thirty-five minutes, I tell the cops where to look.'

Safety first.

We're fucked-up and we're junkies, but we're not dumb.

Except this night. I'd got a new bag of rock. The oily guy I'd got it from told me this batch was intense. And it was. It was something else. Trish got curious, and before I could stop her, she grabbed the pipe, took a puff. Or two. I guess, sitting there watching me the last few days, she'd got the itch. Dang. After that, she couldn't sit still, her legs were bouncing like she was on a trampoline. She said she had to walk for a bit to stop her head exploding. She was gone five minutes when I got a text for a job.

'Trish. Trish!'

Maybe her head had exploded. I couldn't find her to come and take the money and write down the plate. From where I was sitting among the pōhutukawa, I heard the sound of the car horn. I thought about just not going. Or texting the guy to cancel or to come back later. It started to rain. I figured it was a signal. Tāwhirimātea was looking out for me. What can go wrong when you've got the boss of thunder and lightning on your side?

When I got to the guy's car, it was really starting to pour. I hoped Trish had got back to the trees, out of the rain. Just in case, I put my hand up to where the sickle moon was going to rise, and I told the clouds to stop their teardrops falling. There was no reason to be sad, and I wanted my friend to stay dry. The God of Weather must have been on a coffee break. It kept raining.

I opened the door of the car, looked in and smiled the smile I smile at that moment. Every guy has the same look on his face when they first see me: a cross between a frightened little boy and a jackal that hasn't eaten meat in a week. Except, there was no one behind the steering wheel. The car was empty, the headlights on, the engine running.

Huh?

RETURN TO BLOOD

I heard movement behind me. Before I could turn, the bag went over my head. A hand covered my mouth so I couldn't scream. I was lifted up, thrown into the boot. Some kind of tape went round my wrists, tight and strong. Then my ankles.

The lid of the boot slammed shut.

Darkness.

And that was that.

No more sickle moons.

Not ever.

26

HE'S GONE

The images on Hana's cellphone screen are like a found-footage horror movie. Her phone films through thick undergrowth, past dark tree trunks. It's grainy in the low light, and sometimes the screen is just smudgy blues and blacks. Then faces come into focus. Rendall, then two other men, all in dark clothing. Finally, the fourth guy at the gate, working the bolt-cutters, and the chain breaking. He turns to camera for a moment, long enough for the viewer to recognize who it is.

Eyes sits silent, her lips tight and drained of blood. She looks at the face of her son on the screen.

Hana is with her cousin, sitting together at one of the low student tables in the main room of the kōhanga reo where Eyes is headteacher. 'Kōhanga reo' translates as 'language nest'; lessons and pretty much all daily conversations between teachers and the kindergarten-age children are done in te reo Māori. All around the walls are the kinds of images you would see in every early-education classroom, except the picture of an apple is labelled *āporo*, the image of a friendly dog, *kurī*.

Hana was waiting outside the kōhanga as the last child was picked up. She went in and told Eyes there was something she needed to show her.

The footage carries on. Eyes watches her son get into the hot-wired car and drive the stolen vehicle out through the gates, following Rendall's car down the road before both accelerate away, headlights off. The footage ends. Hana's cousin doesn't move. Doesn't speak. She takes the phone and rewinds the footage back to the moment the chain is cut, and Tīmoti turns towards the camera.

She hits pause. Says nothing for a long moment.

'That was his favourite seat.'

Beside her, there's a small wooden chair with a sun hand-painted on the backrest, the word *rā* written beneath.

'My first year teaching, he started here the same day I did. He was so little. One time a new girl came to class. She just cried and cried when her mum left. I tried to pick her up, give her a cuddle. An orange juice and a cookie. She didn't want to know about me. I wasn't her mum. Finally, Tīmoti took her by the hand. Took her outside, gave her a guided tour of the swings, the slide, the sandpit.'

Eyes stares at the sun chair. 'I was so proud of him,' she says.

She rewinds the footage again. Hana watches as she zooms in on the screen, the face at the gate. Her hand unconsciously goes to the scar on her forehead, from when she fell off the bike all those years ago.

'Him and the little girl,' Eyes continues. 'They were best friends after that. They just stayed best mates. Not boyfriend–girlfriend or any of that stuff. Just actual best friends. Last year Cynthia left for university down in Dunedin. She's going to be a doctor. Smart kid. I was really hoping she'd inspire my boy. Maybe he'd go to uni. He tried. Not everyone's cut out for academics, eh.'

Hana can tell Eyes is in automatic mode. Talking but not really thinking about or processing what she's saying. Finally, she looks up from the cellphone screen to Hana. She uses language she'd never use any other time in this room.

'Why the fuck did you have to show me this?'

Hana had dreaded this. But she had to take the footage to her cousin, to try to work out together what to do about Tīmoti. She'd fully expected a whiplash reaction from Eyes. If the roles were reversed, if that was Addison on the cellphone screen committing a crime that could result in a conviction and a police record that would change her opportunities in life from that point forward, Hana's pretty sure deflection, anger and denial would be her initial reactions too.

The footage continues until Hana scrambles with the phone through the undergrowth, hauling herself into the small ditch behind the gorse. Once there, her hand had covered the phone, to stop any light showing. There's nothing to see on the screen. But the microphone still picks up the sounds.

'C'mon, fucker. Make it easy on yourself.'

The sound of Hana's shallow, urgent breathing.

'ARRGGGH!' Rendall's angry outburst.

Eyes flinches. Even via tinny cellphone audio, it's unnerving. When she speaks again, her tone has changed.

'They could have killed you.'

Hana can't remember the last time her cousin spoke to her with anything like this sense of concern. It must be years, half a lifetime.

'The guy with the tattoos is the leader of the gang. Rendall. He's a bully and a coward. If anything went wrong, it'd be Tīmoti caught behind the wheel of the stolen car. Rendall would keep driving. And Tīmoti wouldn't say a word about him to the cops.'

'Snitches get stitches,' Eyes says. A phrase that Hana is pretty sure Eyes never thought she'd use about her own son. Her cousin hands back the phone. She's seen enough. The images are imprinted now.

'He's been staying out. Every other night, most weekends. He suddenly has the money to buy the clothes he was always hassling me for, and I could never afford. He said he was staying with mates. They were lending him money, buying stuff for him. I accepted what he was saying. I thought, he's missing Cynthia. But I knew something was up.'

It's an awful thing to acknowledge about her son. But the truth was there on the screen.

'All day, every day, parents trust me with their kids,' Eyes continues. 'My job is to give them our language. Our beliefs. Our traditions. Our values. And I can't even keep my own son from fucking up his life ...'

In Eyes' face is the same look as the day she fell off her bike. Determined not to shed a tear. But already crying, inside.

'If Mātai was here ... ,' she says.

Her ex-husband is a teacher too, and, like Eyes, a fluent speaker of te reo. A year before Tīmoti was born, Mātai made the commitment to receiving a puhoro – a full-body tā moko* that starts at the thighs and extends up over the buttocks, across the lower back. It's an intense, life-changing process, taking place over two weeks; eight hours a day of tattooing, every day, punctuated by meditation and prayer to help the recipient deal with the pain. Eyes was at his

---

* Tā moko – traditional form of Māori tattooing.

side every day. At the end of the two weeks, Mātai was transformed. His identity, his culture, his whakapapa, everything he and his ancestors carried inside, now proudly displayed on his skin. On the final day, as the last line was tattooed on Mātai's back, Eyes asked the tā moko artist to give her a moko kauae, the small, elegant chin tattoo, customarily for women, using elements of the design from Mātai's puhoro.

When Tīmoti was at primary school, Mātai was offered his dream job. Teaching te reo in a big full-immersion secondary school in Auckland. At first, he came back to Tātā Bay for one night during the week, and every weekend. Then it became every second weekend. By the time Mātai was only returning to the family home once a month, Eyes started to think something was wrong. In his second year at the Auckland school, he told her what was going on. He was in love with the senior teacher of his unit. He moved in with the woman the following week. And that was that. It was hard on Eyes, and on Tīmoti. Eyes was wounded; but even so, she and Mātai would be connected forever. By their son, and by the tā moko on their skins.

'Mātai is the only one Tīmoti listens to anymore. But he's not here.'

Hana can see her strong and fierce cousin is terrified. Terrified she has lost her son, terrified he's going to be another young Māori kid entering the justice system. Terrified that just as his best mate Cynthia starts her life as a doctor, Tīmoti is starting another life, walking in a very different direction.

Hana reaches across the low kids' table. She takes her cousin's hand. Eyes quietly cries.

On the eighth floor of Central Police Station, the most recent available image of Gordon John Weeks is projected on an AV screen. A team of seven CIB detectives and five uniformed officers is being briefed with details of the location of Weeks' flat, the entrances and exits to the apartment block. Weapons have been issued. Kevlar plates have been fitted into BAS* vests. After Jaye gives the statutorily required weapons briefing, Lorraine talks to the arrest team.

'He has a history of mental health issues. When I questioned Weeks, he was emotional and erratic. We've no specific information that leads us to believe the suspect will be armed or will use force to resist arrest, but this arrest is in connection with the most serious possible violent crime. There's reason to believe he is involved in two murders. We're not taking any chances.'

The briefing over, the team gather in the parking area on the ground floor. Four unmarked vehicles

---

* BAS – Body Armour System.

move out, in convoy, Lorraine driving the lead car.

An hour earlier, the results had come back from ESR for the DNA from the blue latex glove found in the sand dunes. The chances that the DNA belongs to any random member of the population that is not Gordon John Weeks are several million to one.

There are only five million people in New Zealand.

Kaikākāriki Junction is thirty kilometres from Tātā Bay. It used to have a couple of hundred residents, most working at the local meat processing plant. A few years ago, the plant was shut down: 'rationalizing operations' was the reason given in the press release. Translated from corporate spin, that meant the overseas owners of the meat company were making several million dollars from writing off the property. But it meant half the town lost their jobs. A dozen businesses closed.

One of them, on the outskirts of town, was a panel-beating workshop. The owner had to walk away. The place was abandoned. A couple of years later Rendall bought the place lock, stock and barrel.

Hana's car pulls up outside the corrugated iron gate of the workshop.

'Stay here,' she says as she gets out of the car.

'Like hell.'

Eyes is already out, and Hana knows there's no

point trying to keep her cousin from walking in there at her side. Rendall's car is parked in the weed-covered forecourt area. They cautiously step through the open rusted-out roller-doors of the warehouse. Inside they find welding machines, metal cutters. There's no sign of the ute taken from the farm buildings. Hana figures the vehicle was probably dismantled, the parts distributed around various willing buyers in Auckland, the evidence gone and profits made, perhaps before the owners of the vehicle even realized it was missing.

At the back of the workshop area, there's the sound of music playing. Hana and Eyes look through a window into an area decked out with couches. They see some cooking gear. And trays of beers, a couple of bottles of Jack Daniels. Some of the profits spent already, then. A half dozen young men are sitting around, smoking weed, drinking. Most of them white.

Apart from Tīmoti.

The unoiled hinges creak as Hana pushes open the door.

Rendall immediately recognizes her. He gives the same smile as when she confronted him outside the dairy. He kills the music. Tīmoti turns to see his mother at the door beside Hana.

'Fuck,' he groans quietly.

If Rendall is disconcerted by the presence of the ex-cop, he doesn't show it. 'If I'd known you were coming,

I'd have got you to pick up some Fanta and chippies from the Hindus.'

Hana walks towards him. Her phone in her hand. She starts the video playing. As the men watch, sharing dark looks as they realize who was there at the farm that night, Eyes stares at her son. Every muscle in Tīmoti's body is telling him to run. His two worlds, so carefully kept apart, are now crashing disastrously into each other, head-on. His mother, *here*. Tīmoti wants to throw up, climb out the window, get the fuck out of there, be anywhere but this place with these people.

'In case you're thinking of putting my phone through a grinder,' Hana says, as Rendall and the others watch the cars racing away down the unlit road on her screen, 'I made copies.'

Rendall looks up from the screen. A cold smile on his face. Begrudging admiration. He gets up from the couch. 'I must have been five metres from you. You got balls. Or did you piss yourself, sheriff?'

He takes a step towards Hana, getting in her face. She reacts, pushing him, hard, the palms of both hands against his chest. He stumbles backwards. The others stand, ready to go for her. Rendall signals them, a wave of his hand, *let her be*.

Hana holds Rendall's eye. Undaunted.

'Stay away from Tīmoti,' she says. 'Stay away from my cousin. Stay away from our whānau.'

Eyes is suddenly at Tīmoti's side, grabbing him by the arm, hard. He tries to shove her away. But now, he's crying. She grabs him harder still, hauls him towards the exit.

'Oh, baby boy,' Rendall says, mocking Tīmoti's tears. 'Fuck off. You were never up to the job anyway.'

Hana waits until Eyes and Tīmoti are out the gate and heading for her car before she speaks again.

'If I hear you've gone anywhere near them, this video goes straight to the most senior cops in Auckland.'

'How come you haven't done that already?' Rendall asks. 'Oh yeah. That'll fuck up little Timmy as much as it does me. That video's not going anywhere.'

'Try me,' Hana says, heading for the gate.

Rendall stands in the open doors of the warehouse. 'Watch your fucking back, sheriff. 'Cos I sure will be.'

In the car, Eyes is in the back seat, still locked onto Tīmoti's arm. Tīmoti sits, trying to be staunch despite his wet cheeks. Hana starts the engine and pulls away. As her car turns the corner, out of sight of the warehouse, her nephew's façade evaporates. His mother's grip on his arm loosens. Her arm goes around his shoulders. She pulls him to her.

Hana drives, her eyes on the rear-view mirror. But no one is following. She's helped her cousin make a first step to winning back her son.

But in the process, she has made herself an enemy.

The curtains of the flat are drawn.

A Delta unit* has been called in to rendezvous with the arrest team at the address, the dog handler deployed at the rear of the apartment block with three CIB and several uniformed officers, in case the suspect attempts to flee. Police vehicles wait at either end of the street, lights flashing.

At the front door of Gordon John Weeks' flat, Lorraine and Jaye exchange a silent look.

Here we go.

Lorraine presses the speaker button twice on her comms radio. The prearranged signal. She knocks on the door. A casual few taps. It could be a courier or a member of the Church of Latter-Day Saints. She and Jaye listen carefully. No sounds from inside. Lorraine taps on the door again, a few more times, a little louder. Still no indication that the occupant has heard. She takes a step closer to the door. Three hard knocks.

'This is the police, open the door please.'

Another three knocks, louder.

'Police. Open this door.'

Lorraine knocks hard and repeatedly. No movement inside the apartment. Nothing. Jaye looks to a uniformed officer with a battering ram who steps forward,

---

* Delta unit – canine squad.

ready to knock down the door. But first, Lorraine tries the handle.

The door swings open. Unlocked.

In unison, her and Jaye's hands go to the Glocks at their waists. Lorraine leads the way through the flat, identifying herself and warning that she is armed, Jaye two steps behind. It takes Lorraine less than twenty seconds to move through the entire small space, checking the wardrobe, under the bed. She comes back to where Jaye stands by the shattered 42-inch television.

She speaks into her handset. 'He's gone.'

Hana waits at Eyes' house for as long as it takes Tīmoti to throw his clothes into a couple of sports bags. In the car, on the road back to Tātā Bay, Eyes had phoned her ex-husband. Tīmoti is going to his place for the next few months. Out of reach of the gang. Mātai is taking accumulated leave to spend time with his son, work with him. Try and find a way forward.

'Maybe we'll get a tā moko together,' Mātai told Tīmoti on the phone.

With Tīmoti packed and in her car, Eyes takes a moment with Hana.

'Cuz,' she starts. But she can't find any other words.

'Haven't called me that for a while,' Hana says, and smiles.

Eyes reaches out and hugs her.

Then she gets into the car, and she and Tīmoti start the long drive to Auckland.

'He quit. This morning.'

Lorraine, Jaye and the arrest team are at the transitional house, speaking to the manager.

'He called in sick the last few days. Finally turned up this morning. Grabbed a bag of his beekeeping equipment. He was all over the place. Never seen him like that. He said thanks for everything, but we wouldn't see him again. He's been here twenty years. Do you know what's going on?'

Lorraine gets on her phone to request a FLINT* be created and posted out urgently to the iPhone of every police officer in the country, to be on the lookout for Weeks and his vehicle. The odds of finding him anytime soon aren't great; New Zealand has a land area larger than the UK and Ireland combined and hundreds of thousands of kilometres of tarmac main roads and unsealed back routes. Apart from a couple of toll motorways, there's almost no licence plate recognition technology; there's just too much road to even hope to monitor all of it.

For Lorraine and Jaye, the disappointment burns.

---

* FLINT – Front Line Intelligence alert.

They'd moved as fast as they could. It hadn't been fast enough.

A small kawakawa bush has been left on the rear deck of Hana's house, the root system wrapped up in wet newspaper. Addison had phoned the night before, to let her know that she and PLUS 1 were driving down. Hana could hear in her voice that her daughter needed more than just a home-cooked meal. She told Addison to come, stay the night if they wanted. And she asked for a favour; that her daughter carefully dig out one of the smaller kawakawa plants from the garden for her. There's a sheltered spot at the side of the wharenui that looks a little bare, and a shade-loving kawakawa will be perfect.

Climbing her steps, Hana can see that PLUS 1's car is parked outside Eru's place, half a mile down the road. After the confrontation with Rendall, she could really use a moment or two to decompress. She'll let Addison and her mate have a bit of time with Eru before she goes over with the macaroni cheese she got ready yesterday evening.

Hana puts the kawakawa in a bucket, gives it a quick spray of water from the hose. Heads in. Makes a cup of tea. There's leftover rice from the curry she made the night before. She goes out to the back deck, tosses it on the driveway for the insatiably hungry local seagulls.

There's something she's been meaning to do. She hasn't quite been able to face it yet. But she can't avoid it any longer. In the lounge she sits down in the big, heavy old armchair she likes to use when she's on her laptop. She opens Google and types in the same search terms she found in Eru's search history.

Early-onset dementia, symptoms, prognosis.

When Lorraine and Jaye get back to Weeks' address, a SOCO team are systematically turning over the small flat, looking for any further forensic or physical evidence to connect him to the two historic homicides, and for any clues as to where he might have fled. In the bedroom, a forensics officer shows the detectives the closet, the cardboard box in the hidden space under the loose floorboard.

But there's one thing that's not as Hana described it. The bracelet with the single star has gone.

In the lounge, a detective trained in digital forensics is working on breaking into Weeks' laptop. There are multiple password-breaking software programs, coded by tech geeks on both sides of the law: investigation bureaus and hackers. Tools developed from very different motivations, but with the same goal. Between the various software apps, digital forensics specialists (or dark-web scammers) can crack ninety per cent of passwords quickly and efficiently. It's only the most determinedly complex passwords that take more work. And there are very few that can resist breaking altogether.

'Are you close?' Lorraine asks the officer working on the laptop.

With nothing found in the flat to indicate where Weeks may have fled, his recent internet searches are the best hope for a clue; whether he has booked accommodation or looked at remote areas to go bush. The detectives are hoping that no international flights were purchased in the brief window between his DNA sample being taken and the decision to arrest him.

'Got it, boss.'

The password on Weeks' laptop isn't complicated. Jaye or Lorraine could probably have opened it themselves with a few dozen considered guesses, given their knowledge of Weeks, his profession and his day and month of birth.

Nectar0511

Lorraine types in the password. The laptop unlocks. She and Jaye stare at the multiple files on the screen, tabs left open in the browser; the things Weeks was looking at in the twenty-four hours before he disappeared.

'Oh god.'

As Lorraine scrolls her way through the open files, Jaye watches, his face grim. Weeks had googled news stories from six months earlier. Stories about a big case, the biggest in many years. The pursuit of Poata Raki, New Zealand's first serial killer. The searches on Weeks' computer focused on the senior police officer who had spearheaded the search for Raki. On his screen, image after image of one person.

The brilliant Māori cop who retired just hours after the killer died at his own hands.

Detective Senior Sergeant Hana Westerman.

27

HARD STEEL

A cushion is sitting on top of the log. PLUS 1 is down on one knee behind it, resting their elbow on their bent leg to support the stock of the rifle, the recoil pad squeezed firmly into their shoulder the way Eru showed them. The barrel of the M1 carbine lies on the fraying floral design of the cushion, an empty Watties tomato sauce can sitting on a tree stump twenty-five metres beyond the rifle's sights.

'Inhale. Exhale. Breathe normally but deeply until you're ready to fire. Focus your eye on the reticle, that sticky-up bit at the end of the gun. Ease the position of your body until the target is lined up behind the reticle. One last deep breath in. Out. It's all about the breathing. And gently squeeze the trigger. Smooth. Slow.'

Addison watches, Boca in her arms, barely

breathing herself, as PLUS 1 squeezes the trigger, smooth, slow. The trigger reaches its end point, up tight against the guard, with a faint metallic click. PLUS 1 takes a breath.

'Ready to try the real thing?' Eru asks.

'You know it, Mr Westerman.'

Eru takes the rifle, loads a round into the chamber, engages the bolt.

'That thing's gonna knock you on your skinny brown arse,' Addison giggles nervously.

For PLUS 1 and Addison, both brought up in the nice central city suburbs, being around a real gun is very unfamiliar territory. A bit shady, a bit exhilarating, more than a little scary. With the safety engaged, Eru carefully hands the rifle back to PLUS 1. PLUS 1 pulls the recoil pad tight into their shoulder. Takes the weight of the stock again on their bent knee.

'All set?'

'Uh-huh.'

Addison watches as her grandfather eases the safety to the left.

'You're now holding a live loaded weapon,' he says quietly. 'This is serious.'

'I understand.'

'Like I showed you,' Eru says.

PLUS 1 eases their body a little to the left, a bit forward, a half inch back. Finally the tomato sauce can sits plumb in their sights.

That morning, as Addison shuffled round the house, getting herself and the puppy ready for the drive down to Tātā Bay, PLUS 1 had stood in the bathroom. Staring into the mirror. They'd bleached one of their longest dreadlocks. Something to do, to not think about the other things. Like the messiness of the last few days, since Addison had found Kiri's bones. And the sick feeling PLUS 1 had felt when Addison had talked about the night she'd spent under the Harbour Bridge with the guy named Dax.

For a moment, I wanted to be with him.

The conversation over scrambled eggs had been tough. PLUS 1 and Addison have carefully defined their relationship for years. Best friends. And that's enough. More than enough. Well that's the agreed line anyway. Neither of them are the kind to fall in love. They've said this to each other a hundred times, all the while writing songs together about falling in love.

There's what you say. There's what you sing. And there's what you actually feel.

PLUS 1 has long since realized: they *are* the kind that falls in love, most definitely, and they've been head over heels in love with Addison for a very long time. The love songs they write aren't theoretical for PLUS 1. They're actual. Those songs are how they feel about Addison. As long as there's just the two of them, flatmates, best friends, a joy-filled musical partnership,

PLUS 1 has been able to live with the pretence of 'we're not the kind to fall in love'. The maths works imperfectly for PLUS 1 if they're being completely honest, but it works just well enough for them to be able to live with it. But what happens when someone else enters the equation?

For a moment, I wanted to be with him.

What happens when it's more than just a moment? What happens when Addison finds out she *is* the kind who falls in love, not with Dax, but with someone else? Someone who's not PLUS 1?

'What are you up to in there?'

'I bleached a dreadlock.'

'Success?'

'Ummmmmm ...'

PLUS 1 studied the dreadlock in the mirror. It was more yellow than white. Maybe not in a good way. Maybe in a way that looks a bit like the fur around the mouths of cats with overactive salivary glands.

'Think I need to rebleach. You guys go.'

'What do you mean?'

Hearing the disappointment in Addison's voice, PLUS 1 looked again at the mirror. *Fuck it*. The second bleach could wait. They needed to just ignore the messy feelings. Make things normal, by being normal. Be in the here and now, with Addison, with Boca. The maths worked well enough. Just got to keep going, cross bridges when they needed to.

PLUS 1 opened the door.

Addison was standing with a dug-up kawakawa bush in her hands, the roots wrapped in wet newspaper. 'Mum wants us to bring this,' she said. Addison looked at PLUS 1's kind-of-white, kind-of-yellow dreadlock. 'It looks great.'

'It doesn't.'

'It really doesn't,' Addison said, smiling, trying not to be unkind, but it was true. 'I'll fix it up when we get home, babe.'

In the clearing in the bush behind Eru's house, PLUS 1 breathes in. Deep. Addison snuggles Boca under her cardigan, trying to cover the puppy's ears. PLUS 1 breathes out. Holds after the exhale. Finger squeezing. Smooth, slow.

A sharp crack.

The bullet hits the tomato can a half-inch high of centre, puncturing a small hole through the second 'T' in the Watties label. The can goes spinning and tumbling off into the bush, as PLUS 1 whoops with delight and Boca gives a nervous yelp, not at all sure what just happened.

'Over-achiever,' Addison laughs.

PLUS 1's physicality, their athleticism, their laser focus: great for diving. Great for the turntables. Now, it seems, great for marksmanship.

Eru takes the gun and reloads it for PLUS 1, his smile a mile wide.

'Well, e hoa.* You're better at target shooting than hairdressing.'

On the websites she's googled, Hana scrolls through the red flags for early-onset dementia.

Memory loss around recent events. Difficulty with problem-solving and complex tasks. Hana thinks about how Eru had to get her to fill in the credit card details for the registration.

In the big armchair, she tucks one leg up into her chest, wraps an arm around her knee. It's a comfort thing she used to do when she was little, when she was upset or afraid about something. If her father's fears are correct, Hana wants to know what's coming for him. She keeps scrolling. Other symptoms from the websites don't seem to fit. An indicator of early-onset dementia is the inability to express emotions. Eru happily talks about his feelings, passionately discussing the things he believes. His vivid memories about Tama, the reasons why he was sure he wasn't a killer. And there's no hint of the change in personality many sufferers experience, not that Hana can see. Her dad is still the warm, loving, unshakeably optimistic guy he always was. *But what if he's carefully curating his emotions?* she thinks.

---

* E hoa – my friend.

Constructing a façade of warm easiness, hiding what he's feeling, from Hana, and maybe from himself?

Through the open sliding doors that lead out to the back deck comes a sudden, jarring sound. The sharp crack of a rifle being fired. Two seagulls in Hana's driveway pause for a moment. Satisfied they're not in any danger, they go back to the leftover rice. Hana looks towards the bush behind Eru's place. Her father must be keeping his promise to PLUS 1. Target practice.

One website says that depression can happen in the early stages of dementia, when the sufferer is still lucid enough to know what's happening and starts to suspect what's coming down the road for them. Depression and acting on depression – self-harm and suicide – is far more likely in the early stages.

Self-harm.

From outside, the sound of another rifle shot. The report echoes off the hills behind. The seagulls don't even bother to look up this time.

Hana thinks about the Vietnam-era gun her father had used to shoot deer, the gun that is part of her mum and dad's love story. Is it time to get rid of it? The shed her dad keeps the rifle in is locked with a small padlock that's nearly rusted through. She could make a persuasive argument, Hana thinks; tell Eru he can't keep hold of an unlicensed, unregistered firearm. What if some local kid breaks in, nicks it and does something stupid?

The crack of another shot.

Hana's phone rings. The caller ID says Jaye. Even as she goes to pick up, the battery dies. With everything that happened with Eyes and Rendall, she forgot to charge it. She plugs it in. The spinning charge logo circles the battery level indicator, zero per cent.

As she waits for enough charge to call Jaye back, she returns to the websites.

'I was a kid when I volunteered. A year or two older than you two are now. I thought it was going to be the adventure of a lifetime. See the world.'

PLUS 1 fired the rifle half a dozen times in all. They hit the tomato sauce can three times. There were a few rounds left, but Addison didn't want to try, uneasy on a whole lot of levels about the idea of holding a gun. Walking back through the bush towards Eru's house, looking at the rifle in her grandfather's hand, Addison asked him about his time in Vietnam.

'I've never really heard you say anything about what it was like, Grandpa.'

'I was just a Māori boy from a small town who liked to go fishing. I wasn't political. Still not, not how you are. Your grandmother changed things for me, though, after I got sent back. She'd be out protesting against the war. Then she'd put on her uniform and head into work and fix up people like me who'd been shipped back with bits missing.'

Eru adjusts his beat-up old bushman's hat. This isn't an easy conversation. It's something he's never wanted to talk about, like so many Māori who came back from the overseas wars of the twentieth century. It still doesn't feel comfortable.

'Two men in my company died. One was a close mate. None of that was any kind of good. But what was even worse was walking through the villages after they'd been hit from the air with those fucking chemicals.'

'Oh, Grandpa.'

It's not just that she's never heard her grandfather use that word before and never expected to. It's the look on his face. His eyes moist, his lips trembling. Reliving things he wants to leave behind but knows he never can.

'I'm sorry, love.'

'It's okay. I asked. I just feel so bad for you.'

She puts her hand through his arm. They walk out from the edge of the bush, crossing the road towards Eru's place. PLUS 1 can see Hana's car parked half a mile away, behind her house, the sliding doors leading off her deck wide open.

'Your mum's made it home.'

They climb the steps to Eru's back door. He carefully puts the M1 Carbine down on the table he uses to gut fish after he's been casting off the rock shelf.

'There's a kitbag in the shed,' he says to PLUS 1. 'Grab it and I'll show you how to clean and oil the barrel and disengage the firing mechanism.'

PLUS 1 heads to the little shed to find the bag.

'The only good part of the whole story: I met a nurse with cobalt-blue eyes and a beautiful singing voice. She spent every day I was in hospital telling me how it was a war no one should've been fighting. Least of all us down here at the end of the world, in little old New Zealand. By the time I could walk again, I was out there on my crutches, protesting with her.'

Addison hugs her grandfather.

Hana powers off the laptop.

It's been a sobering read. The articles from various medical journals and Alzheimer's support sites tell the same story. If Eru is suffering early-onset dementia, the best-case scenario is an unhappy one. The worst-case scenario is heart-breaking. She pushes back into the soft padding of the armchair. Sips the last of her tea. It's only just lukewarm now.

With her cousin Eyes, the decision was simple; Hana had to show her the video, face the bad news with her. With Eru, it's way more complex. He's a proud man. He's her father. He has decided not to tell her about his fears. Maybe he's already talked to his GP, maybe he's been referred to a specialist, maybe he's waiting until he has some kind of confirmation, so that he feels a sense of ownership over his world; so that he is able to make a plan and find the right time to share it with Hana and Addison. It's his life, his health, his mind, after all. Is it Hana's place to know better, to think she can decide that he has to share everything with her, before he's ready to?

Hana has no idea what the answer is to any of these questions.

She looks at her phone. Back to five per cent. She presses the power button.

Beep-beep-beep-beep-beep.

Five missed calls. All from Jaye. Has there been a development, something to do with Gordon John Weeks? She presses *return call*, and Jaye picks up immediately.

'My battery died. Something wrong?'

'We went to arrest Weeks this morning. He'd left his house in a hurry. Quit his job. He's disappeared.'

Hana feels a familiar tension in her spine. Already running through scenarios in her head, starting to work through the matrix of possibilities for where a suspect like Weeks could have gone, as she would if this were her own case. But it's not.

'Why are you telling me this? I'm not supposed to be in the loop.'

'Hana. His computer is full of photos of you.'

Her jaw tightens. 'I don't understand,' she says.

'Me either. When you went into his flat, is there any way Weeks could have known? Could he have seen you?'

In her driveway, the two seagulls have finished the rice. As they flap away, Hana thinks back to sitting in her car, outside Weeks' flat, after her lucky escape. Sebastian got out, she remembers, and she watched in the rear-view mirror as he walked back to his own vehicle fifty metres down the road. Then she started her car. As she was about to pull away, did she look back at the ground floor apartment for a moment?

She did.

She remembers looking across. She saw the curtains were still drawn. She's certain of that. But was there a crack in the curtains? As she looked back at the flat, could Weeks possibly have been looking out? Could he have seen her, somehow recognized her?

'I can't answer that question, Jaye.'

'But is it possible?'

'Yes. It's possible.'

With her laptop powered off, the screen is now black and reflective. Out of the corner of her eye, Hana catches a glimpse of something in the dark, shiny surface.

Movement.

Something behind her.

By the time she realizes it's not some*thing*, it's

some*one*, someone rushing towards her fast, it's too late. She tries to pull herself out of the armchair, but already she feels the sickening cold of hard steel on the soft skin of her throat, slipped around her from behind. Her hands rise to protect herself. Her phone falls to the floor. The flat of a long steel blade pulls hard against her windpipe, forcing her backwards against the armchair, pinning her there.

A foot kicks the phone away to the other side of the room.

Struggling to draw breath, Hana looks to the laptop. Reflected on the screen, a face. A face she hasn't met up close in real life before. But it's a face she knows well, a face she has sketched. Bushy eyebrows, blond hair greying at the temples.

The face of the man who lived in the caravan on Mountain Road.

28

THE DUNES

After what happened that night, twenty-one years ago, Gordon John Weeks went home.

The night he killed the girl, Paige.

He went from the dunes to the place that felt like an actual home to him, much more of a home than the small, mildewy, aluminium-walled caravan with the VHS player and the movies about angry young men like him and what they did to frightened girls. Much more of a home than the small house he'd lived in with his mother, the place with the cupboard in the hallway where she kept the leather belt.

He went straight back from the dunes to his friend's house. Tama would know what to do. He showed Tama the bracelet.

He still remembers the look on the older man's

tattooed face. Weeks had seen people fishing on the beach at Tātā Bay, casting out their long surf rods. He would watch as they'd pull in a snapper or a kahawai.* The fish would fight and fight for what must have seemed like an eternity to them, a lifetime, but the hooks were in their mouths and there was no escape as they were dragged through the breakers and up into the shallow water. One time Weeks got close enough to see the eyes of a beached snapper. There was nothing there, in the fish's eyes. There was life, but only barely; nothing else. No fight left. Everything gone.

The same look came to his friend Tama's face when Weeks showed him the bracelet.

Two weeks before, after he'd chased the religious girl with the scarf around her head, he'd gone from the dunes to Tama's house, shaky and wired, blood coming from where she'd hit him with her hockey stick. 'I wasn't going to hurt her,' he told Tama. He tried to explain about why he chased her. To scare her. That was all. To feel the things the young men felt in the VHS movies. To see what it was like to make someone feel afraid. To make a girl feel fear.

He thought the old man might understand.

And Tama understood. He knew exactly what was boiling up inside the younger man. And he knew what he had to do.

---

* Kahawai – a breed of ocean salmon.

It was the only time Tama hurt him.

He pushed Weeks up against a wall, slapped him with an open hand, hard. Once, twice, three times.

It was so different to when his mother took the belt from the cupboard. In Tama's face there was no anger. Only pain. Hating that he was hurting Weeks. But doing the only thing he could, the thing he had to do to jolt Weeks out of this moment, to make him listen, to make him understand that he had to fight the feelings inside him, he had to fight those dark impulses with every fibre of his being.

It worked; that is to say, it worked when Tama was there, to talk to him, to get him to focus, to see the colour blue behind his eyes. While Tama was there, everything was okay.

But Tama wasn't there, two weeks later, the night it happened.

Tama had gone to a hospital in the city for treatment. Left alone in his caravan, Weeks put one of the VHS movies into the player. The new meds that Tama had asked the local doctor to prescribe for him made him feel sluggish. He hated the feeling. He went to Tama's place, found a bottle of cheap sherry. Anything not to feel that way. He drank the sherry under the tree out the back of the old man's house. He took a bunch of his old meds that always made him jittery, hyped. But at least they made him feel alive. He went back to the caravan, played one of the movies. It was his favourite;

one he'd played so many times there was almost more static than clean videotape. But his favourite scene was on the bit of the tape that was still kind of okay. A close-up of the pretty girl. She'd just realized the angry young man was following her.

In her eyes, fear.

Weeks took the nearly empty bottle of cheap sherry, and he walked out into the night. Telling himself he was just going for a walk. Just going for a walk.

In his mind was the image that was paused on the screen.

A pretty girl with fear in her eyes.

The plastic cable tie is a metre long.

Weeks uses the extra-long cable ties on the hives, to fix the mouse guards to the bottom of the stack of bee boxes, to make sure even the most determined rodent won't ever squeeze its way between the layers and into the honey beyond. With the flat of the knife's blade hard against her throat, he drops the cable tie into Hana's lap.

'Put it around your wrists.'

She considers pushing back, trying to knock Weeks off his feet, but though her armchair is solid enough, there's nothing to lever her legs against to push the heavy thing backwards. She can't see the blade; can't see what kind of weapon it is. Against her windpipe it feels solid, hard and wide.

A machete?

'Around your wrists.'

Weeks came prepared, with the tapered end of the cable tie already threaded through the catch, the resulting loop just wide enough to go around a person's wrists. Hana takes a half moment, running through her options. Pushing back against the armchair isn't going to work. Going in the opposite direction, diving forward, would mean pushing the most vulnerable part of her body against the blade at her throat. That's pretty much where the options end. She really doesn't want to put that cable tie around her wrists. Anything but that.

She looks at the phone on the floor on the other side of the room. If it hasn't disconnected, if Jaye is still listening, she needs him to know who is in her house.

'Put the knife down. Please, Mr Weeks, put the knife down.'

The steel pulls back against her throat, harder still.

'Your wrists. Do it. Now.'

The worst option is now Hana's only option. She slips her hands through the hard plastic loop. She knows these things; she's used them. The plastic might look thin but it's impossible to break.

Weeks has thought this through.

He's had time.

After she'd been in his flat, after he'd seen her

through the gap in the curtains, he wracked his brain for days, trying to remember where he'd seen that face. The more he fought to place her, the more the memory became like a puff of smoke from his bee-smoker, wafting away in the breeze. Then the detective with the lipstick came to take his DNA. The walls were closing in. When the cops left, he sank to the floor among the shattered glass of the big-screen television, not even caring if the shards cut his legs. Given up. Defeated.

Like the snapper hauled up onto the beach.

All hope gone.

And then, as if the very act of trying to remember had kept the memory at bay, it came to him in a rush. When he stopped trying, realization flooded in to fill the void.

He'd seen the woman's face in the papers, on the news broadcasts.

The cop who'd hunted New Zealand's first serial killer.

He spent the next few hours googling the case, learning her name, searching for everything he could find about her. She'd left the cops, but there was nothing to indicate where she lived now. Then he found an article from a small weekly regional newspaper. A good-news story about a programme at the Tātā Bay marae, to help young drivers get their licences. There was a photo of the locals running the programme. Eru Westerman, and his daughter.

Now he knew where Hana was.

And how to find her.

It took him less than an hour driving around Tātā Bay to find the car he'd seen across the road from his flat. He waited in a place in the dunes where he could watch the house it was parked outside. When Hana drove away, he found a window he could force open. He climbed in. Violating her privacy. The same way she'd violated his. He found the cupboard where she kept the vacuum cleaner, leaving the door open just enough of a crack so he could see out into the living room.

And he waited.

'Tighten it. I'm not going to ask again.'

'I only have two hands,' Hana manages to gasp, hoping he'll use one of his to tighten the loop, then maybe she can strike out against the one remaining hand holding the knife.

'Your teeth. Use your teeth.'

The blade pulls against her throat, tighter still. Struggling to even breathe now, Hana has no choice. She raises her hands, grips the plastic between her teeth, pulls, tightening the loop. But she keeps her wrists slightly apart, trying to leave enough wiggle room so she might be able to slip one hand out.

'I see what you're doing. *Tight.*'

The steel blade is so hard against her throat that it's cutting off her windpipe. She can't black out. She bites down on the cable tie again, pulling it tight, pulling harder and harder still, until the plastic cable is indenting the hard muscles around her wrists, as tight as it can go.

Finally, Weeks releases the blade from her throat. She gasps air into her lungs.

He comes to the other side of the armchair. Facing her. He reaches into his pocket. Pulls something out.

A delicate silver bracelet. An interlocked chain, with a small star hanging from it.

When he tries to remember that night twenty-one years ago, it's like a VHS tape with more electronic drop-out than footage. He remembers bits. Then there's static. He remembers finishing the bottle of sherry as he went down to the township. Then static. Then he remembers passing the dunes, just as the girl Paige ran past, athletic shoes and running gear. She smiled at him. So pretty. So young. Blonde, like the girl in the movie.

What would she look like not *smiling?* he wondered. *What would she look like terrified?*

She ran past, heading into the dunes.

He followed her.

Then static.

Then it's like the videotape reaches a clean bit again. Weeks is deep in the dunes. Ahead of him, she's aware that he's following her. She runs faster. Then static.

Then the static clears again. Now he sees her eyes looking at him. Not smiling. Now he has what he's been wanting for so long. The chance to see if he can make a girl feel what those girls in the movies felt. To see if he can have power. The power to make someone afraid. He tightens his grip around her throat.

Then static.

Then when the videotape hits a good bit again, he's standing above her body. Covering her with sand. There's still one hand emerging from the dune, pale flesh against the black iron. On the girl's wrist, the bracelet. He unclasps it. Puts it in his pocket. And he covers her hand with sand.

Then static.

Then, he remembers being back at the old man's house. Tama had just got back from the hospital, pale and gaunt from the treatment. Weeks showed him the girl's bracelet. Told him what he'd done.

The look in Tama's eyes. Like the snapper dragged in, through the waves. Still alive, but only barely. All hope gone.

Tama had been quiet for a very long time. Staring at the bracelet.

'I'll take care of this,' he'd finally told Weeks.

And he did.

'You found this,' Weeks says, holding the bracelet with the dangling star. 'You found it when you broke into my house. Don't lie. I saw you. That's why they came and took my DNA.'

Hana looks at the distance between them. He's a body length away from her, the open sliding door behind him, the large blade hanging at his side in one hand, Paige's bracelet in the other. Even with her own hands bound, she could still try and regain control of the situation. She could pull herself from the armchair, throw herself across the distance between them – it would take perhaps a second or two to get to him – her arms locked straight, her bound fists like a battering ram with all her weight and momentum behind them, aimed straight at his face.

But a second or two is also enough time for him to raise the knife. And for her momentum as she threw herself at him to drive the blade deep into her torso.

She can see her phone on the floor. If Jaye has heard the confrontation, the local cops will be coming. There's a rural police station thirty kilometres away. Or the AOS squad might be on the way from Auckland, dispatched on an Eagle helicopter. But either way, it will be a good thirty minutes before help arrives. And what if the phone had disconnected, and Jaye had assumed that the only thing amiss was that Hana's battery had died again?

'Please, Mr Weeks. There's nothing I can do. I'm no

threat to you, with this round my wrists,' Hana says, wanting to give Jaye as complete a picture as possible, if he is still listening. 'Talk to me. Let's sit at the table, work this out together.'

She goes to rise from the armchair, slowly, slowly.

'Don't move an inch.'

His voice is low. Anger burning in his face. Hana knows he's not about to de-escalate. If anything, the opposite. She lowers herself back down into the armchair.

'None of this would've happened,' Weeks says. 'If it wasn't for you.'

His eyes move to the stretch of land in front of Hana's house, leading down to the ocean.

To the blackness of the sand dunes.

The sand dunes.

Twenty-one years ago, Tama Hall knew that it would take at most a day for the cops to be at his door once Paige's body was found. Maybe there were other people in the Tātā Bay community who had criminal records. But Tama was pretty sure nobody would have the history of violent crime he had. The Māori guy with the tattoos and the convictions for grievous bodily harm, assault with a weapon. One plus one was always going to equal two.

The young fella wanted to go to the cops himself. Confess to what he'd done. But Tama made a decision.

'They'll come for me. Let them.'

He was dying. A couple of years to live at best. There was one thing left he could do that might mean his life was of some value. And that was to give something to a boy Tama believed had good inside, even though he'd been so badly fucked up by his upbringing and his internal chemistry; to give that boy a chance to start again. Tama phoned the transitional house in Auckland, the place he'd gone to after he'd come out of prison, the place that had helped him so much. He begged them to find a job for the boy. Tama knew it was a place where there were no women. It was a place where Weeks would be taught about the Bible.

When the cops knocked at his door, Tama already had his bags packed. Two days later, after the old man had confessed and been arrested for the murder of Paige Meadows, Weeks caught a bus and left Tātā Bay and never returned.

Until today.

Weeks looks back from the dunes. His eyes meet Hana's.

'Twenty-one years ago, I made a terrible mistake. I've spent the rest of my life since making amends.

Living a decent life. Trying to help others be better men than me. Telling them about the bees. How it's the job of the workers to protect the queen. How it's a man's job to protect women. I learned the Bible. The scriptures. They teach about sacrifice. My friend gave himself up for me. I changed. But then, you turned up. You came into my house. You ruined everything.'

The rhythm of his speech is hastening. His eyes flick about with anxiety and adrenaline. Hana knows that things are fast approaching a tipping point.

'Know why I kept this?' Weeks holds up Paige's bracelet.

'I think so.'

Hana remembers the things the Australian murderer kept hidden in the ceilings and walls of his house: the sleeping bags, camping stove, clothes. The tusk a big game hunter keeps after shooting an elephant.

'A souvenir,' she says.

'No. You don't know,' Weeks says. 'You think you understand. You have no fucking idea.'

For the first time, Hana glances at the knife in Weeks' hand. It's a strange-looking thing. If it's a machete it's one she's completely unfamiliar with, the long flat steel blade curved slightly where it connects to the wooden handle. Hana's eyes rise from the blade.

She sees something over Weeks' shoulder.

Movement on the driveway, unseen behind him.

Hurrying quietly down the road that leads to his

house, her father. Addison and PLUS 1 close behind him. In Eru's hands, his rifle.

Weeks is completely unaware.

'Tama made me keep her bracelet. A reminder. Something I had to look at every day. To see again and again and again what I did. What I could do again. To remind me every day of my life what I was capable of. So I would never do it again.'

With the gun raised, aimed at Weeks, Eru moves carefully towards Hana's house. Step by step. The recoil pad squeezed tight against his shoulder, how he'd shown PLUS 1.

In the moments after Weeks rushed Hana and her phone fell to the ground, Jaye heard enough to understand that the man they were hunting as a suspect in two homicides was in Hana's house, and he was armed with a knife. And from what Jaye could hear of the rapidly escalating confrontation through the still-connected phone, he knew the time it would take to get police to her door would be too long. Instead, he called Eru. Eru took the gun he and PLUS 1 were cleaning and oiling, loaded a new round into the chamber, told Addison and PLUS 1 to go inside and lock the door, and ran for his daughter's house. But Addison and PLUS 1 weren't going to let Eru go there alone.

Hana sees her dad climbing the stairs to her rear deck, step by step.

'None of this had to happen. Why did you do it?' Weeks asks.

'You killed Paige, Mr Weeks.' She talks fast, worried that if she leaves a silence, he might hear her father approaching. 'And I think you hurt Kiri.'

Weeks' eyes flare. He raises the strange knife, stepping forward. 'That's bullshit, why are you doing this to me? Why are you doing this?'

As Weeks walks towards Hana, from behind him—
'Put down that fucking knife!'

Weeks spins and sees Eru at the open sliding door, the gun in his hands. It takes a moment for Weeks to understand what's happening. A moment is all Hana needs. She leaps from the chair, launches herself at him. She and Weeks go sprawling to the floor. Her cable-tied hands grab the knife, and they wrestle back and forth. Weeks manages to turn Hana over and seize back the knife; he rises over her, the blade grasped in his hands.

Boom.

Gordon John Weeks flinches. Falls. The knife drops from his hand. He's been shot through the upper back; blood seeps through his shirt, a stain spreading fast over the carpet. As Eru reloads, keeping his gun trained on Weeks, PLUS 1 rushes forward, kicks the long-bladed knife out of reach. Hana hurries to kneel at the wounded man's side, looking at his injury.

There's a lot of blood.

'I need something to stop the bleeding,' she says.

Addison pulls off her sweater. With her wrists still bound, Hana uses it to staunch the man's wound.

On the floor, Weeks stares up at her. The wild anger that was in his eyes only moments before, gone. His pupils dilated with fear.

'I didn't kill Kiri Thomas.' His voice grows weaker. 'I never met her in my life. I never met her.'

Hana holds the sweater to the wound in the injured man's back, as Weeks slips into unconsciousness.

29

RAINBOW'S END

The service is held in a beautiful little chapel that stands overlooking a lagoon on the edge of Auckland Harbour. At the front of the church, Kiri's casket is white. White was chosen so everyone who loved her could decorate the sides and top, using her favourite spray can colour, seafoam green. The casket is a gorgeous tapestry of doodles, messages of love, broken-hearted farewells.

In the pews, Kiri's adoptive family, and a big turn-out from her birth whānau. Hana is there, with Eru, Addison and PLUS 1. Friends and teachers from Kiri's school. Lorraine and Jaye and a number of other cops and social workers who worked with her.

Kiri's friends from the Youth at Risk group are in the front row. Trish is at the front of the chapel, beside her friend's casket.

'We used to go to Rainbow's End, Monday mornings. No normal human being goes to an amusement park on a Monday morning. We were always the only ones there. Her favourite ride was the rollercoaster. To me it was just noisy and awful and made me want to throw up. Not for Kiri. She loved the thing.'

Trish smiles sadly. Dax is standing at her side, holding her little boy as she speaks.

'There's this moment in the ride that she loved most of all. Coming down the dip of the loop-de-loop. The perfect moment, she called it. Heading back towards solid earth, but you're not quite there yet. Floating. Weightless. Free. Kiri always wanted that perfect moment to last forever. But the ride would finish. Our feet would be back on solid earth. The moment would be gone. And we'd go eat a hot dog.'

Around the congregation, smiles. And a lot of wet eyes.

'Where you are, sweetheart, I hope it's always Monday morning. I hope you have all the rides to yourself. And I hope every moment is perfect and weightless and free.'

Trish takes her son.

Dax's hand rests for a moment on Kiri's casket. A silent goodbye. Then he returns to his seat.

Sitting between PLUS 1 and Hana, Addison blinks away tears.

Three days earlier, the helicopter landed on the road outside Hana's driveway, five black-uniformed AOS officers onboard, including a sharpshooter. When it was determined the suspect was no longer a physical threat, the helicopter became a stand-in rescue chopper, flying a handcuffed Weeks to the nearest emergency facility. As they waited for the ambulance to take Hana to hospital, to make sure there was no damage from the confrontation, she hugged her father.

'I wish you hadn't had to go through that, Dad.'

'It's not me anyone needs to worry about. Your neck, your wrists. You're sure that arsehole didn't hurt you?'

Eru gently raised Hana's chin. She could feel his hands shaking as he looked at the skin on her throat. It was reddened and bruised, but not broken. There were lacerations on her wrists where the plastic cable tie had cut, but nothing serious.

'Mum,' Addison whispered.

Hana held her daughter as Addison started to cry, giving in to the terror she'd felt seeing her mother incapacitated, a weapon to her throat, and watching her grandfather raise a gun and shoot a man. The fear coming out in unstoppable sobs. PLUS 1 came to Addison's side; Eru put his arms around all of them.

'I'm so sorry,' Hana said quietly.

'It's not your fault, Mum.'

But for Hana, there was a question mark. Was it her fault? She had wanted to find the truth of who had killed two young women, and she had followed a trail that led to the door of Gordon John Weeks. But in the process she had brought fear and danger into her world and into the worlds of those she loved most. Hana had walked away from the cops because she couldn't live with the darkness anymore.

But the darkness had followed her.

And it had followed her family.

Weeks was flown to Middlemore Hospital in South Auckland, rushed into surgery.

It had been half a century since Eru had used a gun in a confrontation with another human being. Despite the passage of time, his training had kicked in. If a bullet hits the middle of the torso, the site where all the important organs reside, they're going to go down and they're very probably not going to get up, ever again. If you go for the mass of muscles and nerves in the shoulder area of their dominant arm, the arm that holds the gun or the bottle or the knife or whatever they're using, they'll go down, it will be intense and agonizing, and most importantly they won't be able to pick up the weapon with that hand again.

But they're much less likely to die.

Eru's training had worked. At Middlemore, the bullet was removed from Weeks' upper back. The wound wasn't life-threatening. When Weeks regained consciousness a few hours later, cuffed to his bed in the recovery room, Lorraine and Jaye were waiting, along with an armed uniformed officer. Medical staff checked Weeks' vital signs, confirmed his responsiveness. When they'd done their job, Lorraine approached the bedside.

'You are under arrest for the murders of Paige Meadows and Kiri Thomas. You have the right to remain silent. You do not have to make any statement. Anything you say will be recorded and may be given as evidence in court.'

On the hospital bed, Weeks stared at the ceiling.

'You have the right to speak to a lawyer without delay and in private before deciding whether to answer any questions. Police have a list of lawyers you may speak to for free. Do you understand your rights as they have been read to you?'

He made no reply.

In the chapel, Lorraine is one of the last to speak. She talks of Kiri as the bravest person she ever met.

'I only wish, sometimes, she'd been more afraid.

Maybe she wouldn't have found herself in the places she did. But I've come to understand, that's not something you can teach someone. Everyone who knows Kiri knows, that's who she was. Someone incapable of fear.'

After the ceremony, as the hearse leaves the chapel, Eru gathers his whānau down by the water. He blesses each of them, to remove the tapu* of the funeral ceremony, to return them back to the world of the living. Sitting by the lagoon, Addison talks about the dreams.

'She's always there, at the crossroads, along from the vintage shops. Just standing there. The red man never turns green. Kiri can't cross the road. The look on her face.' Her eyes shine with tears. 'Like she knows she needs to go. But she can't.'

The sun is setting over the lagoon. Eru takes Addison's hand in his.

'Your great-auntie Oha. You never knew her, she passed thirty years before you were even born. She had a big sister, Marjorie. When Oha was six years old and Marjorie was ten, Marjorie went missing in the forest behind the family house. The family looked for her for hours. Darkness had fallen, it was the middle of winter and the weather was about to turn very bad. The little girl was only wearing thin clothes. A night out in the open, in a storm, in winter. She wouldn't

---

* Tapu – state of sacredness or spiritual restriction.

have had a chance. There was a candle Marjorie kept on her bedside table. Standing on the edge of the forest, looking out into the darkness, Oha saw the candle. Off in the distance. She told her father and her brothers. No one else could see it. But Oha could. And beyond that candle, another. And then, another.'

'Leading into the forest?' Addison asks. Eru nods, *exactly*.

'Oha followed the trail of candles. The rest of the family followed Oha, deep into the forest, two hours' walking, into an area they never would have thought to search. The final candle that Oha saw was at the top of a long slope. They got to the edge of the slope and heard a voice crying out. They found Marjorie, just as the rain started to fall. She'd gotten lost and fallen down the slope, broken her ankle.'

Eru gestures to Hana to sit with them. Hana moves closer to Addison, puts an arm around her.

'Matakite* is in your ancestry, in our bloodline,' Eru continues. 'From way back. But when religion came, the family agreed, that was done. They were Christians now. The old ways had to be left behind. But you can't stop what you are. It's nothing spooky, nothing freaky. It's just what it means to be Māori. The veil between the physical world and the world beyond is thin. When someone needs to communicate, sometimes they

---

* Matakite – special intuition; a visionary.

reach out. Kiri reached out to you. There were things that needed to be answered. And now, they've been answered. We know who hurt her. And he's going to pay the price.'

As the sun falls below the horizon, they return to the cars.

'Can you drop Addison and PLUS 1 back to their place?' Hana asks Eru. She's arranged to have a drink with Lorraine and Jaye, the time-honoured cop tradition for dealing with the aftermath of a difficult case.

As the others get into the car, Addison stays with Hana for a moment.

'You okay, love?' Hana asks.

'The dreams. The guy that killed Kiri has been arrested. But Kiri's still coming to me. Every night.'

'The same dream?'

Addison nods her head, *yes*. The same dream.

'She still can't cross the road, Mum.'

30

LAST DRINKS

'The last time I saw her face, it was blurred.'

After the service at the little chapel, Hana and Jaye went back to Lorraine's apartment in a leafy neighbourhood in the middle of town. They ordered in beers and Thai takeaway. Three former colleagues unwinding.

It's late. The food's been demolished, the beers, almost demolished. It's that time of the night. Everyone is exhausted and emotional. Especially Lorraine.

'I knew it was Kiri, straight away,' she says. 'Her face was blurred, they do that on those ads, but I knew it was her. An online escort ad. The same ad I knew she used to put up before she went through rehab and we got her on the programme. "Brown-skinned Teen Angel." Jesus Christ...'

Lorraine's apartment is in a small block. High ceilings. A great view over the city centre. The kind of place a single person without kids and on a senior detective's salary can afford. Lorraine's grip on her beer bottle is tight. This memory is difficult.

'We knew she'd gone off the rails. She'd disappeared from the group. Dax told us what happened between them. The break-up, her smashing up his scooter and his nose. I was worried she'd gone back to old habits. And gone back to sex work to pay for those habits. I saw the ad, the night Kiri disappeared. I wanted to curl up and cry. The idea that that was how I last saw her. I just hate it.'

They're on the balcony of the apartment, looking towards the waters of the harbour in the distance. Jaye uncaps the last three bottles of beer. Hands them around.

'Most cops feel strung out just dealing with the day-to-day stuff,' he says. 'The things you did for those kids, Lorry. You should be proud.'

Lorraine sips her beer. Hana can see there's far more pain than pride there, especially tonight.

'When you asked me to come in and meet the group,' Hana says gently. 'I could see how much they meant to you. I was kind of worried about you, to be honest. You had a lot of skin in the game.'

Flying in low, an Air New Zealand 787 rumbles over the inner-city suburbs, heading south to make its final approach towards Auckland International Airport. The engine noise fades away into the distance.

'I failed her.'

'Bullshit,' Jaye says. 'I'm not going to listen to that. You gave her a chance.'

A knock at the door. Marissa, come to pick up Jaye, her girls with her. Jaye had moved home a few days previously, and as he goes to greet his family, Hana watches the girls cling to his hands.

Marissa hugs Lorraine. 'You must be glad you found the guy,' she says.

Then she turns to Hana. It's the first time they've seen each other since the meeting with the counsellors.

'Are you all right? Your dad? Addison?'

'We're okay.'

'What a thing to go through. I can't imagine.'

Marissa hugs her, and Hana can feel it's not perfunctory. The embrace is genuine.

'The girls miss Addison,' Marissa says, pulling out of the hug.

'I'll tell her to visit.'

'We miss you too.'

Marissa kisses Hana and heads out the door with Jaye.

There's a photo of their graduating class from police college on a shelf. As Lorraine brings in the beers from the balcony, Hana takes it down.

'God. We were so young.'

In the photo, Hana's long black hair is tied in a tight regulation plait. Her eyes look directly at the camera. Serious. Jaye is on the same row as her, but he's placed himself a discreet distance away. They were together by then, had been seeing each other since one particular Friday night in the go-to bar near the police college when quite a few tequilas were consumed, but they were keeping it quiet. Late nights spent sneaking into each other's apartments trying not to wake flatmates; they were waiting to graduate before making things official. In the middle of the group, between Hana and Jaye, Lorraine's platinum-blonde hair is tied up in her usual scraggly workaday bun. Her lipstick just a shade redder than strictly allowed, but somehow she always got away with it.

'Not a wrinkle between us,' Hana says. 'They seriously let us babies out into the world?'

Lorraine takes the photo. 'A tribe of young idealists,' she muses. 'Thinking we were gonna come out and save the world. Then the world got in the way.'

Hana knows what she means, especially tonight. Lorraine tried so hard with the kids. With Kiri.

'Maybe it doesn't matter that we're never gonna save the world,' she says. 'Maybe what matters is, we try.'

'That's philosophical for a Thursday.'

Lorraine clinks Hana's beer bottle with hers. A

warm, silent moment. Hana takes her bag, gets out her phone, requests an Uber.

'I'm gonna head off.'

'Through this whole thing, Hana, I've been watching you pull together threads piece by piece that no one else ever would have thought to.'

Lorraine puts the picture of their graduating class back on the shelf.

'You left the cops,' she says. 'I'm not sure the cops left you.'

'Who's the philosopher now?'

Lorraine opens the door for Hana. 'Are you really where you should be? Or where you need to be?'

Hana doesn't know the answer. 'Goodnight, Lorry.'

'Don't be a stranger.'

As Hana hugs Lorraine goodnight, she sees the sadness in her friend's face. A sadness that isn't going away any time soon.

Efeso is 5 minutes away

Hana waits for the Uber at the bottom of the stairs leading up to Lorraine's apartment.

She'd come up to Auckland early that day, a few hours before Kiri's service, and headed to the little West Auckland house that had had part of its roof ripped off in the freak weather event. When the young mother

Sandra handed her back the insurance form, Hana saw that there was now no claim for a ruined iPhone. She dropped in to see Seb Kang, gave him the paperwork for the insurance claim job.

And she told him what had happened with Weeks.

'Oh God,' he said, wrapping her in a hug.

The emotion of his response was surprising, but not unwelcome. Hana was reminded again of the ease and warmth she feels in Seb's company. She'd been moved, floating out in the middle of Auckland Harbour, when he'd told her he couldn't take the emotional toll of being a cop anymore. She doesn't know another male officer who would show their vulnerability in that way. Maybe once she has her feet firmly on solid ground back in Tātā Bay, maybe in six months' time, say, she might give Seb a call, suggest he comes down for a swim at the black sand beach. She'll make him tacos with fish bought at half the city prices, fresh from one of the little local fishing boats. Seb would get on well with her dad – Hana is sure.

Unless she's reading the situation completely wrongly, she thinks Seb would be agreeable to the idea. But not just yet. Too much change, too fast. Hana's still catching her breath. When she left to go to the service for Kiri in the little chapel by the water, she leaned in and gave Seb a kiss on the cheek.

Surprising them both.

'See you next time,' she said.

Efeso is 4 minutes away

Hana takes another sip of beer. Thinks about the last few days.

A killer. Stalking her, hiding in her home, subduing her with a weapon. She saw her father shoot the man, with the very gun she'd been considering taking out of his reach, to protect him or others, if he had early-onset dementia. But what none of them had known at that moment: their lives had never actually been in danger from Weeks. The long-bladed knife in his hand was a beekeeper's uncapping knife, designed to scrape honey from trays. It was not a tool you'd choose to kill someone. But at the time, with the large, shiny metal blade pressed hard and cold against her throat, Hana had known none of this.

Efeso is 2 minutes away. Get ready for your ride

Weeks had come to her house in a deep rage. Hana had seen it in his eyes, and it had been frightening. He'd believed he was about to be put away for the two homicides he'd committed and, until that time, gotten away with. The cops discovered later that he hadn't taken his stabilizing medications for days. It was a volatile collision of factors that had led him to Hana's house.

But, the knife.

Hana still can't get her head around that knife.

She'd seen other knives in Weeks' flat when she was there, some with blades that would have done serious damage to another human being. But the knife Weeks chose to confront her with could never have seriously harmed her.

Efeso is arriving now

The silver Prius pulls up, silently, like they always do. Hana's never got used to that. It's eerie and disconcerting. She takes a final sip of her beer, finishing the bottle. She opens the yellow lid of the recycling wheelie bin, the movement setting off the security light at the bottom of Lorraine's stairs. She drops the beer bottle in. She closes the lid.

She stops.

Hana opens the lid again. The intense beam of the security light fills the interior of the bin. Hana looks again at what she's seen inside. She blinks. Realization hitting. She goes to the Uber and apologizes to the driver, handing him a twenty-dollar bill.

'I have to cancel.'

Lorraine is in her pyjamas, ready for bed, when she answers the knock at her door and finds Hana there.

'Something I need to talk about,' Hana says. 'Is that okay?'

Lorraine slips on a robe. Guessing that maybe Hana needs a friendly ear, that she is looking for a confidante to share something personal with, maybe something to do with Jaye, or Marissa, or life away from the cops. Or perhaps, after a couple of beers, she wants to talk about the private investigator guy she occasionally works with and sometimes mentions. Lorraine has felt a bit of emotional subtext in the way Hana smiles when she talks about Sebastian.

But that isn't why Hana climbed the stairs back to Lorraine's apartment.

'Remember our first year at college?' she asks. They are back out on the balcony; Lorraine has made a pot of tea and is pouring it for them. 'In one of our first classes, they got us to say why we signed up for the cops. I talked about the teen girl from my high school who'd been murdered. How much that affected me. You heard that story then. You knew about the dead girl in the dunes.'

'I think I remember you mentioning it.'

'You said so. The night Addison found Kiri's bones.'

Lorraine nods, *okay then*. As she sips her tea, Hana sees her jaw tightening. She takes a deep breath and continues.

'When you saw Kiri's escort ad again. Her blurred face. What did you do?'

'I cried. Like I said.'

'What else did you do, Lorry?'

'I don't know what you're asking. Or why you're asking it.'

The atmosphere has shifted. Imperceptibly. But it has shifted.

Hana takes a sip of her tea. Happy to wait for Lorraine to speak again.

'What could I do?' asks Lorraine. 'Kiri was back out on the streets. I knew it was going to be a long hard haul. Find her, try and talk her into returning to the group, start again. Even if she agreed to come back, if she'd decided to start using again, she'd last a day and then go back for another hit. And on and on. It just broke my heart.'

Lorraine pulls her robe closer around her. 'I don't know what else to say. I saw her photo in the ad. I crawled under my sheets. And I cried.'

'I don't think you curled up under a blanket, Lorry. I don't think you're even capable of doing that.' Hana takes a long moment. What she's about to say, to someone she's known for years, someone who she counts as a friend, she'll never be able to walk back from.

'I think you got up and you did what you do. You went and tried to fix things.'

Across the balcony, Lorraine's eyes rest on Hana's.

'What would that look like? How would I fix things?'

'In the church today. You said, "I only wish she'd been more afraid." I think you tried to make her afraid. To make her see the danger of what she was doing. Tough love, Lorry. The amazing things you did with them. Like the boxing in your family's gym. Making those kids confront the pain, feel the brutality of their decisions, a strong hard slap in order to make them face themselves.'

To her surprise, Hana's hands are trembling slightly. In her former life as a cop, facing someone she suspected of committing a crime, she'd never let her emotions slip in this way. But this isn't a suspect in an interview room.

Lorraine is a friend.

Hana consciously folds her hands in her lap. Straightens her shoulders.

'You knew tough love worked for Kiri. I think you grabbed her. Wanting to give her a fright she'd never forget. Show her she could really get hurt. But I think something went wrong. Badly wrong. And when it fell to pieces, you remembered my story. Took the body to those same dunes, knowing it was a place far away. Deserted. Knowing that if she was ever found, it might look like some kind of copycat.'

'Are you accusing me of murder? Manslaughter? Because I heard a story you told in our first year at police college?' Lorraine's words aren't aggressive. She seems genuinely bewildered. 'We found Gordon John Weeks' DNA, Hana. In the glove near Kiri's body.'

'This was in your recycling bin.'

Hana opens her bag, takes something out that she has wrapped in a tissue to prevent contamination. She carefully unwraps the tissue. Inside, a small heavy glass bottle. An individual-serve mānuka honey health drink. Manufactured in Taiwan.

'Weeks drinks these. There are boxes of them in his flat. I think you took this from there. A used one that he'd drunk from, that would have traces of his DNA. I think you introduced some of his DNA into a glove, the same kind he used with the bees. Knowing that in a latex glove, DNA could survive a few years in the sands. Then you went back to the dunes, buried it, and the next day called in a team to sift for evidence. To find what you'd left there.'

The two friends hold each other's eyes for a long moment.

Then Lorraine turns away. She goes to the railing, looking out over the city and the harbour.

A few minutes earlier, looking into the recycling bin, seeing the empty mānuka honey bottle, everything had fallen together for Hana. When Weeks had been lying on her floor bleeding, after Eru had shot him, he'd already confessed to killing Paige. He had nothing to lose; he very probably believed he was dying. But he'd said, 'I didn't kill Kiri Thomas.'

He'd turned up with a knife that was only good for scraping honey, not for hurting someone.

And that afternoon at the lagoon, what Addison had said while she was leaving. Her dreams had continued after Weeks was arrested. Kiri still couldn't cross the road.

On the balcony, Hana carefully wraps the mānuka honey drink bottle in the tissue once more and returns it to her bag. She goes to stand beside Lorraine at the railing.

'You're a good cop, Lorry. You think through all the angles. You knew after Kiri's body was found there was a chance, however slim, that it could come back to you. And you knew that Weeks had killed Paige. You were pinning the crime on someone you knew had killed before and who had got away with it, who deserved to go to prison anyway. No one loses, right?'

Hana puts her hand on Lorraine's shoulder. Despite everything, a gesture of connection. An acknowledgement of their history. Hana can feel that her friend's shoulder is rigid. More like steel than muscle.

From the balcony, there's a clear view of the harbour in the distance. They can see the stretch of water below the pōhutukawa trees, near the candy-striped swimming pool where Kiri was abducted.

'What killed Kiri was years of drugs,' Lorraine says, quietly. 'The fucked-up choices she made. The fucked-up choices she went back to.'

'That's how you justified it to yourself. That's what you had to believe, to keep going. But it's bullshit. She was a seventeen-year-old girl, Lorry.'

'I'm not going to beg,' Lorraine says. 'You do what you have to do.'

Hana picks up her bag. Heads for the doorway.

As she opens the door, Lorraine turns.

'The irony is, recycling comes round in the morning. If I'd asked you for drinks one day later . . .'

Hana walks out the door, closes it behind her. Starts down the stairs. The security light above the yellow recycling bin turns on as she passes.

She walks away into the night.

31

REFLECTIONS

On her days off, Lorraine Delaney drives down the Southern Motorway from her apartment in the city centre, takes the Māngere offramp, and goes and opens up the family boxing gym. First thing, 5am. It gives her dad a chance to have a bit of a lie-in, an extra hour's sleep before he turns up with bad takeaway coffee and pastries from the local gas station.

The gym is in Lorraine's heart, and in her soul.

She unlocks, flicks on the big fluoro lights, starts up the treadmill machines. She turns on the music that feeds out from the big speakers that hang from the ceiling around the gym. With no one else there Lorraine gets to turn the volume up. Old-school South Auckland hip-hop, the music she grew up hearing, blasting out from the huge, bass-heavy speakers behind the front grilles of the cars belonging to the young Tongan and Samoan men and women who came to train at the gym. A driving beat. The kind of rhythm it's good to pound bags to.

She gets out the mop, fills a bucket with hot water and disinfectant. The main boxing ring stands raised in the middle of the gym, where the up-and-coming boxers get to spar. Every month, exhibition matches are held so the young fighters can invite their families and friends and show them why they've been spending every spare moment working out and running the streets and coming to the gym.

She mops the canvas floor of the main ring. Then the two lower rings at either end of the gym.

The full-length mirrors are always the biggest job. They encircle the space so the fighters can watch their stances as they spar, check the defensive position of their gloves, make sure their jaws aren't exposed and just begging to get broken. Lorraine moves from one big mirror to the next, using a stepladder to get to the highest corners, carefully using glass cleaner and paper towels.

With the mirrors done, she looks up at the stencilled motto high on the wall, the words she's read a thousand times.

BLOOD MAKES YOU TOUGH
SWEAT MAKES YOU STRONG
TEARS MAKE YOU HUMBLE

Lorraine remembers her father talking about the one trip he'd ever made out of New Zealand. As a young man, he'd been a good fighter himself. He'd gone to the United States to work as a sparring partner for a rising contender for the world middleweight belt. He met the legendary trainer whose words are painted up there above the main ring. The guy was a drunk. He smelled of cheap whiskey and body odour. But in the five minutes he worked with Lorraine's dad, talking in a broad New York Italian drawl that sounded like he was auditioning for a black-and-white movie from the fifties, the trainer taught him more about boxing than he'd learned in twenty years back home.

Then her dad shattered ten bones in his hand in the ring. Fighting career over.

He came back to Māngere determined to pass on to the locals in his community the things he'd learned in his year in the States. He found an old warehouse going cheap. He got a loan, converted it into a gym. He painted the motto on the wall. And he set about trying to change the lives of young people.

He gave his daughter the same values and goals.

The last thing Lorraine cleans are the skipping ropes. The ropes hang from a series of hooks on a rail at the back of the gym. She takes each one, carefully checks it for fraying, makes sure the swivels are turning smoothly, sprays disinfectant on the handles and wipes them down. Then she returns the rope to the hook, moves on to the next.

In the polished surfaces of the full-length mirrors, the reflections of flashing lights.

Blue and red.

Outside the gym, police cars pull up. Jaye gets out of the lead vehicle.

The gym has two dozen skipping ropes. Lorraine is down to the last two. She's going to finish the job. She checks the swivels of the second-to-last rope. Sprays the handles with antiseptic. As she wipes off the spray, she gives a rueful smile. She's known Hana for nearly twenty years. After Hana left her apartment the night before, Lorraine knew what decision her friend would make. Because she knows exactly who Hana is, who she will always be.

A good cop.

Lorraine finishes the last skipping rope and hangs it back on its hook. She turns to the nearest mirror. A crack runs vertically down the length of the glass, almost from the ceiling to the floor. Lorraine's been meaning to call a glazier and get the thing fixed. She adjusts her carefully messy bun. Freshens her lipstick. From this angle the crack in the mirror runs through her face, cutting her reflection clean down the middle.

Lorraine looks at herself for a long moment. Her face looking back at her, splintered in two.

She should've got the mirror fixed.

She walks out the front door of the gym. Locks it behind her.

And she goes and gets into Jaye's police car.

32

AFTER

The initial interview takes place in Counties Manukau's regional HQ, 25 kilometres south down the motorway from Auckland Central Station.

When the plans had been finalized for the arrest of the suspect, in discussion with the commissioner of police, DI Jaye Hamilton decided that it would be an intolerable disruption and threat to the morale of the arrested officer's colleagues if she were held and questioned in the precinct where she had served for the last twenty years. She was driven in an unmarked police car to Counties Manukau where Jaye transferred custody to Detective Inspector Elisa Williams, his equivalent rank in that region's CIB.

In the interview room, the suspect ignores her lawyer's caution that she has no obligation to speak to the interviewing officers. She begins the interview by stating that she is very familiar with the information needed at this initial stage of an arrest; she will willingly provide all relevant details required for the police to prepare the necessary charges. The suspect proceeds to give a detailed summary of the events leading up to and on the night of Kiri Thomas' death. She talks about the progress Kiri had made in the Youth at Risk scheme, getting sober, building her goal of a career in which she could use her love of words. She explains how when Kiri's relationship with a young man in the scheme broke up, Kiri abruptly dropped out of the programme and disappeared. Believing it was likely that Kiri had returned to drug use and sex work to pay for the drugs, the suspect began monitoring the online sites Kiri used to attract clients. On the Saturday evening in question, Kiri posted an advertisement, which the suspect immediately saw. She made the decision that an assertive intervention was necessary, employing the kinds of wake-up-call tactics that Kiri had responded to previously in the Youth at Risk scheme, giving her a shock-and-awe moment of realization regarding the dangers she was placing herself in. Texting with a burner SIM card, the suspect posed as a client, arranging a meeting at the car park where Kiri was working. When Kiri approached the vehicle, the suspect deployed what she knew Kiri would believe were the textbook tactics of a kidnapper, forcing a thick bag over her head, restraining her hands with heavy-duty duct tape, throwing her into the boot. She drove out of the city, to the south, to a deserted industrial area she knew of. Her plan was to pull Kiri from the boot, leave her in the empty factory for a few hours, cold and alone, expecting the worst. At dawn she'd remove the restraints. The suspect expected Kiri to lash out, that it would be confrontational, awful.

'But that was how I knew I'd finally get through to her.'

When the suspect opened the boot of the car at the deserted factory, Kiri wasn't moving.

'She'd vomited and choked. Probably within minutes of going into the boot. I found out later that Kiri had purchased a new supply of narcotics, of unusual purity. The vomiting was likely a reaction. I tried CPR for nearly an hour. She was gone.'

Faced with the certain loss of her career and lengthy imprisonment, the suspect made a decision.

To dispose of the body.

She chose a place nearby where she knew another young victim had been dumped years earlier.

The interview lasts twelve minutes. Before being taken to a holding cell, from which she will be transferred to a high-security unit at Auckland Region Women's Corrections Facility, the suspect's police identification card is taken from her. As the formal questioning ends, Detective Senior Sergeant Lorraine

Delaney asks the interviewing officer if she can say one more thing.

'I only wanted to save her.'

Addison and PLUS 1 have dragged the couch out into the backyard. Surrounded by the small rainforest of Addison's mother's native trees and shrubs, a fire is burning in the kitchen sink firepit.

It's the day after Lorraine was arrested. That afternoon Addison and PLUS 1 had picked up Stan in their crappy car and gone to some quiet suburban back streets so he could try driving with his new prosthetic limb. It had gone well. They'd dropped him home, and when they got back to the house, Hana was waiting. She told Addison that an arrest had been made. It would be in the papers soon enough – she couldn't tell her daughter about what had really happened yet – but she wanted to put Addison's mind at rest that the person who'd killed Kiri had been detained.

'I dreamed about her again last night,' Addison says, staring at the flames.

'The same dream?' PLUS 1 asks.

'Mostly. I walked past the same shops. She was wearing the cardigan, like always. Waiting at the intersection. The red man standing still up on the lights. But this time, when I got to her, it was different.' Addison tucks one leg up into her chest, wraps her arm around her knee. The same way her mother does, sometimes.

'This time, she turned. Kiri looked at me. She didn't say anything. But she seemed okay. Not happy. That's not the right word. But okay.'

PLUS 1 reaches out, takes Addison's hand.

'The red man turned green,' Addison continues. 'Kiri walked across the street in her blue-and-white cardigan. I turned around. And I came home.'

Their fingers entwined, Addison turns towards PLUS 1. 'I've been a mess. Sorry. Thanks for not giving up on me.'

'It was a lot for you,' PLUS 1 says. 'I think that's the last time you'll dream of her.'

'Kiri and me – I think we could have been friends.'

'One hundred per cent. Friends that are more like sisters than friends. Like us.'

Addison thinks about this for a moment. 'Is that what we are?'

There are words you have to be certain about before you give them voice; if you change your mind, if you realize you didn't really mean what you said, everyone gets hurt. You have to be certain, or it will ruin everything.

Addison is certain.

'If Kiri was my friend. If she was my sister. I know what she'd tell me.'

The puppy snuffles on the couch between them. Her

paws twitch in her sleep; maybe she's seeing a rabbit in her dreams and readying for a frantic pursuit. Addison rubs Boca's ears. Her paws stop twitching.

'Kiri would say don't do what she did. Don't be afraid to accept love for what it is. She'd tell me, don't be a dick. Don't be scared to love and be loved.'

Addison puts her head on PLUS 1's lap. Easy, loving, comfortable.

'We say we're not the type that falls in love,' Addison says. 'We say it all the time, and we're lying to ourselves. I want to stop being scared, babe.'

Addison looks up at her friend. 'Do you feel the same?' she asks.

PLUS 1's eyes shine in the firelight.

Both already know the answer to the question.

In Tātā Bay, Hana is with Eru and Jaye looking out over the sand dunes. In the darkness, a sea of candles burns.

There was a service that evening, led by Eru and Chloe Purchas in her role as a minister of Eternity Farm church. Several members of her faith came to pay their respects. At sunset, karakia were said for Kiri, and for Paige. The area was blessed, so locals could once again return to the beach. Jaye came in dress uniform, to represent the New Zealand police, and to express formal sympathies to the community. The last of the locals have placed their candles in the sand and gone home. It's late.

'I'll head off. See you tomorrow, love,' Eru says. 'Thanks for being here, Jaye.'

Before the service that evening, as Eru was getting dressed in his good suit, Hana took Jaye out onto her deck overlooking the dunes. She quietly told him of her worries about her dad. The Google searches she'd found. Jaye couldn't hide his concern and sadness.

'He's a warrior,' he said quietly. 'He wants to find out what the threat is. If the enemy is real. When he's ready, he'll ask you to stand by him and help him fight. Give him the right to decide when that happens.'

Now, a few hours later, with the service finished, and as the candles flicker in the empty sand dunes, Hana watches Jaye hug her father goodnight. She sees in Jaye's eyes how hard he is fighting not to show the raw emotion of the last few days, the sadness at what Hana has told him about her fears for her dad. When a relationship of many years ends, sometimes you look at your ex and wonder why the hell you were together. Hana knows why she and Jaye were together. And that they will always be a part of each other's lives.

'Okay then,' Eru says, extracting himself from Jaye's hug with a smile. 'Drive home safe, Jaye.'

After Eru has left, on the dunes, Jaye holds his dress uniform cap in his hands. The wind is picking up.

'This place is your home. Your iwi,'* he says to Hana. 'But the cops are your iwi too. Blue is in your DNA, as well as brown. I know you think you have to choose one or the other. That's not true. You can be both. What you can do, no one else can do. Your job is there, waiting for you. The moment you want it.'

Hana watches as Jaye walks to his car and drives out of the car park, turning down the road that heads back to Auckland. Black sands, tossed by the building gusts, sandpaper her bare feet and shins.

Heavy rain and winds are forecast for the next day. A good day for the fearless young surfers in their thick wetsuits. Or for sitting inside with hot chocolate, playing Monopoly.

Hana watches the candles across the dunes flicker as the onshore wind rises.

---

* Iwi – tribe.

33

GUESS HOW MUCH I LOVE YOU

At first, there was the void. Te Kore. The great big nothing.

No inside, no outside. No left, no right. No up, no down.

Nothing.

Then came Te Pō. The darkness.

And in the realm of eternal darkness, movement.

The Sky Father. The Earth Mother.

Between them, their kids. Squished. Unhappy. Crushed like when you accidentally sit on a bag of chips. Like when you're tossed into a car boot and it's slammed shut.

The kids, stuck in the darkness, questioning why they were there.

Wanting to be free.

They were over it.

They pushed their parents apart, those mischief kids, and they created the sky and the earth. They brought into being Te Ao Mārama, the World of Light.

The naughty kids became gods.

And the parents wept.

The rain falling from the sky, the tears of the father.

The mist rising from the earth, the heartbroken sighs of the mother.

One of the gods tore out their own eyes and crushed them up and tossed them into the heavens to make a sacred constellation for us down here to navigate by.

In the city we don't have stars. We've forgotten the language of the sky. We make our own heavens out of what we have here. The lights on the Harbour Bridge. Headlights reflected on the water. We don't know our gods, we can't see the crushed-up eyes to navigate by, so we ride around on a rusty moped and dodge rainbows and call ourselves *The Gods of Auckland*.

The streets swallow us whole. We forget where we're from.

We decide it's easier to be fucked-up.

And the parents weep.

I have a memory.

I don't know if it's a real memory or something I made up out of bits and pieces people told me. I remember a woman, beautiful, dark hair and dark eyes. She smelled of the yellow flowers that grow when the lawnmower is broken, and the grass gets too long. I remember a man with a beard that was a little bit scratchy when he kissed me on the forehead. It was scratchy, but I liked it, and I can see his big beaming smile as he buckled me into the car seat, whispering.

'E kō.'

My baby girl.

I have other memories. Lots of them.

These memories are one hundred per cent real.

My adoptive parents. My mum, with her warm, tender eyes, always reading to me, teaching me to fall in love with words. My favourite book that I'd make her read again and again about the long-eared daddy hare who was always asking the little baby hare to guess how much he loved her.

And the little hare could never guess just how much she was loved.

My adoptive dad, big and strong, who would toss me up, like the daddy hare in the book, throw me so high it felt like I was going to fly away, but then he'd catch me, and I'd hold onto him with my arms wrapped round his neck and kiss him and never want him to let me go.

I wanted a kid of my own.

Not at seventeen, are you kidding?

But one day, when I got my shit together. I would've been a good mum, I bet. Like Trish is a great mum. The kid would have green eyes. In bright sunlight, their eyes would be seafoam green. I'd love that kid like no one ever loved a kid.

Which is to say, I'd love her or him, the same way my parents loved me.

The same way all my parents loved me.

My real parents.

And my adoptive parents.

Like how Dax loved me. In his fucked-up, big-nosed, teen-junkie way. He told me I had god eyes and he loved me. He fucked a girl and I wanted to put a knife in his head for it. But he did it 'cos he was scared of loving and being loved. Just like me.

Maybe after I calmed down, after Dax got a new moped to replace *The Gods of Auckland* after I drove Trish's car into it, after his nose got better, I reckon we would've found our way back to each other.

I would've found my way back to my family.

Who knows, maybe it'd be me and Dax who would have that kid.

He was always kind to little kids, Dax. Maybe because no one was ever very kind to him.

We'd get a really good car seat, even if we couldn't afford it, and at night in our bed, our kid would lie between us and push at me with its feet, and Dax and me would hold onto each other and the kid, and it would be warm, and it would be good.

That poem I wrote on the rock face, the night I rode

around the city with Dax. My poem has a beginning and a middle but no ending.

Sometimes, I guess, that's just how it is.

I love you to the stars and back, the big hare said, in my favourite book. But the little hare was asleep.

And she never guessed just how much she was loved.

ACKNOWLEDGEMENTS

Writing a novel is equal parts wondrous and terrifying, a journey of discovery through unmapped lands, searching for the stars to guide you along the way. Doing this job is a privilege, and the greatest privilege of all is the generosity of the wonderful people who have my back and walk beside me.

Tuatahi rā, me mihi ka tika ki a matua Ngamaru Raerino. It is with deep sadness that I acknowledge the passing last year of my friend and mentor, Ngamaru Raerino. Matua Ngamaru was Pou Matua for my first novel, and has been an inestimable support to me and to so many other Māori writers and creators for many, many years. For those of us who were uplifted by his aroha and by his tautoko, Ngamaru pushed us to tell our stories with integrity and authenticity and manaakitanga.

I am humbled to work again with Katherine Armstrong, my brilliant editor, who always brings out the very best in my ideas and in my work, and does so with passion and kindness and care. Ngā mihi aroha ki a koe, e hoa.

Tim Worrall (Ngāi Tūhoe), thank you e hoa, not only for your cultural and language guidance with this manuscript, but for your Yoda-esque advice and breathtaking range of knowledge. Te Aranga o Otene Kane Hopa (Ngāpuhi, Ngāti Whātua, Waikato) is Pou Matua for this novel; ngā mihi for your support and your deep insights and your generosity.

Craig Sisterson is by a country mile the fiercest and most passionate advocate for we down here in Aotearoa who love crime (in a literary sense). I am blessed to have you as a friend, and as my agent.

Ngā mihi to George Gibson of Grove Atlantic, for your fervent belief in these characters and this series. Ngā mihi also to Amy Fletcher and the Simon & Schuster rights team, and to the publishers and editors and translators and narrators who are taking this book into other languages, and into other forms of media.

My aroha and unending gratitude to so many friends and whānau for your generous insights and support and advice – Steve Brewer, Miriama McDowell, Cian Elyse White, Detective Constable Turi Bennett, Tajim Mohammed-Kapa, Matariki Bennett, Māhina Bennett, Sandra Noakes and the team at Harper

Collins NZ, Deb Brewer, Ezra Dyer, Rebecca Henry, Alison Elston, Niki Bennett, Chloe Fergusson-Tibble, Nicola Ngarewa, Tīhema Bennett, Lily Cameron, Awa Puna, Harriet Crampton.

Sian Wilson designed the stunning cover. The beautiful Māori designs on the cover and throughout the book are the creations of Māhina Bennett. Matariki Bennett shared her extraordinary recent poems, which are the inspiration for Kiri's poem, and which echo in Kiri's voice throughout the book.

Georgina Leighton is the project manager. Thank you for the commitment and care and impeccable taste you bring, it is such a joy working with you.

The copy-editor is Maddy Hamey-Thomas and the proofreader is Gillian Hamnett. Ngā mihi ki a kōrua.

Ngā mihi to Creative New Zealand, the Arts Council of New Zealand Toi Aotearoa. The writing of this book was made possible by their generosity.

My dad and mum gave me the belief and courage to pursue my dreams. My love of writing came from my mother, and it's a joy to have her words alongside mine in this book; I know she is smiling at her mussel and courgette recipe turning up in these pages.

Arohanui to Jane Holland, for everything and for always. Without you the characters in this book wouldn't exist. Without you my world wouldn't exist.

Better the Blood

**WINNER of the Best First Novel Award
at the 2023 Ngaio Marsh Awards
FINALIST for the Best Novel Award at the
2023 Ngaio Marsh Awards
SHORTLISTED for the Jann Medlicott Acorn Prize
for Fiction, Ockham New Zealand Book Awards
LONGLISTED for the CWA John Creasey New Blood Dagger
SHORTLISTED for Audio Book of the Year at the
Capital Crime Fingerprint Awards**

**A DETECTIVE IN SEARCH OF THE TRUTH.
A KILLER IN SEARCH OF RETRIBUTION.
YOU CAN'T HIDE FROM HISTORY.**

Detective Senior Sergeant Hana Westerman is a tenacious Māori detective juggling single motherhood and the pressures of her career in Auckland's Central Investigation Branch. When she's led to a crime scene by a mysterious video, she discovers a man hanging in a hidden room. With little to go on, Hana knows one thing: the killer is sending her a message.

As a Māori officer, there has always been a clash between duty and culture for Hana, but it is something that she's found a way to live with. Until now. When more murders follow, Hana realises that her heritage and past are the keys to finding the perpetrator.

But the killer's agenda of revenge may include Hana – and her family . . .

AVAILABLE NOW IN PAPERBACK, EBOOK AND AUDIO